THE RAVEN SONG

HIDDEN NORFOLK - BOOK 11

J M DALGLIESH

First published by Hamilton Press in 2022

ISBN (Trade Paperback) 978-1-80080-089-2
ISBN (Hardback) 978-1-80080-349-7
ISBN (Large Print) 978-1-80080-179-0

EXCLUSIVE OFFER

THE RAVEN SONG

PROLOGUE

THE WHITE LIGHT on the horizon blinked on and off as the sash window rattled with yet another fierce gust of wind driving against it. Moments later, a spatter of rain carried in off the sea. Searching the growing gloom for the speck of light, it reappeared momentarily before vanishing a fraction of a second later. Were the crew hunkered down inside, safe against the ravages of nature hammering the ship, or were they battling to keep afloat, to stay alive?

The howling wind dissipated for a second. A moment of quiet calm descending on the room. Had the storm passed? The window shrieked again making her jump, accompanied by a squeak passing from her own lips.

"Come away from the window, darling."

She remained where she was, staring out at the passing ship whose lights were, once again, winking at her from the darkness. In that moment she wanted to be on board that vessel – wherever it was going – rather than here in her bedroom. Would someone be on that ship staring at the lights from her home atop the headland, envious of the safety and security that the mainland had to offer?

It wasn't any safer here.

"Are you going to come and read?"

She looked back, smiling at the man lying on top of the duvet, feet crossed with an open book in his hand. With one last glance towards the ship out at sea, she crossed the room and climbed over her father and slipped under the duvet.

"Don't you want to close the curtains?" he asked.

"No." She stared out into the black of night. "I want to see the stars if I wake up during the night."

"I don't think there will be any stars tonight, darling. This storm won't pass until tomorrow morning."

She shrugged. "I don't care."

Nestling into her father, he held the book open with his right hand and put his left arm around her.

"Now, where did we get to last night?"

"There," she said, pointing to a break in the text at the top of the right-hand page. Her father paused, rereading the section before.

"Yes, you're right."

"Tim is searching for his brother... and everyone has heard about him, but no one knows where he is."

"Right... I remember," her father said quietly. "I think."

"I can tell you..." She offered, nervous. "If you like?"

"Yes, thank you."

How he could have forgotten, she didn't know. They'd read three chapters the previous night, far more than the one chapter they usually read. That was probably down to today. Neither of them had been looking forward to today, attempting to put it off as long as possible. But as night follows day, it had come. There was no way of avoiding life, or death, as it transpired.

"Tim has died... and now he is looking for his brother in the afterlife." She hesitated.

"What is it darling?"

"Tim… he can walk here… he can run?"

"Yes, that's true. It's a good thing." Her father shifted in the bed so he could look sideways down at her and read her expression. "Isn't it?"

"Yes, of course… but…"

"But what?"

"He isn't in pain anymore. He is… normal."

The weight of that last word sounded heavy as she spoke it.

"Yes."

"And… in the afterlife… that's how it is?" He looked at her quizzically. "I mean, if you are ill in real life, you don't carry that across with you?"

"No… it's a fresh start… sort of, but with all the memories, thoughts and feelings of your life carried over with you."

She thought about it for a moment, reluctant to ask the question although she could tell he was preparing himself to hear it.

"And what about Mummy?"

"She is there too."

"And she isn't… hurt anymore?" She was scared of the answer. Whatever he said, it wouldn't take away the pain she'd felt all day, but it might, at the very least, offer a crumb of consolation.

"No," he said quietly, "she isn't in pain. Not anymore."

She teared up, burying her face in the side of her father's chest to hide the tears from him. He had been upset enough already and she didn't want to add to his burden. Yesterday he'd walked in on her as she wept and his smile had rapidly faded and within minutes, as he consoled her, he was in tears again. She couldn't remember the last day that passed without her seeing him cry. She resolved not to be the cause of yet more upset. She couldn't bear it.

"And she can run, like she used to when I was small?"

She didn't look up, but she could hear the emotion in her father's voice, cracking as he spoke.

"Yes... she can run as fast as she likes... and for as long as she wants to."

He leaned into her, stroking the back of her hair and kissed the top of her head. She said nothing, images coming to mind of people dressed in black, stern faces and tears... lots of tears.

The organist played a sombre piece while they all filed out of the church. Looking at her hand, she could almost still feel the discomfort in her fingers, her father's grip so tight that she thought she might scream as they left the church. This was her experience today, being led around by the hand, passed between adults, no one really knowing what to say to her. She did get a lot of smiles, affectionate strokes of the hair and gentle touches, but the sense that everyone was keen to move on as soon as possible wouldn't leave her. They were protecting her father, giving him a break.

Where were these people when Mum really needed them, when she really needed them?

Their expressions were all so similar today... pity in their eyes... sorrow in their smiles. Artificial. Forced.

Now she pictured her mother running along the golden sand, the sunset behind her as the waves broke upon the shore. She couldn't quite believe it was her mother... because she had never seen her mother that way. She couldn't run, even if she had wanted to.

"Why couldn't it be different, Papa?"

Her father choked back tears as he drew her closer to him, but he didn't speak.

She looked up at him. "Why do these things happen?"

He took a deep breath before answering. "Things happen in life... things that are beyond our control. And we have to accept them."

The answer was unsatisfactory, but truthful.

"And where Mummy is now, with Tim and his brother, bad things don't happen?"

"I like to think not, no."

"I hope I find her one day," she whispered.

"I'm sure you will, darling," her father said, tightening his grip around her. "I'm sure we will."

CHAPTER ONE

ERIC COLLET GLANCED sideways at his wife, Becca, her expression set in a scowl at the lady in front of them in the queue. Becca was in a state of agitation, and it was growing. She muttered under her breath, drawing a brief shift of the pharmacist's eye in their direction. George grumbled in her arms.

"Do you want me to take him?" Eric asked.

She shook her head, adjusting the baby in her arms to make it more comfortable for her.

"It's okay. I don't mind."

"I said no, Eric."

She shot him a dark look and he averted his eyes from hers.

"Forget I mentioned it," he said quietly. Becca looked back at the counter as the lady accepted her bagged items from the pharmacist.

"Finally," she said quietly.

They stepped forward and were greeted with a warm, if slightly forced, smile.

"Good morning. How can I help?" the pharmacist asked,

aiming the question at Eric which seemed to encourage Becca to bristle.

"It's our son, George," Eric said, gesturing towards the baby cradled in the crook of his mother's arm. "He's running a temperature and his eyes are all swollen... and gunky."

The woman looked at George, Becca offering him up a little towards the counter so she could get a better look. Becca's demeanour noticeably shifted to one of outright concern for her child.

"His temperature is over thirty-nine degrees... and has been through the night."

"I see," the pharmacist leaned in a little, inspecting the corner of George's eye where it was oozing a vivid yellow pus. On cue, he started grizzling which developed into a full-blown wail within moments. Eric was strangely comforted by that sound as George had been remarkably subdued overnight, and to make such noise now he saw as a good sign rather than a bad one.

"And what have you given the little man?"

"Paracetamol," Becca said. "He had one dose last night and his last at 5 am, but it doesn't seem to have brought his temperature down at all."

"Any ibuprofen at all?"

Eric shook his head. "I thought better not, seeing as we'd already given him the—"

"Not at all," the pharmacist said. "You can give him both at the same time should the need arise."

"But..." Eric looked at Becca, her scowl returning and focussed directly on him now, "I thought it was dangerous to combine—"

The pharmacist shook her head. "Usually, I would advise staggering the doses to give you ample coverage throughout the twenty-four-hour period, which would help with your sleep patterns as well," she glanced at Becca and smiled supportively, "seeing as it looks like you've all had a long night."

Becca's stance softened. Eric thought she was about to cry.

"Oh," he said quietly. "I didn't realise."

"First child?"

Eric nodded.

"It's a steep learning curve, isn't it?"

"Yes," Becca said, gently rocking George from side to side to try and calm him. It didn't work. "So, you think we should give him ibuprofen?"

The woman behind the counter turned and lifted a small, orange-coloured box, containing a 100ml bottle, from the shelf behind her and placed it on the counter before them.

"The key thing is to try and bring his temperature down. This will help. Be careful with the dosing intervals. Give it half an hour and check the temperature again and if it hasn't started to come down, then you should call the NHS helpline."

"But... won't giving them both together cause an issue?" Eric asked. Becca rolled her eyes and he suddenly felt self-conscious, silly. "I mean, I don't want to hurt him."

"As I said, it is not something to do as a routine matter of course, but, with an elevated temperature like this, then I think it would be okay. I must stress though, if his temperature doesn't drop then you should call the helpline."

"We should have done that hours ago!" Becca mumbled.

"I didn't want to cause a fuss," Eric protested. "The services are stretched as it is—"

"Whatever," Becca said dismissively.

Eric frowned. The pharmacist looked at him sympathetically.

"It is hard to know what to do for the best sometimes," she said. Becca scoffed.

"What about his eyes being all puffy and stuff?" Eric asked.

"A bit of conjunctivitis, I should say. Babies will rub their eyes after rubbing their noses and it can easily lead to a little infection there."

"What can you give us for that?" Eric asked.

"I can't, I'm afraid." Eric looked confused. "Because of his age. A GP would need to prescribe something for him."

"I told you we should have called the out-of-hours number, Eric," Becca snapped.

Eric was about to reiterate his point that he thought he was doing the right thing but changed his mind when he saw the fire in her eyes. The pharmacist came to his rescue.

"It's nothing to worry about. More often than not it will clear itself up in a day or two. If you boil some water, let it cool in a clean bowl and gently wipe his eyes clear with a cotton wool pad, that should help. If you do it regularly, then it will stop his eyelashes sticking together."

"Or we can go and see a doctor and get something to treat it," Becca said with a hint of accusation.

"Yes, you could also do that."

Eric smiled awkwardly, appreciating that Becca's tone was a little spiky. He was used to it. He took out his wallet and made to pay for the medicine, reaching across the aisle and picking up a pack of cotton wool pads and placing them down alongside the box of ibuprofen. He smiled at the woman. She returned it as Becca walked away, leaning into George and kissing his brow. He had settled slightly.

"It really is hard to know what to do for the best sometimes."

Eric nodded vigorously. "Becca doesn't mean to be rude… it's just—"

"I know, don't worry. We've all been there," she said. Her tone was reassuring, and he felt the tension in his shoulders relax a little. "But don't hesitate to call 111 if his temperature doesn't drop after you've given him this," she said, tapping the top of the box before putting it into a paper bag along with the receipt.

"I will."

Eric put his wallet away, thanked her for her help and hurried to catch up with Becca as she approached the door. He pushed it open for her and they stepped out into the fresh morning air. A stiff breeze was coming in off the sea and the cloudless sky saw bright early morning sunshine streaking between the high street's buildings and promising a pleasant, if chilly, day.

Becca didn't say a word as they walked the short distance to the car, whispering soothing words to George who, mercifully, appeared to have gone back to sleep.

"She said to call 111 if his temperature doesn't come down after taking this," Eric said, holding the bag aloft like a trophy as he unlocked the car and opened the rear door for Becca to gain access to the child seat.

"Well, we'll be phoning 111 as soon as we get home, Eric."

He was confused. "But she said—"

"And I don't care what *she said*, Eric. I want him looked at by a professional."

"A pharmacist is a professional."

"Oh, please!" Becca, hunched in the rear of the car having drawn the seat belt over and connected it, looked up at him with disdain. "Filling bottles with tablets and dispensing emergency lip balm does not make you a professional. I think a doctor is preferable, don't you? You know, someone who studied medicine for more than a term. Fair enough?" she asked, holding out her hand. Eric looked at it, then made eye contact before realising she was asking for the medicine. He took it from the bag, opened the box and passed her the small bottle and a syringe. "How much should I give him?"

In the rush to seek medical help, Eric had forgotten to put his contacts in. Holding the box at arm's length, he tried to read the print. It was impossibly small.

"Eric?" she asked, irritation in her voice.

"2.5 ml," he said at last, "no more than four doses in a twenty-four-hour period."

He rested one hand on the roof of the car, watching as Becca carefully drew out the measure and slipped the end of the syringe into George's mouth. He accepted it and seemed to like the taste. It was strawberry flavoured and Eric guessed it had a fair bit of sugar in it. If it worked, then he didn't care.

Eric heard an excitable shout from some distance behind him. He looked over his shoulder to see a group of men rounding the corner, coming from St Edmund's Terrace, and crossing the road in front of the bus station towards him. He felt his chest tighten.

"Well, if it isn't *politically correct Collet!*" one man shouted, much to the amusement of several others. Eric looked away.

"Who's that?" Becca asked under her breath, taking the box from him and putting the medicine bottle and syringe inside. Eric shook his head, stepping back to allow her to get out of the car.

"No one. It doesn't matter."

The group came closer. Eric could see they looked slightly the worse for wear and seemingly intoxicated through drink or drugs, more likely both, seeing as they were still full of energy at 9 am on a Saturday morning. Dressed as they were in clothes to hit the town, they must have been on it all night.

"Not in uniform today, Constable?" the first, and loudest, newcomer asked him as Eric opened the driver's door. Becca glanced across the roof of the car from the other side as she got in, keen not to engage with the party.

Eric sniffed. He should just get in the car, but he felt challenged and to back down was to lose face. He'd done enough of that.

"I'm not in uniform anymore, Jonny. I'm a detective now."

He spoke with confidence. With pride, puffing out his chest. The group responded with a chorus of derisive catcalls.

"We'll have to come up with a new nickname then, won't we?" Jonny said to his friends, two of whom nodded along.

Still surrounding himself with sycophants, Eric thought.

"*Dim Constable Collet*. How's that?"

Eric glared at him.

"Eric!" Becca called from inside. He ducked down to look at her. "Let's go."

"In a sec—"

"No. Now, please!"

Her tone wasn't harsh, more concerned. Eric frowned, glancing up at his tormentors. It wasn't the first time he'd come across them and had to hear their nonsense. It was far worse a while back on a Friday night when the pubs closed, and he was on duty policing the town. Although, he'd barely come across them since he'd left uniform and joined CID. He should be unaffected by it, unfazed by their jibes, and maybe on a normal day he would be, but today wasn't a normal day and their attention – the disrespect – bothered him. Something in his expression must have conveyed his anger because Jonny, the de facto leader of the group, as he'd always been, pursed his lips and quietened the others down.

"Don't mean anything by it, Eric lad, you know that," he

said, looking at the baby in the back seat. George was starting to grizzle again. "Your boy, is it?"

Eric nodded. "Yes. He's not well."

"Shame. I guess that's what happens when you play it safe, marriage, career and kids and all that. Me and the lads have been on a cracker. Just heading home now. I know which I'd rather be."

"Congratulations." Eric wasn't sure what he was supposed to say. He didn't really want to say anything at all. Jonny appeared annoyed. What did he expect, to be lauded for the achievement of a night out?

"You look shattered, mate," Jonny went on. "At least we've had the night before to ruin us, hey boys?" The others cheered, celebrating their experience, and then jeered Eric with artificial joviality. "We're off home to bed. Maybe I'll pop in and see the missus first, who knows?"

"Yeah, well..." Eric said. He'd had enough now and regretted engaging, wishing instead he'd done as Becca requested straight away. "Nice to see you boys again." It was far from a heartfelt statement.

"Hey, Eric," Jonny said as he made to get into the car. He looked at him. Jonny flicked his left hand towards George in the back seat. "You let me know who knocked her up and I'll take care of him for you!"

The group laughed as if it was the funniest comment in the world. Eric felt anger and frustration in almost equal measure, but he said nothing and got into the car, swiftly closing the door, a little too hard as it happened which set off George towards another level. At least now, the laughter was muted.

"Oh, Eric, do be careful," Becca said. "Who were they anyway?"

He shook his head again, drawing his seatbelt across him.

His hands were shaking, his chest tight, and he gripped the steering wheel so hard the whites of his knuckles showed.

"Eric?"

"Just... the idiots from school. Nothing to bother about."

"School was a long time ago."

He sighed. "For some, yes." He met her eye, then shook his head. "It looks like they haven't exactly moved on since graduating either."

"Nice bunch," she said, reaching across and touching his leg supportively. He smiled at her. The group had moved off up Westgate, crossing the road in front of oncoming traffic and cheering as the drivers sounded their horns in irritation at the road being blocked by their crossing. The action only seemed to make them more vocal.

"Muppets," Eric muttered under his breath. "Let's go home, yeah?" he said, looking in the rear-view mirror and adjusting it to see George. His mobile rang before Becca could answer. It was Tom.

"Hi, Tom, what's up?"

"Eric, sorry to do this but I need you in."

Eric looked across at Becca and he could read her expression. She knew what had been said without needing to ask. Her kind, supportive expression dissipated, and her demeanour darkened.

"Uniform are at the scene of a suspicious death and by all accounts it's looking like a murder."

"Righto," Eric said as casually as he could, already thinking of what he would say to Becca.

"I'll text you the address. See you soon."

The call ended but Eric kept the phone against his ear as if he was still listening. He could feel her eyes burning into the side of his head.

"Yes, I understand," he said, frowning.

"Eric, I heard him say goodbye."

"Oh... right. Sorry. I have to go in."

"So, I gather. Is it too much to ask for you to have a weekend off?"

"I'm on call. You know I am," he protested, sensing her reaction was about to be delivered with full fury.

"This bloody job..." she said, shaking her head and staring straight ahead. George began to wail.

"It'd be worse if I was in uniform. I'd be working almost every weekend the way numbers are these days."

"Well, at least we'd know and could plan for it," she said. "I suppose I'll have to manage on my own now then. You could have told Tom that George was ill."

Eric looked over his shoulder at George. "The pharmacist wasn't too worried. It's not serious—"

That was the wrong thing to say. Becca glared at him.

"I mean, he's ill... which is serious, but you know..."

"No, Eric. I don't know! When did you graduate from medical school exactly?"

He took a deep breath, knowing that whatever he said next would only lead to another outburst.

"Look, I'll take you both home... and I'll call 111 and see what they say. If they think it's serious— if he needs to see a doctor, then we'll sort something out. I won't just leave you to it. Tom will understand. Maybe your mum could come over?"

"No," Becca said flatly.

It was true, their relationship had been strained of late. Becca's father split from her mother when she was young and then remarried. This left Becca with a foot in two familial camps, one large through one parent who went on to have a second family whereas the other remained very small. The close bonds of the large group meant everyone pitched in and helped, offered advice whether it was desired or not, and the other, smaller group largely took care of themselves. Becca felt more comfortable with the latter, resisting her mother's advances to help which Becca repeatedly saw as intrusive.

"Okay, well... we'll sort something out." Eric reached across with his left hand and touched the back of hers. She withdrew it from his reach which saddened him. George was in full voice now.

"Just... drive, would you?"

Eric turned the key in the ignition and pulled away.

CHAPTER TWO

VICTORIA AVENUE in Hunstanton was a narrow residential street, lined on either side by a mix of Victorian terraces, semi-detached and detached properties. Few of them had off-street parking which exacerbated the issue regarding the width of the road leading to cars parked bumper to bumper. During the traditional workday much of them were gone, but this day, Saturday morning, the majority of residents were still at home.

Eric had to park on neighbouring Northgate, a wider road with larger, more imposing properties. Rounding the corner, he saw several curtain twitchers observing proceedings from their front rooms whereas others, concerned locals and no doubt a handful of friends, were milling around the police cordon, little more than a uniformed constable and a line of tape across the short path leading up to the front door.

PC Marshall stood stoically at the gate, professionally batting away inquiries from anyone who asked. He spotted Eric's approach, greeting him with a grim smile as they met, and the two men stepped out of earshot of those gathered.

"Hey, Eric."

"Morning." Eric looked beyond the constable towards the house, indicating it with a tilt of his head. "What's the score?"

"We had a call this morning from a local carer doing her daily visits. Kerry and I found her inside. She's pretty upset."

Eric frowned. "Is it bad?"

Marshall shrugged. "Seen worse... a lot worse! The DI is upstairs with the body, in the front bedroom."

He looked over his shoulder and Eric followed Marshall's gaze up to the large bay window above them overlooking the street. One of the curtains was drawn aside allowing light in. Eric took a deep breath and entered the house.

The entrance to the house was much as he expected. From the size, Eric presumed it was a two-up, two-down with the kitchen at the rear. The stairs rose from the hall directly in front of the door and he cast a quick glance along the hall towards the kitchen, but no one appeared to be downstairs. The floorboards squeaked above him, and Kerry stepped into view on the half-landing at the turn of the staircase above him. She smiled, but it was artificial and forced, in stark contrast to the rest of her expression.

"Hi Eric. We're up here."

He made his way up to her. PC Kerry Palmer turned and stepped up onto the landing, where he joined her. She gestured towards the front of the house and Eric saw movement in the front bedroom, guessing it was Tom.

"You look tired," she said, eyeing him with apparent concern.

He smiled. "George is unwell, he's not been sleeping."

"Oh, I see. Nothing serious, I hope?"

Eric shook his head. "No, just the usual colds and whatnot that children pick up in nursery and stuff. He'll be fine."

"Is that all?" she asked.

He met her eye, trying to read the question behind the question. If there was one.

"How do you mean?"

"Just... you look... sad." Kerry smiled supportively. They'd been friends for years, passing through training together.

"I do?"

"Yes," she said, touching his forearm. "It's in the eyes. You can't hide it there."

Eric looked away, suddenly self-conscious, feeling himself flush.

"I'm sorry. I didn't mean—"

"No, no. Don't worry," Eric said. "I'm just tired." He gestured to the front bedroom and stated the obvious to change the subject. "The DI through there, is he?"

First donning a set of forensic gloves as a routine matter of course, Eric eased the bedroom door open, and DI Tom Janssen glanced over at him standing at the threshold. His gaze lingered on him momentarily.

"Everything all right, Eric?"

Eric exhaled. "Yes, why does everyone keep asking me that?"

His tone was perhaps sharper than he intended, and Tom shouldn't be the one at the point of the rapier.

"Do they?" Tom asked, perplexed.

"Sorry," Eric said, feeling sheepish. Tom waved the apology away and Eric's gaze was drawn to the bed where a young woman lay. He was struck by how young she was, most likely a similar age to himself, mid-twenties perhaps. The angst of the morning forgotten; Eric looked around.

"Tell me what you see, Detective Constable," Tom said, attracting his attention. "Walk me around the scene."

Eric took a deep breath and examined the room. His

tendency in the past was to speak too soon, engaging his mouth before his brain had finished calculating. He waited, clearing his mind, much as Tom had taught him.

There was no obvious sign of disturbance in the room; no broken glass, items discarded on the floor or anything that appeared to have been used either as a weapon of attack or one of self-defence. A dressing table was set in front of the window. It was old style, from what period he couldn't tell, but certainly one that he figured would belong to someone much older than a woman in his own generational range. Various toiletries were standing upon it, all laid out in front of a set of mirrors, three of them with the outer two attached through hinges. The dresser was untidy but that looked like the normal state rather than the result of anything untoward.

"No sign of a struggle," he said aloud. Tom agreed.

Eric eased open a door on the wall opposite the bed. It was a cupboard space being used as a wardrobe. The space was narrow and chock full of clothes, both on hangers and neatly folded on shelving. Two stacks of shoe boxes rose from the floor, but Eric chose to leave the exploration of those to the crime scene technicians when they arrived. Turning back to face the room, he approached the bed.

Tom was standing off to one side, observing Eric intently. The woman, little more than a girl in his eyes, lay on her back on the bed, atop the duvet with her head resting on two pillows. The bed linen was white, or off-white, ivory might be more apt, and it was clean with no staining of blood or anything else as far as Eric could make out unless hidden by the body. There was a small side-table, with one drawer and storage alcove beneath it, at the head of the bed. A half-empty glass of water was set down beside an old book; the edges of which were dog-eared, the spine so damaged the title and author's name were now illegible. The lamp standing upon it was on, casting a bit of light over the body.

"Was this light on when uniform got here?"

"I believe so, yes."

Eric looked on the floor, but he couldn't see anything. Leaning around, he peered down the back of the side table. "What's this?"

Tom came around to see, evidently he hadn't spotted it, and was curious but he couldn't get close enough. The space was too tight.

"What is it, Eric?"

"A bottle. Prescription meds by the look of the label. The lid's off though. It looks empty."

"Okay, better leave that for Scenes Of Crime to look at. Can you read the label?"

Eric shook his head. He turned to the woman lying on the bed.

Standing up, he moved closer, examining her. She was brunette, with hair hanging to her shoulders, straight, and he guessed that was helped by the application of straighteners. Becca's hair looked similar when she'd made herself up to go out for the evening and he could see the signs. Hair wasn't naturally that straight. It had been a while since they'd been out, mind you. Pushing thoughts of his wife aside, he cast an eye over her body. She was fully clothed, wearing a long red dress that carried past the knee. Eric would class it as an evening dress, not quite figure-hugging but stylish. It looked classic or vintage. The material had a sheen of velvet to it and was thicker than anything he'd ever seen Becca wearing, and he considered her choice of outfits to be of higher quality than the average. Not that he knew a great deal about such things.

The dress wasn't low cut or particularly revealing, with two thin straps looping over her shoulders. She was made up, but not overly so. Her lipstick was a close match to the colour of her dress, and he glanced at her feet, half expecting to see matching shoes but she wasn't wearing any. Her feet were covered by tights, or stockings, he couldn't tell. Returning to her face, she looked so serene, as if she was sleeping and Eric couldn't see any injuries to her features. Her arms were bare and uncovered, and here Eric found bruising between the elbow and upper portion of her right arm. He quickly looked across at the other arm and nodded. Glancing at Tom, he gestured to them.

"Indicative of force," he said quietly.

Tom nodded. "When?"

Eric looked again, biting his lower lip, deep in thought. The bruising was a deep colour, literally blue through purple and into black. Whatever inflicted them had been done some time ago.

"Two, maybe three days," he said, meeting Tom's eye for approval.

"I'd say so, yes. Anything else?"

Eric frowned, glancing around. "It all looks... normal."

"Doesn't it just," Tom said with a nod.

"Too normal."

"How do you mean?"

Eric's frown deepened and he cast an eye around the room once more.

"Don't worry. It's not a trick question," Tom said.

"It's just... so well presented," he said. "No sign of a struggle. The room is clean and as tidy as you might expect. It's far tidier than my place... and yet..."

"So, why do you think uniform called us in?" Tom asked.

"The bruises... her age?" Eric shook his head. "Cause of death?"

"Which you think might be?"

Eric exhaled heavily, looking around. "Without the empty bottle of pills, I'd be stumped... Do you think it might be suicide?"

Tom Janssen tilted his head to one side. "That's a bit of a leap at this stage, wouldn't you say? But keep it in mind."

Kerry appeared at the door, waiting patiently. Tom nodded to her.

"I've brought her in, sir. She's downstairs in the kitchen."

"How is she?" Tom asked.

"Still shaken... worried."

"We'll be right down," Tom said. Kerry smiled and left. "Unless there's anything else you can think of to note, Eric?"

Eric felt a pang of anxiety. He knew Tom wasn't putting him on the spot, but at the same time he wanted to show he was up to the job and suddenly he was fearful there was something he'd missed. He still didn't know why uniform would call CID in to see this one.

"No... I don't think so. Is that... okay?"

"Yes," Tom said. "You did well."

Eric felt relieved. "So, why did uniform call us in?"

"The carer found her."

The penny dropped for Eric, and he looked back at the bed. *Why did she need a carer?* He couldn't see anything wrong with her. Tom placed a hand on his shoulder and steered Eric out of the room and along the corridor. They stopped at the entrance to the second bedroom and Tom nudged the door open. Eric looked in.

It was far narrower than the main bedroom, sharing almost half of the property's width with the bathroom and the landing. Evidently it was a child's bedroom. A little girl's. The far wall had unicorn wallpaper on it, although it was peeling at the corner where it met the exterior wall and the ceiling. Eric spied some black mould growth in the area, and he could smell damp, now that he'd tuned in his senses. A bed was placed beneath the window overlooking the rear. There was a raised guard on the one side to prevent someone rolling out and falling to the floor and it looked as if the bed itself could be raised to elevate the occupant into a seating position if desired. To the side was an adjustable table, similar to those found in hospitals that could be wheeled in and out of place to help a patient with eating.

A chest of drawers was just inside the door and on top of it was a lot of medical paraphernalia, the likes of which Eric had largely never come across. There were contraptions with plastic cylinders attached to tubes and pumps alongside various packages, boxes of disposable aprons and gloves. Eric saw an oxygen bottle leaning against the wall beside the bed. A tube led to a mask with an elasticated strap that lay on the carpet. On the end of the bed was an assortment of cuddly toys, a bear, a blue dinosaur and a panda among others.

"The carer was here to see her?" Eric asked, aware that the question didn't warrant an answer.

Tom nodded.

"And where is she?" Eric asked.

"I don't know. And that's why we're here."

The front door opened and the sounds from outside carried in. Cars were manoeuvring around one another. It would appear scenes of crime were here along with the forensic medical examiner, all of whom were struggling with the nature of the access.

"Hello, Tom!"

They both looked down to see Dr Fiona Williams climbing the stairs to join them. She was already wearing her white disposable coveralls and carrying her medical case.

"Good morning, Fiona."

"Forgive me for already having covered up. I understand this is a lost cause."

"Yes, I'm afraid so," Tom said, glumly. "She's cold. I reckon she died sometime in the early hours—"

Dr Williams touched Tom's forearm as she came alongside him on the landing.

"I do so love you dearly, Tom, but perhaps you should leave the medical analysis to me."

Eric smiled, despite the grim nature to their all being present. The doctor was only teasing the detective inspector, he was quite sure.

"The tax on your car is up to date, is it?" Tom asked with the hint of a smile.

Fiona Williams winked as she passed him. "This way is it?" she asked over her shoulder, puffing and panting at the exertion of carting her kit up the stairs.

"I'll be downstairs," Tom called to her, and she waved with her free hand, not looking back, "keeping out of your way."

CHAPTER THREE

TOM LED Eric into the kitchen where Kerry Palmer was sitting around a small circular dining table in the corner next to the door leading to the rear garden. Opposite Kerry was a woman, most likely in her early thirties and dressed in a light blue uniform denoting her as a home-carer. Her mousey-brown hair was scraped back from her forehead and tied in a bun, loose strands escaping in all directions. She looked pale, more so than just a result of her natural complexion. It was more likely to be shock. Her eyes were red and looked sore. She'd obviously been crying and was still clutching a screwed-up tissue in the fist of her right hand.

Upon hearing them enter, Kerry stood up, gently tapping the woman's hand as she rose. The woman acknowledged the gesture with a forced smile and a brief nod of thanks.

"Sir, this is Katie Watkins," Kerry said to Tom who smiled at the woman seated. She returned it but it was fleeting, and she wiped at the end of her nose with the tissue trying to steady herself. "She was the first to arrive this morning and found Scarlett upstairs."

"Scarlett?" Eric asked.

Kerry nodded. "Scarlett Turnbull. She lives here with her daughter, Maggie."

Katie looked up at Eric, recoiling from him, eyes wide. Tom looked at Eric and realised she'd noticed the forensic gloves that he hadn't removed yet. He inclined his head down at Eric's hands and the detective constable turned away and took the gloves off, quickly stuffing them into his pockets behind Tom's back.

"Hello, Katie. My name's Tom," he said, slipping into the seat Kerry had just vacated. She pursed her lips, trying to smile again but failing. Tom was well aware of his own physical presence and being well over six feet in height with a body mass to match, he knew he could be intimidating, and he wanted to set the woman at ease. Usually, he preferred to give the first people on the scene a bit of time to settle before questioning them, but something told him in this case he didn't have the luxury. "What time did you arrive this morning, Katie?"

She took a deep breath. "A little after nine. I was supposed to be here between half eight and nine, but I was running late." She looked at him apologetically. "I had to drop my eldest at his football match before I could come over and... people wanted to chat. When I got here... I–I... found Scarlett upstairs."

She looked down at the table, wringing her hands as she spoke.

"It's okay, Katie. Take all the time you need," Tom said as reassuringly as he could. "How did you get in?"

Katie looked up at him, her eyes brimming.

"I mean, was the house unlocked? Was the door open?"

She nodded vigorously, her eyes drifting to the back door. "There's a side access gate to the garden from a path that runs along the back of the houses in the street."

Tom glanced out of the window. The garden was narrow and not deep with a fence running the full width at the foot of the space. He saw the gate at one side.

"The street outside is always packed, especially on the weekend," Katie said. "You can never get parking, so I park on the next road and come in the back way. Scarlett leaves the door unlocked unless she's going out and I let myself in." She looked up, fearful that she'd done something wrong. "It's what we've always done, pretty much since I started caring for Maggie."

"And Maggie is Scarlett's daughter?"

She nodded, wiping her left eye with the back of her hand and sniffing hard. She proceeded to fondle the tissue with both hands in her lap. "She's one of my regulars. I come in most days to help."

"What support does she need?"

"Maggie or Scarlett?"

"I was thinking of Maggie, but..."

"Oh, they both need my help in one way or another," Katie said, shaking her head. "Don't get me wrong, Scarlett is an absolutely wonderful mum... she dotes on that little girl like nothing else I've ever seen. Maggie is her entire life as far as I can see, but it's hard for her, so, so hard."

"What is... wrong – sorry, terrible choice of word – the nature of Maggie's condition?"

Katie sank back in her chair, shaking her head. "The poor thing. She has so much to cope with... needs round-the-clock care. I'm not a doctor, obviously, but Scarlett had multiple issues during the pregnancy. Maggie was premature and spent weeks in an incubator. I don't think she was given much hope of survival, but she's a real fighter that one. She made it. The knock-on effect for her has been a struggle though, hence why they need me."

"Maggie has ongoing problems?"

"I'll say so, yes," Katie said. "She was starved of oxygen in the womb, hypoxia I think they call it, and was born with cerebral palsy, the extent of the associated brain damage only becoming apparent as she grew."

"I see." Tom glanced at Eric. "I'm not familiar with the effects. Can you elaborate a little for me, please?"

"I can... but her symptoms are quite extensive. Maggie has trouble with muscle control, eating, language and communication skills... is prone to seizures... has only about twenty percent of her visual acuity and has trouble eating along with the subsequent processing of her food. She is a handful; I can tell you. But she is also one of the most affectionate, wonderful children I am privileged enough to work with," Katie said, her face lighting up as she smiled warmly. "She's a delightful little girl." The smile faded.

"How old is Maggie?"

"Seven. Although she looks much younger. She's small for her age which is unsurprising bearing in mind her condition."

Tom took the information in, weighing it carefully. He could see a wheelchair in the next room which was probably a dining room but now doubled up as a playroom judging on the coloured pictures on the walls and toys he could see on the floor.

"How mobile is she?" he asked.

Katie raised her eyebrows. "On a good day, she can scribble some crayons on a piece of paper or hug her cuddly animals... that sort of thing." She looked at him intently. "Is that what you meant?"

"I was wondering if she would be able to leave the house under her own steam?"

Katie shook her head. "No, I very much doubt that."

"Besides yourself," Tom said, "who else does Scarlett have

in her support network? Any family or Maggie's father perhaps?"

She scoffed. "The father? No, I think he's out of the picture entirely from what I can gather."

"Do you know him or have his name at least?"

"No, sorry. I can't help you there. Any time he came up in conversation with me, Scarlett always referred to him as *the sperm donor*. She has her father, though. Alan. He's lovely, very kind. I've met him here quite often. He lives in town. Nearby, I think but I couldn't tell you where."

"That's okay. We'll find him. Do you know if Scarlett was dating or had any close friends who might shed some light on her life?"

Katie thought hard, her brow furrowing. "I think she had been dating recently but we're not close enough to share that kind of stuff really. I know she's good friends with a lass across the way there," she said, gesturing randomly through the walls with a wave of her hand. Lives at number thirty-two. Joanne, I think her name is."

Tom made a note, nodding his approval. "Was there anything that stood out for you when you arrived this morning?"

"How do you mean?"

Tom shrugged. "Anything unusual. Anything that might have struck you as odd or out of the ordinary, however small it might seem."

Katie blew out her cheeks, looking around. "I suppose I found it unusual that Scarlett wasn't up and about... but I soon found out why." Her head lowered and she fought back tears.

"I understand," Tom said quietly. "I know this is difficult, but even the slightest observation could help us."

Katie nodded. "I know. I'll try." She steadied herself,

letting the damp tissue drop into her lap and then she rubbed at her cheeks with the flat of her palms. Exhaling, she drew another breath and let it out slowly. "The house is... tidy. Much tidier than I usually find it." She looked around the kitchen. "Particularly in here, I must say. Often, Scarlett will wash up from the night before while I'm bathing Maggie upstairs. Then we'll have a cup of tea once Maggie is settled into the playroom, watching her morning cartoons." Her eyes adopted a faraway look as she seemingly remembered an image, smiling. "She loves her morning cartoons does Maggie."

"But it was all clear this morning?"

"Yes, all done, which I think is odd, now that you mention it."

"Why?"

"Well, yesterday, Scarlett was really upbeat. She said she was going out. It was the first time in ages she'd mentioned actually going somewhere."

"Was it a date? With her boyfriend perhaps?"

Katie shrugged. "No idea. But... she was a bit weird about it."

"Weird how?"

Again, she didn't know and shook her head. "I couldn't say. I don't even know where she was planning to go. She was a bit coy. I'm sorry, that's probably not very helpful, is it?"

"No, on the contrary, it is very helpful. Did she say if she was going alone, or was Maggie going too?"

"Didn't say either way, but if Maggie was going then I very much doubt it was a date."

Tom thought of Scarlett lying on the bed upstairs, the dress, the make-up. She looked as if she'd been on a date to him.

"Has Maggie ever stayed over at anyone else's home do you know?"

Katie shook her head. "I doubt anyone would be able to cope. I know Scarlett has been in touch with a local charity who do offer to have people come in overnight to provide support. This then gives the parent an opportunity to go out for the evening or away for a night. I'm not sure if Scarlett ever took them up on the overnight stay or not. I doubt it, though, to be honest."

"Why would you say that?"

"I don't know really. I don't think Scarlett was the type of mum who would entrust Maggie's care to anyone else. At least, not beyond a few hours or so. Certainly not for the whole night, no matter how stressed she was in managing everything. She would have mentioned it, I'm sure. Scarlett loves – loved – that little girl so much. Like I said, she was her whole life."

Tom could recognise the passion Scarlett must have had for raising her daughter. Katie was evidently impressed and that was something a person could fake but only for a brief period. The reality would shine through in the end, and he had no reason to doubt Katie's analysis.

"So, you were here yesterday. Was that at the same time?"

"A little earlier," she said, nodding. "The children head out to school at eight and I'm on my way shortly afterwards."

"And how was Scarlett when you were here, apart from excited about her night out?"

"Oh, I wouldn't say she was excited exactly... it was more that she was looking forward to it, but I wouldn't say she was skipping around the room or anything."

"My mistake," Tom said, smiling. "How was she?"

"Well... I would say. Much improved."

"Improved? Has she been different previously?"

"Oh yes. She's been finding it hard. Not that she complains to me, but I see enough people on a daily basis that I can see through the veneer, you know? You must find that in your job?"

Tom bobbed his head. "True. So, she was... what? Upset before? Tired?"

"Definitely tired. Maggie doesn't sleep particularly well. She gets a lot of pain in her muscles and is often uncomfortable, which leads to a poor night quite regularly... for both of them. There is medication, but... drugs can only do so much, can't they? And Scarlett wasn't one to pump her child full of every medication going just for the sake of it."

"So, she was struggling?"

"Yes, I think so," Katie said before raising a hand and shaking it, fearful of having said too much. "Not that she wasn't doing right by Maggie, you understand—"

Tom held up a hand to reassure her. "Don't worry. That's not how I took it at all. You would say she was strained? Is that fair?"

"Yes. Strained. That's very apt."

Raised voices were heard coming from outside and all of them turned towards the front door. Figures could be seen moving beyond the obscured glass inset on the door panels. Kerry Palmer made to leave the kitchen and Tom indicated for Eric to go with her and the two picked up the pace to see what was going on outside, the muffled voices seemingly growing ever more tense as the seconds passed.

Katie looked past Tom and when he turned to her, she was concerned.

"I'm sure it's nothing to worry about," he said but she wasn't convinced, which intrigued him. "Is there anything else you'd like to add at this point, Katie?"

She was hesitant.

"Anything at all?"

She bit her lower lip and then shrugged off her reticence. "The bruises. You saw the bruises, right?"

"We did, yes. Do you know how she came by them?"

Katie shook her head and Tom thought it a genuine response.

"No. But… I don't think it was the first time. I've seen them before."

"On Scarlett?"

"Yes… but I swear I don't know who was responsible. I did ask her once."

"And what did she say?"

"Brushed it off." She sat forward in her chair, leaning towards Tom. "But it was the way she did. I've seen it before. I recognise the look."

"The look?"

"The look of someone desperate to keep it from others… what's going on, I mean. You hide it, bury it… and dismiss others' concerns when they raise it."

"You're speaking of domestic violence… spousal abuse?"

"I am." Katie sank back, but she held Tom's gaze and her eyes gleamed with defiance. "Believe me, I've been there. I've seen the look in the mirror many, many times and I know what I saw in her face. You hide it, lie about it and hope people stop asking questions. It's a cycle that is so, so hard to break."

Any further conversation between them halted as Kerry re-entered the house through the front door, a concerned look on her face. Tom smiled at Katie and asked her to stay where she was and he got up, heading into the hall to meet the PC.

"I think you should come outside, sir. It's all getting a bit heated and… everyone's watching."

CHAPTER FOUR

STEPPING out into the warm sunshine, Tom was confronted with an unpleasant scene. A man was attempting to force his way past the gate and up the path, currently being restrained, albeit with minimal force, by PC Marshall with Eric's assistance. The man's temper was fraying, his cheeks were flushed, eyes wide and he was determined to pass them. Despite repeated attempts at engagement, he was hell bent on reaching the house and had no truck with any form of conversation. The gathering locals were watching on in a mixture of bemusement and horror.

"Now, what's all this then?" Tom said coming to stand before the three men, pushing and shoving.

"Let me in, damn you!" the man said, attempting to free his right arm from the uniformed constable's grip. It didn't work. Both PC Marshall and Eric had a firm hold of him and they were both half the man's age and perhaps more. He was a tall man, slim, with a thinning shock of white hair wafting back and forth on the stiff morning breeze. He was in no mind to relent. "I said... let me through!"

Tom made eye contact, the simplest and most effective

communication tool at his disposal. Once he'd garnered the initial engagement, he was able to calm the situation down and try to speak with him.

"Sir… I'm Tom, Tom Janssen. If you could take a moment to breathe and then we can—"

"I want to see my daughter!" he yelled, but the anger didn't match his posturing. The exertion of the brief struggle seemed to have taken a lot out of him. He was breathing heavily, his breath ragged.

"Your daughter lives here?" Tom asked.

"Yes," he said quietly as Tom gestured for Eric to loosen his hold. He did so and Tom saw realisation cross Eric's face. This was Scarlett's father. "I want to see my daughter."

In the man's current state of mind, there was no way Tom was going to allow him into the house but, at the same time, they couldn't talk outside in such close proximity to the community. Not only could it compromise the investigation, but it was unfair on the man for him to share such anguish in public.

Tom held the man's gaze as he tried to look past him towards the house.

"Alan, isn't it?"

At mention of his name, Scarlett's father focussed on Tom, nodding.

"I've just been speaking to Katie about you," Tom said, glancing over his shoulder, "inside. She said you're a kind man."

Alan Turnbull's expression softened ever so slightly, the anger dissipating to be replaced with a mix of fear and trepidation. "I just want to see my daughter."

"Alan!"

Tom looked to his left, a young woman was crossing the street and coming over to them, pressing her way through the bystanders. She looked between Tom and Alan, nervously.

"I'm sorry, I didn't see you arrive, or I would have come out sooner," she said, gripping the man's upper arm supportively as she came alongside him. Eric let go and PC Marshall did the same. Alan visibly shrank at the connection with someone he knew. He looked into her eyes, his own brimming.

"They won't let me see her," he said quietly, his voice cracking.

She looked at Tom, desperation in her eyes, nodding and squeezing Alan's arm that bit tighter.

"Can I ask who you are?"

"Joanne..." she said, forcing a smile. "I'm a friend of the family... of Scarlett's."

Alan's head sank at mention of his daughter.

"I see," Tom said, looking around, keen to get them all away from the watchers. "Do you think we could speak in private?" Joanne looked at Scarlett's house but something in Tom's expression conveyed they wouldn't be going in there and he guessed she knew why.

"We could go to mine," Joanne said, pointing at a semi-detached house on the other side of the road.

"That'd be great, thanks," Tom said, gesturing for her to lead the way. Alan Turnbull allowed himself to be guided and they moved off. In the meantime, Tom leaned in towards Eric. "You go with them, get him settled down and I'll be across in a minute."

Eric nodded and trotted after the couple, joining them as they met the pavement on the far side of the road. He offered to hold the gate open and Tom saw Joanne lead them into her home. Once the door closed behind them, he turned away, left PC Marshall to assume the management of the onlookers and went back inside with Kerry. She went through into the kitchen where Katie Watkins was sitting patiently. Tom took the stairs two at a time up to the landing and hovered outside the bedroom as Fiona Williams turned to him, her coveralls crinkling as she crossed the room to join him.

"Was that a relative?" she asked, indicating towards the window with a nod.

"Father."

She sucked air through her teeth, grimacing. "That's a shame. I'm sure that's not how you prefer to meet the next of kin."

Tom shook his head. "Certainly not. Other than him walking into this very room, I can't think of a worse situation. I know you've not been here long, but I'm keen to hear anything you have prior to speaking to the family and friends. Sorry for being pushy."

She waved the comment away, looking at the clipboard in her hands and reading through her notes. "Not at all, Tom. I'll give you the obvious; no signs of a physical altercation, no defensive wounds, blood, cuts or such like."

"What about the bruising?"

Dr Williams paused. "Two to three days in the making with that level of discolouration. By the angle of them, I wouldn't be surprised if someone had taken a hold of her and given her quite a violent shake, a strong person no doubt, but not contributory to her death. At least, not directly."

Tom understood her meaning. The same person could very well have been involved with her death, but they would be two separate instances.

"By saying *not directly* are you viewing this as suspicious?"

"Absolutely I am, yes."

Tom was caught a little off guard by her directness. He looked at the body and then at the doctor inquisitively. He too

hadn't seen any defensive wounds, considering Eric's suggestion of a suicide as quite plausible. Dr Williams encouraged
him into the room and he came to the other side of the bed
where she leaned closer to Scarlett's body. With the tip of her
pen, she pointed to the eyelids.

"They are masked by the eyeshadow, foundation and the
running of the mascara, but if you look closely, you can see the
petechiae; the small spots, no larger than a pin head, caused
by the bursting of the capillaries beneath the skin. Hidden by
her make-up, you can see the raised bumps—"

"She suffocated to death," Tom whispered, irritated with
himself for missing such an obvious indicator.

"You will have to wait for the pathologist's confirmation,
but that's my best guess, yes."

Tom cast his eyes to the ceiling, pursing his lips, before
searching the room with a different mindset, that is to say one
primarily looking for evidence of murder.

"Something as simple as a pillow would be my guess,
Tom," Fiona said.

There were no extra pillows cast aside but Scarlett was
lying with two beneath her head. Her arms were folded across
her stomach, her hands interlocked. Aside from the running of
her mascara and the smudging of her foundation, there was
nothing indicative of her struggling under the weight of
someone smothering her. Tom knew that the process wouldn't
be quick, it was an inefficient method of killing regardless of
what it looked like in television and film depictions.

"The poor girl," Fiona said, shaking her head. She looked
over at Tom. "It's always harder when they are so young,
isn't it?"

He nodded. "Can you estimate the time of death?"

"Sometime between midnight and two in the morning, I
should think. It won't be much either side of that."

"Eric noticed an empty bottle of pills down the back of the bedside cabinet. Did you spot it?"

"I did, but I can't see enough of the label to give you any information. I'm sorry. That will be one for the forensic fellows."

Fiona sighed, staring at the lifeless form of Scarlett on the bed. "It's a lovely dress."

Tom nodded. "We thought so."

"I wonder why she got into it?"

"Excuse me?"

Fiona read his confused expression and she waved her hand in the general area of the bed.

"It's odd that she got into the dress, especially if she was going to bed."

"Apparently, she'd been out for the evening."

Fiona scoffed. "Not in that dress she hasn't."

Tom's brow furrowed. She smiled.

"The material is absolutely lovely, high quality. It's a vintage piece, the dress I mean, and it still looks like it came off the rack yesterday, but I'll tell you this for certain, she wasn't wearing that out. It's immaculately pressed. Had she been out in the evening, wearing it just for a dinner date, then it would show."

Tom cast an eye over the body once more before meeting Fiona's eye once again. "You're sure of that?"

"Trust me, I'd know. This girl changed into that dress when she got home... or someone else did it for her." Fiona nodded forcibly as if to emphasise the point. "Mark my words. And if she was smothered until death, then someone took the time to put a brush through her hair afterwards, too."

"They presented her to the world."

"Maybe in the way he – or she, let's not be sexist – saw her.

That's my opinion, Tom," Fiona said, raising her eyebrows. "For what it's worth. You're the detective after all."

Tom gently stroked his chin, thinking through the permutations. He heard a vibration alert from a mobile phone, and he exchanged a glance with Fiona.

"It's not mine," she said. "I left it in the car."

"Not mine either," he said, looking around the room. They hadn't come across a mobile phone. Tom lowered himself down onto his haunches, scanning the carpet. He bent down and looked under the bed; a mobile could be seen in the shadows. He took a new forensic glove and used it to reach under and bring out the mobile. The screen was locked but still lit up with a text message notification. The number was visible and evidently belonged to someone not saved in the contacts list. The message was short and therefore entirely visible, reading *Thanks for last nite x x.*

The screen background was a shot of Scarlett with her arms around a smiling young girl, presumably her daughter, Maggie. The screen switched off, back to black and the image disappeared. Tom stared at the blank screen for a moment longer, acknowledging this was most likely Scarlett's mobile. He was keen to know who she'd been out with the previous night and wondered if this was the last person to see her alive, aside from, perhaps, her killer.

CHAPTER FIVE

PC Marshall stood aside allowing Tom to leave the property and cross the road to the neighbour's house where Eric was waiting with Scarlett's father. A car picked its way through the crowd which appeared to have grown while Tom was inside speaking with Dr Williams. At the end of the road he saw a van turn off Cromer Road and head towards them. It was an outside broadcast van judging by the small satellite dish mounted on the roof. *Word is travelling fast,* he thought, picking up the pace and approaching the house.

He rang the bell and waited patiently. Movement from beyond came a moment later and the young woman he'd seen step forward to comfort Alan Turnbull revealed herself. She didn't want to meet Tom's eye, averting hers from his gaze.

"Joanne?" he asked.

She nodded with a slight smile and fully opened the door, wide enough for him to pass. The hallway was narrow and very similar to Scarlett's house, although in place of a fitted carpet, Joanne had what Tom guessed were the original Victorian floor tiles arranged in a geometric pattern of blue and white.

"Alan and your detective constable are in the dining room," she said softly. "I'm really sorry, I didn't think."

Tom cocked his head. "Sorry? Think about what?"

She hesitated. His eyes narrowed as he looked upon her as she glanced back into the house as if she could see Alan and Eric in the back room.

"I called Alan... you know, once I heard what had happened. I thought he'd want to know..." She shook her head. "And I figured better coming from someone he knew rather than... well..."

"A policeman knocking on the door out of the blue?"

She nodded, grimacing. "Yeah... but if I'd known he'd react like that..."

Tom smiled. "Don't worry. You weren't to know." He lowered his voice. "How is he?"

"Shaken up, no end. Beside himself really." She folded her arms across her chest, hugging herself tightly. "Aren't we all?" She looked at Tom intently. "Is it true?"

"Is what true?"

"What they're saying outside," she said with a flick of her head towards the street beyond the door. "That Scarlett... that she's... you know, killed herself."

"Is that doing the rounds among the locals?"

"That's what they're saying, yeah. Is it true?"

"I don't think anyone can conclude that at this time," he said.

"That's just police talk for yes," she said.

Tom raised an eyebrow and Joanne backtracked.

"I mean, you see it on the telly all the time." She inclined her head. "Too early to say. Keeping all options open... and all that sort of stuff."

"We don't like to give much away, that is true," Tom said.

"But, in this case, it really is too early to say. Who told you Scarlett had been killed?"

Her face was a picture of concentration. "Morag… she lives at number fifty-six."

"And how would she know? Was she friendly with Scarlett at all?"

Joanne laughed, but the humour faded very quickly.

"She heard it from Davey," Joanne said. Tom gestured for her to continue. "Davey Bullen. He's her neighbour. He hangs out with Scarlett sometimes… or he used to at any rate."

"Did they fall out?"

Joanne appeared reticent, avoiding Tom's eye. He didn't let up though, allowing the silence to hang until it became uncomfortable for her. She shrugged.

"Davey… has a certain lifestyle that… well, it doesn't fit well with single parents and," she scoffed, "certainly not single parents of kids with special needs."

"Were they an item?"

"No, I don't think so. They went way back to their school days as friends. I have the impression Scarlett was pretty wild back in the day, but she's calmed down a lot since then. Had to, I guess."

"Because of Maggie?"

She nodded, a glum expression fixed on her face. "Poor Maggie. Where is she now?"

Tom stared at her.

"I mean, who's looking after her." She looked over her shoulder. "Alan's here, so… who's got her?"

"We can talk about that in a bit, if you like, but for now," Tom said, reluctant to give her the information until he'd had a chance to pick her brains. "When did you last see Scarlett?"

"Oh, last night. I was babysitting for her while she went out."

Tom was surprised. "I see. Is that something you do for her often, look after Maggie?"

Joanne shook her head, relaxing her arms a little but they remained crossed. "I mean, I would do it more if she wanted but she didn't tend to go out very much. Sometimes she'd go for a walk along the seafront for an hour or so, just to clear her head. I'd sit with Maggie and watch cartoons and whatnot. Lovely little girl. My husband works shifts, and he was work-ing, so I had nothing else to do anyway and Maggie usually sleeps for the first part of the night without issue. It's only in the early hours where she plays up." A look of horror crossed her face and she reached out a hand and grasped Tom's fore-arm. "I'm sorry, that sounded awful. I meant that she suffers more later in the night and the pain wakes her up... not that she's a problem as such—"

"That's okay don't worry. Who was Scarlett out with last night and do you know where they went?"

"No, sorry. She never told me," Joanne said, disappointed. "I thought she might be on a date... she was all dolled up."

"To go dancing... or out to dinner?"

"She had a little black number on, eye shadow and lashes to match. She looked stunning... and quite intimidating to most men I would say!"

"How was she around people, would you say?"

Joanne thought on it briefly. "Confident, although it was largely for show. She is quite a vulnerable little soul under-neath her outward projection of strength." She sighed. "I think she had to be quite bullish because of her daughter. That little girl wants for nothing if Scarlett could get it for her or if she was entitled to it. People would fob her off; you know how it is these days when you're trying to get what is rightfully yours, but she'd keep going if it was for Maggie."

"So, last night was something of a one-off?"

"Yeah, I think so. She texted me Thursday afternoon, just after lunch, asking if I could watch over Maggie for her. Like I said, the husband was working anyway—" She suddenly checked her watch. "Oh... speaking of whom, he'll be home soon and... he'll want to get to his bed."

"That's okay, we'll be out of your way soon enough."

"Thanks. He's a bit of a grump when he's been working nights and it's been a long week for him." She shrugged. "Mind you, with all of this, he'll probably struggle to get to sleep anyway."

"He was friends with Scarlett too?"

Joanne laughed but it was without any genuine humour. "No. They didn't like one another *at all*. Chris thinks Scarlett is a bit of a scrounger."

"Is she?"

Joanne waved the comment away. "Chris thinks anyone who doesn't work is a scrounger. Like, what's she supposed to do with little Maggie? She can hardly leave her at home, can she? It's a full-time job for Scarlett. I think Chris should stop spending his time on Facebook and the like. There are some proper weirdos on there with some very funny ideas, don't you think?"

Tom inclined his head. "Yes, social media really isn't my thing either."

"Oh, it's definitely mine, don't get me wrong. I just know decent people and Chris... well, his friends are all wallies!"

Tom smiled. "You say you thought it might be a date Scarlett was going on?"

Joanne nodded.

"Did Scarlett have a boyfriend that you're aware of?"

"She had been seeing someone, yes," Joanne said, her expression darkening. "I think it was off and on, by all accounts. *More off* the last time Red mentioned him."

"Red?"

"Oh, sorry. It's my nickname for Scarlett."

"Right. The boyfriend?"

"A bit rough to be honest. I've seen him coming and going, passed him once when he was leaving the house. Ignorant so and so. I don't know what she ever saw in him."

"Do you have a name?"

Her forehead creased in thought. "Jim something, I think. I heard her refer to him as Jimmy once, but I don't know his last name. Sorry." She tilted her head at Tom. "I expect you'll have him on file somewhere."

"You think?"

"I do. Proper layabout. Chris would hate him too, but at least it would be justified. I expect Davey up the road will know him. I've seen them speaking on occasion while on my way in or out of the house. I tell you, he's a surly piece of work." Her expression changed, a lightbulb moment Tom would call it and she snapped her thumb in the air, pointing a finger at him. "Not Jimmy... it was Jonny. Yes, that was it."

"Thanks. We'll look into him." Tom was almost done. Now he would have to speak to Scarlett's father. It was never a great experience at the best of times and now, having to do it like this, it would be even worse. However, he was sure Joanne had called him with the best of intentions. "One more question, if you don't mind?"

Joanne nodded. "Sure."

"What time did Scarlett get home last night?"

"A little after ten o'clock," Joanne said. "I was through the door myself before the news finished on the telly. I didn't stick around for a drink or anything. We had a bit of a natter in the hall, me telling her what Maggie had been like – which was lovely – and then I left."

"And she was alone?"

"Yes. She left the house by herself and came back alone as well."

"Right, and what was she like in herself?"

"You mean depressed and that?"

Tom shrugged. "Whatever comes to mind."

"She was in good spirits I thought. She was all smiles; said she'd had a fun evening. The best in months, she said."

"But not where she went or who with?"

"No. But she did call me during the evening to check on Maggie." She thought about it, cupping her chin with thumb and forefinger. "That must have been around eight, eight-thirty, I think. She didn't say where she was but there was music, and I could hear other voices in the background."

"Loud voices? Shouting? Drunk or happy?"

"General background noise, I would say. More like a restaurant or a busy pub than a club or gig, if that helps?"

"I should think so. Did she use her mobile?"

"Yes, she called from her mobile. She said she was having a good time but then lowered her voice and ended the call quite abruptly. Come to think of it, someone was shouting at that point."

"At her, do you think?"

"Ooo… um… I couldn't say for sure either way."

"No matter. But you think she was in good spirits when she arrived home. Had she been drinking?"

"A little, yes," Joanne said but was quick to add, "not too much, though. I could smell alcohol on her but I wouldn't say she was drunk by any means."

Tom smiled warmly. "It wouldn't be illegal if she was."

"No, I guess not. What I mean is, she was social, but I never once saw her drunk. Not ever. She had too much responsibility on her shoulders." She looked concerned. "What will happen to little Maggie now?" she asked barely above a whisper, clearly concerned Alan would overhear them.

"That... remains to be seen," Tom said. "And what time did Scarlett go out last night?"

"Seven o'clock, on the nose."

"Walking you said, right?"

Joanne nodded.

"Okay, thanks for the information. You've been very helpful. Perhaps you could take me through now?" Tom asked, holding out an open palm for her to lead him through the house.

"I'll see you in and then go and put the kettle on." She tilted her head towards the room, where presumably Eric was waiting with Alan Turnbull, listening. She still spoke in a hushed tone. "I think he's calmed down now. I'm afraid I wasn't much help to your colleague."

"I'm sure a familiar face was reassuring for Mr Turnbull."

"I think a cup of tea is in order, don't you?"

"You're very kind, Mrs...?"

"Lester. But please, call me Joanne."

The front door opened and a man entered. "What's with all that lot outside?"

He pulled up as he saw Tom, viewing him suspiciously. Joanne stepped out from Tom's shadow.

"Hello, love. This is a policeman—"

"Police? What's going on?"

He was still suspicious, but concern was evident in his expression.

"It's Scarlett, Chris. She's... she's died."

He stared at his wife, his lips parted, but there was no other reaction. Then his forehead creased and his left cheek twitched.

"Scarlett? Are... are you sure?"

Tom nodded. "I'm afraid so. She was found this morning."

"Well... can't say as I'm surprised—"

"Chris!"

He held his hands up defensively. "Just saying..."

"Why would you say that?" Tom asked, casually inspecting the man. He was big, not as big as Tom himself, but comfortably over six-foot. He was athletic with a powerful upper body. It was clear he visited the gym three or four times a week. There was no way he could have that physique otherwise. He had dark patches beneath his eyes but, if he'd been working night shifts all week, that was understandable.

Chris Lester looked apologetically at Tom, shrugging. "I don't mean much by it. It's just Scarlett... I've known her since she was a kid. Always seen her around town... and for it to end like this... I'm just not all that surprised."

"End like what?" Tom asked.

His lips moved but no words emanated from his mouth. In the end he shook his head. "Nothing... I'm just tired, that's all."

He averted his eyes from Tom's. Was that embarrassment or was he fearful of digging himself a deeper hole and afraid that he wouldn't be able to clamber out of it? Joanne was clearly disgusted with her husband who looked past her, peering into the kitchen at the rear.

"Any chance I can get my dinner?"

"Sorry, love. I haven't had a chance to make anything what with all of this going on. Alan's in the dining room with Eric."

Chris Lester frowned. "Who's Eric?"

"My detective constable."

"Ah... right. I'll just grab something from the fridge."

The couple exchanged a glance, Joanne staring hard at her husband before rolling her eyes. Chris shrugged.

"I've been at work all night."

"What is it you do, Mr Lester?" Tom asked.

"I work down in Lynn... maintaining the refrigeration at an agri-packer."

Tom nodded along as if he knew what that entailed whereas, in reality, he had no idea.

"Right, well don't let me keep you," Tom said. "We'll be out of your way as soon as possible."

"Okay. No problem... take as long as you need."

He looked at his wife once more as he slipped past them both and wandered into the kitchen.

"There's leftovers from last night's tea in the fridge if you fancy it," Joanne said. She smiled awkwardly at Tom. "Sorry. He's not the best straight after work anyway, and he was never a big fan of Scarlett, as I said."

"Not a problem," Tom said, allowing her to lead him through the house to the dining room. He glanced into the kitchen as he walked along the hallway. Chris Lester had his head in the fridge, rummaging through it. Something about him troubled Tom; perhaps the slightly callous manner with which he greeted news of Scarlett's death irked him. To be fair to Chris, the cause of death most people in a small town like Hunstanton would reach for was unlikely to be murder, but to assume an air of inevitability around her passing, especially at her age, was troublesome to Tom. Reaching for something to eat straight after hearing the news was also odd, even if he didn't like her.

CHAPTER SIX

ALAN TURNBULL LOOKED up as they entered and upon seeing Tom, he rose from his chair on the other side of the dining table. Tom gestured with a flat palm that there was no need to get up and Alan slowly lowered himself back down, both hands resting flat on the table before him.

"This is DI Tom Janssen," Eric said. Alan glanced at Eric and then back to Tom, smiling a weak greeting.

"Hello, Mr Turnbull," Tom said, drawing out a chair and sitting down opposite him.

"I'll make some tea," Joanne said to no one in particular and backed out of the room.

Tom smiled his thanks at her and she'd barely left the room before Alan sat purposefully forward and spoke.

"Inspector... where's my granddaughter?" His eyes searched Tom, desperate to hear positive news. "Where's Maggie? I need to see her!"

Tom gently held up a hand, appreciating his desire for news. "At this time, Mr Turnbull, we honestly don't know but I assure you, my team are doing, and will do, everything in our power to find her."

He held Tom's gaze, probably judging his sincerity above all else. He nodded almost imperceptibly, his shoulders sagging a little, the tension in his body easing if only slightly.

"To that end, I need to ask you a few questions, if you feel up to it... about your daughter and her life. Is that okay with you?"

"Y-Yes," Alan said, sniffing hard and touching the end of his nose with a shaking hand. "Anything I can do to help." He glanced sideways at Eric. "This... young man told me... that my daughter is..." He looked at Tom, lowering his shaking hand to lie flat on the other one on the surface of the table. "She's gone... isn't she?"

There was no way to break such news, the best way in Tom's experience was to be straight with people and not dance around the subject. "Yes, I'm afraid so."

Alan Turnbull swallowed hard, the whites of his knuckles visible as he squeezed his hands together and raised his eyes to the ceiling drawing breath and fighting back tears. He'd been holding everything in and despite Eric confirming Scarlett's passing, the gravity of hearing the news from the lead detective threatened to overwhelm him. Tom allowed him the time to process the information, to steady himself. Taking a deep breath, Alan lowered his gaze as he exhaled and bit his lower lip.

"What happened to her?" he asked quietly. "What happened to my little girl?"

Tom felt an emotional stab to the chest, images of Saffy coming to mind. How would he cope were he to wake up one morning and find she'd died during the night? Not when she was backpacking across hostile terrain or in the service of her country, but at home, alone in her bed where she should have the right to feel safe. Everyone should be safe in their own home.

Alan's eyes brimmed with tears; both his arms were now shaking as if the involuntary action was spreading throughout his body to the extremities.

"We are investigating Scarlett's death, Mr Turnbull, and at this time we believe it did not come as the result of a natural or accidental cause." He was careful to keep his tone clear and even, so as there would be no potential for misunderstanding.

"You are saying somebody killed her?"

"Yes. I believe that is the case."

Alan's head sank forward and for a moment, Tom thought he might be passing out, but he lifted his hands to his face and let out the most heart-wrenching of sobs. Tom noticed Eric turn his eyes away, dropping his head. Alan was wracked with sobs and Tom had to give him the time to let out the emotion. He was grateful for Joanne's return with a tray of mugs and tea for everyone. She set it down on the table and placed a hand on Alan's back, gently rubbing it supportively. He looked up at her, wiping the tears from his eyes with the heels of his palms. His cheeks were flushed, his eyes red-rimmed and hollow.

"I'm so sorry," he said. "I–I don't know what came over me."

His breathing was ragged, and Tom wondered if this was the right time, but with Maggie's whereabouts unknown, he couldn't leave this line of questioning until later.

"That's quite understandable, Mr Turnbull. I appreciate it's a lot to take in."

He nodded, drawing himself upright and taking a deep breath. His voice was now all but a whisper. "What can I do to help?"

Tom looked at Eric who took out his notebook.

"When was the last time you saw or spoke with your daughter, Scarlett?"

Alan smacked his lips and exhaled, thinking hard. "Yesterday. I spoke with her on the telephone…" he shook his head, "it must have been a little after two o'clock. I'd eaten a bit later than usual and the lunchtime news had finished a while before I called her, so yes, around then."

"And how was she?"

He shook his head, shrugging. "Okay… no, better than that, she was quite lively. I thought she was having a good day."

"How often do you speak with her?"

"I see her most days, Inspector," he said, sitting forward. "Maggie, you see. It's tough for Scarlett. Some days are better than others, but you never know what you're going to get with her, so we all take it one day at a time."

"You all?" Tom asked. He nodded. "Is that you, Scarlett… your partner and… Maggie's father?"

He shook his head emphatically. "No, it's just me and Scarlett." He lifted a hand along with a correction. "As well as the help we receive from Katie," he pointed to Joanne, "and others who are very supportive."

Joanne appreciated the compliment, looking at him sideways from where she'd sat down alongside him, smiling. He forced a brief smile at her before turning back to Tom.

"No, it's largely just the two of us. My wife passed away some time ago."

"I'm very sorry," Tom said.

"Thank you, but it was a long time ago. Scarlett was a little girl herself back then. Not much older than Maggie is now, I think."

At mention of his granddaughter, he raised a balled fist to his mouth. Joanne reached over and placed a hand on his other forearm, offering him a gentle squeeze.

"What of Maggie's father. Is he involved in her life at all?"

Alan's expression hardened. "Bloody reprobate that one. No good for anything, never has been," he sneered. "They're better off without him, both Scarlett and Maggie."

"So, he's not involved?"

"No! Absolutely not. He hasn't been around for years. Why do you ask?"

"We're just building a picture at this time, Mr Turnbull. Any and all the background we can gather will help us get to the bottom of this as soon as possible. What can you tell me about him?"

Alan shook his head, seemingly reluctant to speak of him but at Tom's insistence, he relented. "Tony. Tony Slater." Alan nodded in the direction of Hunstanton town, as if he was pointing to the man's house directly. "He lives in town. I see him around from time to time. Waste of space. A complete and utter waste of oxygen."

"How does he get on with Scarlett?"

Alan shrugged dismissively. "No idea. They have no contact anymore as far as I know. Haven't done for ages. Scarlett was no angel... in the past, you understand? But she cleaned up her act once Maggie came along... jettisoned the garbage that'd been hanging around her for the previous couple of years."

"You're referring to Tony Slater?"

"Yes, absolutely. He led her astray," Alan said, shooting Tom a fierce look. "Don't get me wrong, Scarlett was one to know her own mind, and by no means an angel, but when those two got together, bad things tended to happen. The best decision she ever made was getting shot of him when she did." Alan lifted a hand, wagging a finger in the air. "You know he went to prison shortly afterwards. That helped her no end, it really did. It got rid of him and gave her the chance to make things right."

"What did he go to prison for?"

"Drugs... selling, growing... whatever." He shrugged. "He was a nasty piece of work. Used to get pretty heavy with his fists, too." Alan sat bolt upright, putting his shoulders back. "If I was a few years younger, I'd have swung for him, I really would. The things he did... the things he put my daughter through."

"I see," Tom said. "And Scarlett has no involvement with him these days as far as you know?"

He shook his head. "No. Absolutely not. He was never interested in Maggie, and she knew they were better off without scum like him in their lives. Good riddance to him I've always said to her, even if that means I have to step up and fill the gap left by that... animal."

Tom caught Eric flinching at the last comment, hesitating as he noted down all that was said. Alan Turnbull had no love for Scarlett's ex and what he described made this man someone Tom wanted to speak to, bearing in mind the bruises on Scarlett's arms. Alan's anger subsided and he looked a little sheepish under Tom's watchful eye.

"I'm sorry."

"What for, Mr Turnbull?"

"It's... him... Tony," he said, shifting in his seat. "He brings out the worst in me. I shouldn't let him get to me, and the fact he does lessens me as a person."

"I wouldn't say so," Tom said reassuringly. "When people hurt the ones we love it is only natural to feel a reaction, to want to protect them."

"Yes, well. Even so... I'm sorry."

Tom shifted the conversation back to the present. "Are you aware of anyone else currently in Scarlett's life?"

Alan cocked his head. "A boyfriend?"

Tom nodded.

"No, there isn't."

He sounded sure but the text message received on Scarlett's mobile earlier suggested otherwise.

"Are you certain?"

Alan frowned. "Yes. At least, not that I am aware of. I don't see how she could have had the time. Little Maggie has been quite ill recently which has made things difficult... for all of us."

"Difficult? How?"

"Maggie has had trouble breathing, not for the first time, and she's been taken into A&E on several occasions. For all the good it does." He read Tom's quizzical expression. "Maggie's needs are complex, Inspector. It isn't fair to scold the emergency department doctors too harshly. They are neither trained nor experienced in her... condition to be able to help. Maggie would be shunted off to the Children's' Ward as quickly as possible and then bounced through the registrars and consultants who happened to be on shift at the time. Each and every one of them with a different take on what should be done. In the end, once she was stable, they would send her home where she was no longer their problem." He splayed his hands wide in front of him. "To be fair, what else could they do? In the end, it came back to Scarlett and myself to handle... with a lot of help from the likes of Katie and," he flicked a hand towards Joanne along with a warm smile, "and good friends in the community."

"What about friends, confidants? Is Scarlett close to anyone in particular?"

He shook his head. "Scarlett is..." his voice lowered "... was a popular little girl. She had such an infectious personality that people wanted to be around her, when she was on form anyway."

"On form?"

Alan looked glum. "She had her problems did Scarlett. Mentally. Emotionally," he said, shaking his head. "Nothing that required serious intervention from medical people as such, but she has always been troubled." He sighed. "You see, we lost her mother when Scarlett was very young and... I never remarried. I tried to plug the gap left by growing up without a mum in her life but, I guess, I didn't get over her mother's passing myself and made a spectacularly awful job of helping Scarlett to do so. I think that's why she ended up with the likes of Slater; taking drugs and numbing herself to the world, to her thoughts and feelings."

"Try not to be too hard on yourself," Tom said, recollecting his own experience of his father's premature death. "It's tough being a parent at the best of times, let alone when you're doing it by yourself and trying to process your own sense of loss."

Alan looked at Tom, appearing to be reading his face. "That sounds like the voice of experience."

Tom didn't wish to elaborate. "You were saying about Scarlett's popularity?"

"Yes, yes... she was. But the dark shadow that followed her everywhere she went would sometimes envelop her and she would become difficult, miserable and," he shook his head with a knowing smile, "that isn't what inspires people. Not at all. The friends drifted away, got on with their lives and she spiralled downwards into depression. I saw it happening yet I was unable to stop it. And, believe me, I tried *everything*, I really did. The people she spent the most time with were the same people she needed to steer clear of... and when she cleaned herself up, she did just that. I think she mentioned she'd been in touch with some of her old school friends in recent months... through social media and so on." He looked thoughtful. "I don't recall her saying they'd agreed to meet up or anything, but I know she was quite buoyed by that."

"Thanks. We'll look into her social media," Tom said. Alan's expression darkened and he looked fearful.

"Where is Maggie?"

"We are trying to ascertain that, Mr Turnbull. Is there anyone you can think of who Maggie might go to if she needed to—"

He scoffed. "Maggie couldn't go anywhere by herself!"

"Was there anyone who would offer to take Maggie, perhaps on short notice?"

"No, of course not," Alan said, dismissing the notion out of hand. "With Maggie's needs, she would have to be cared for at home. They couldn't even cope with her at the hospital, and they're medically trained. No, if anyone had Maggie, then they came to Scarlett's."

"And you can think of no reason for someone to collect Maggie, her father for instance?"

"No! Like I said, Tony Slater has had no interest in Maggie for the past six or seven years. Why would he show up now?" His eyes narrowed, staring hard at Tom. "That's the second time you've mentioned him. Do you think... he had something to do with this? Do you think that—"

Tom held up a hand. "No. We are just trying to understand the complexities of Scarlett's life, that's all. Every piece of information we have will help us to find Maggie as swiftly as possible, which is our immediate aim here."

Alan settled, bobbing his head. "I'm sorry."

"No need," Tom said. "I would be grateful if you could give DC Collet here," he glanced at Eric, "as much information as you can regarding who Scarlett spent time with: names, phone numbers if you have them, who had access to the house, to Maggie... anything at all."

"Y-Yes, I can do that," Alan said, looking at Eric. "You will find out what's happened, won't you?"

"We will do everything…" Tom said, sitting forward in his chair, "absolutely *everything* in our power to find Maggie as soon as possible and get to the bottom of this, Mr Turnbull."

The powerful intonation in Tom's pledge caused Alan to choke up and he offered his thanks, choking up as he spoke.

"C-Can I see her?" He implored Tom with his eyes. "I *need* to see my daughter… please."

Tom took a breath. "I will arrange it, but it will take some time."

Alan looked at the wall, as if he could see beyond it. He wanted to cross the road and see her immediately, Tom was certain. That wasn't possible. He would have to wait until after a forensic analysis was completed on the property and Scarlett could be transferred into the care of the pathologist and only then could an official identification take place.

"It would be later today, this afternoon or evening at the earliest, Mr Turnbull."

Alan visibly shrank before him, his head sagging into his hands. "I understand," he whispered.

"We will do it as soon as possible." Tom rose, glancing at Eric and offering him the vacated seat.

"Could I have a word first?" Eric asked, inclining his head towards the hall. Tom nodded and as they stepped out, Joanne sat down next to Alan, placing a comforting arm across his shoulder. He leaned into her, reaching for her hand. He squeezed it and began to cry.

CHAPTER SEVEN

"WHAT'S UP, ERIC?"

He looked back into the room, reaching for the handle and closing the door. Chris Lester was still in the kitchen munching his way through a sandwich and apparently scrolling through social media on the mobile phone lying on the table in front of him.

"Don't mind me," he said. "I'm off to bed in a minute."

Tom led Eric away, comfortable they wouldn't be overheard when they got to the front door.

"What is it?"

"I heard you chatting to Joanne," Eric said, "earlier, before you came into the dining room. She mentioned a potential boyfriend called Jonny."

"And?"

"I used to go to school with a guy called John – John Young – and he went by the name of Jonny."

Tom frowned. "It's a common name, Eric—"

"Yeah, yeah, yeah, I know... but he's the right age, local... and I saw him this morning."

"Where did you see him?"

Eric casually pointed a finger in the direction of Hunstanton town centre, barely a two-minute walk from where they were now. "And he'd been out on a bender last night. It was obvious."

"Did you speak to him?" Tom asked, still dubious as to the relevance but also acknowledging the coincidence shouldn't be dismissed.

"Yeah," Eric said, shrugging and then grimacing. "Sort of."

"Sort of?"

"As much as I ever spoke to him. Jonny was, and still is, pretty much a bit of a..." he hesitated "... of a wally."

"A bit of a reach, though, Eric. There's nothing to link him."

Eric was disappointed, and then he recalled the man's right hand. "Except he had fresh damage to his right hand."

"What kind of damage?"

"Scuffs, scratches... they looked fresh, too."

Tom was still unconvinced.

"Jonny Young, you say?"

Both of them turned to find Chris Lester standing less than six feet away leaning against the door to the cupboard under the stairs. Tom was annoyed with himself for not keeping their conversation private.

"Like I said, don't mind me," Chris repeated, picking a bit of food out from between his teeth. "But Jonny has been in and around Scarlett for the past couple of months. Seen him coming and going."

"Do you know him?" Tom asked.

He shrugged. "It's a small town. I know him enough to know I don't want to know him more, if that answers your question?"

Chris pushed off from the side, stifling a yawn.

"Now, can I get some kip or...?"

"By all means," Tom said, moving aside and allowing him to pass.

At the foot of the stairs, Chris stopped, looking sideways at Tom and shaking his head, said, "I never liked Scarlett, that's true, but she was a nice enough girl... just... I could see trouble following her around, you know? Mixing with the likes of *Rubber Jonny Young* would do little to make her life better, nor Maggie's for that matter."

He held Tom's gaze for a moment longer, then glanced at Eric, smiled in resignation, and set off up the stairs to find his bed.

Once he was safely out of earshot, for certain this time, Tom turned to Eric.

"Right, I'm going to call the DCI and fill her in on what we've got here. I'm going to need to raise as many bodies as we can and start going house to house; we have to search every garden, garage, shed... allotment... find every potential eyewitness we can." He looked up the empty stairs where Chris Lester had just gone. "He's right, this is a small town and someone must have seen or heard something."

"Right," Eric said. "I'll get as much as I can from her father."

"Good. Let him know I'm going to assign Kerry as family liaison. Reassure him we won't leave him alone to deal with all of this by himself."

"Will do."

Eric went back to the dining room and Tom stepped out into the sunshine. It felt warm on his skin and a good counter-measure to the darkness surrounding the new investigation. They had a missing girl to find, not to mention a killer. He hoped that the two weren't connected but, in his heart, he somehow knew they would be. Hanging around the front door, well away from the small gathering across the street, he took out his mobile and dialled Tamara Greave's number. An automated message proclaimed the number was unavailable and passed straight to voicemail. He sighed and left a message asking for her to call him back as soon as she could.

TAMARA GREAVE SHIELDED her eyes from the glare of the sun, angling her mobile away from the direct light and checking the reception coverage. No bars were visible, and the dreaded X struck through the icon confirmed her fears. The breeze whipped her hair across her face, and she swept it aside, tucking it behind her ear but the solution lasted a matter of seconds when she turned to look up the road from where she'd just come. The sunshine spread across the fields surrounding her as the clouds drifted by but there was no sign of civilisation. She was properly out in the wilds of Norfolk.

She hadn't seen another motorist in quite some time.

"My fault for taking the scenic route," she told herself.

Although the sun was out, and it was indeed a beautiful morning, the stiff breeze cutting across the landscape made the sweat on her skin feel cold. Leggings, a sports bra, and a loose-fitting T-shirt were a sound choice for her weekly, Saturday morning yoga class but certainly not the correct attire for standing at the side of the road.

Walking to the front of the car, a little steam still drifted up and away from the engine bay. She sighed, peering down between the grille and the radiator, hopeful of coming up with a solution she'd not yet considered. The pool of water at her feet, currently receding as it soaked into the mud and gravel beneath her, suggested that she had no card to play.

Leaning against the nearside wing with her feet on the embankment, built up against the hedgerow, she cursed.

Holding her mobile aloft in a vain hope she'd catch a signal, she bit her bottom lip. It didn't happen. Another car rounded the corner at the base of the rise, accelerating out of the bend. She thought about flagging it down but the pick-up of the engine suggested she'd never get in front of it in time.

Tamara moved, but the burgundy BMW sped past with the driver staring straight ahead, shifting through the gears and paying her no attention whatsoever. *Maybe Mum's right, and I'm approaching the top of the hill, if not quite over it,* she thought, watching the car crest the rise and disappear from view. Exhaling heavily, she calculated how far she was from the nearest telephone. There was a farm building in the distance, perhaps three miles or so away, but on the weekend would anyone be working there? She'd have to try it.

Standing at the side of the road, miles from anywhere, she realised that was the best option. Another car came over the hill, this one descending towards her at a more sedate pace. She turned to face the driver, taking a half-step into the road and raising her hand. The car slowed, the left indicator started flashing and the driver pulled up in front of her stricken vehicle. A man got out, and with a broad smile he approached her.

"Having a bit of trouble?" he asked, glancing sideways at the car, avoiding direct eye contact.

"A little, yes. I was hoping—"

"Yes, of course. I can take a look for you."

"No, no, I was just thinking—"

"What happened? Did she die on you or was there a give-away?" he asked.

Tamara cast an eye over him. He seemed genuinely interested in trying to help. He was fifty-something, slim for a man of his age but life was catching up on him, and he was a little taller than her but still well under six feet. Maybe five-nine or ten? His hair was cut close to mitigate the sparseness of foliage on top and what hair he sported was flecked with grey. This matched in his close-cut beard, speckled with grey and white flecks. He was dressed in a desert-coloured corduroy suit with a pale blue shirt beneath, unbuttoned at the collar; certainly not the clothing to be tinkering beneath the bonnet of any car, let alone one leaking water and burning oil at a rate of knots.

"Lovely car," he said, looking along the length. "Great condition. How long have you had it?"

Tamara shrugged. "A while now, but I can't take credit for the restoration."

She had purchased the car from a widower whose husband had laboured over the classic for years; a rare opportunity that she couldn't pass up. Still, it was nice for a stranger to recognise it.

"What is it, a Sprite?"

A flicker of irritation must have shown in her expression because his demeanour changed a fraction. This car was definitely not a Sprite and anyone who knew classic cars would know that.

"Guess not," he said, smiling awkwardly and glancing into the engine bay.

"It's a Mark III, Austin Healey," she said, internally chastising herself for being touchy where it wasn't warranted.

"Ah… yes, of course," he said.

The man had no idea. He was also apparently unwilling, or unable, to listen. Carefully placing his hands on the front wing, he peered into the bay, frowning. Tamara saw how he positioned himself so as not to get his palms dirty. Having decided to let her Samaritan do his thing, she decided not to let him know she'd already diagnosed the problem.

"So, she lost power all of a sudden?"

"Overheated," Tamara replied, unfolding her arms from across her chest and stepping back to reach into the car and take out her hoodie. Having cooled down, she was now feeling the chill.

"Right, I see. It might be... um..." he said, tentatively squeezing the top of the ignition leads connecting to the distributor.

"A hole in the radiator," Tamara said, trying to keep the condescension out of her tone.

He looked up at her, nodding. "Yeah, right." He stood up, surreptitiously checking his sports jacket and fingers for dirt, rubbing his hands together. "Not a great start to the weekend," he said, smiling apologetically. "Can I call someone for you?"

"Oh yes, that's a thought," Tamara said, smiling. "Please could I borrow your mobile because mine doesn't have signal out here."

"Ah... good point." He looked at his car, pointing towards it. "Let me grab mine and let's hope we're not on the same network." He walked back to his car and reached inside, gathering his mobile phone from the centre console. "Great news! I have a bar."

He held the mobile aloft, returning and passing it to her. Tamara thanked him, already searching the contacts list on her mobile for a number. She'd never been good at memorising mobile numbers. Who was? Tapping the number into his phone, she pressed the call button, putting the mobile to her ear and smiling gratefully at him. Her dad answered.

"Hi Dad, it's me."

"Tammy? Everything okay?"

"No, the blasted car has sprung a leak and overheated."

"That's a shame. Do I need to come and get you?"

"Please. There's a tow rope hanging in the garage."

"Right you are. Where are you?"

"Somewhere on Langham Road," Tamara said, looking

around for a notable landmark. There wasn't one, just fields and hedgerows. "Towards the Blakeney end I reckon."

"Okay, love. I'll be along as soon as I can."

"Thanks. Love you!" she said, hanging up and passing the phone back with an appreciative smile.

"Your husband on his way, is he?"

"Nope," she said, grinning. "No husband. Father to the rescue. It's like I'm seventeen again."

He laughed.

"Oh, to be seventeen again," he said. "It'd be great, wouldn't it?"

Tamara's instant reaction was *hell no!* She liked who and where she was in life and wouldn't want to revisit that period again.

"Not me," she said. "I'm sure I'd still make the same choices all over again."

"Even the bad ones?"

Now it was her turn to laugh. *"Especially* the bad ones."

He grinned, looking down at the car again. "This really is a lovely car."

"Yes, I love her," Tamara said. "Are you into classic cars?"

"Me?" He nodded, raising his eyebrows. "Absolutely, yes. I... like... um..." inclining his head at the car, he pointed with his forefinger.

"Austin Healey," she said.

"Yes, Healey. Definitely not a Sprite," he said bashfully.

She smiled. "You're not really into classic cars, are you?"

He nodded again before the action morphed into a firm shake. "Yes... no, not really. I'm not a car man at all... know nothing about them and I much prefer bikes, if I'm totally honest." He looked apologetic.

"Motorbikes?" She was intrigued.

"Heavens no. Dirty, gas-guzzling things like…" he indicated her car with his hand. Tamara found herself mildly amused. "Push bikes…" he blurted, "and not those mountain cross things or anything like that… he looked at her, interpreting her unenthusiastic expression. "Which, I appreciate, is rather dull to…"

"A petrol head?"

He flushed. "I wasn't going to say that, necessarily."

"That's okay." She waved away his embarrassment. "I agree… broadly. Besides, I don't know how long I'll be able to keep this on the road. Every time they change the fuels we can buy, it adds another nail in this one's coffin," Tamara said, stroking the car with a light touch.

"Sounds like she is a part of your family," he said. "Like one of your children."

"No children either," she said, beaming.

He flushed a deeper shade of red. "Well, I'm just knocking them out of the park this morning, aren't I?"

This time, they both laughed. He checked his watch, tutting and chewing his bottom lip.

"You're late for something aren't you?"

Taking a deep breath, he nodded. "Yes, I have a thing… at Blakeney Harbour Room and," he frowned deeply, "I was already running late."

"Took the scenic route, hey?"

"Yes," he grinned, "exactly that. Where were you off to?"

"I had my class… yoga," she said.

"Fitness instructor? Well, you're obviously in shape." Tamara raised her eyebrows at the comment and his face reddened. "No… I meant you *must* be in shape if you're a fitness instructor. Not that… I'm… looking—"

"It's okay," she said, putting him out of his misery. He was embarrassed. She saw fit not to correct him having no desire to tell him what she really did for a living. "You don't have to stay. I'll be fine."

"Of course, yes. I didn't doubt it," he said.

Her tone was sharper than intended. There was something about the chivalric notion of saving a damsel in distress that had always bothered her. Fiercely independent, she was in no need of a chaperone.

"But I do appreciate the gesture...?"

"David," he said in answer to the intonation. "And you are very welcome...?"

"Tamara."

He offered her his hand and she smiled as they theatrically shook hands.

"And you're sure you'll be all right."

Tamara leaned forward ever so slightly. "Yes, I'm absolutely certain I'll be fine. I can take of myself."

"Good, good," David said, clicking his tongue on the roof of his mouth nervously and looking back at his car. "In that case, I'll... erm... be off." He gestured towards his parked car with a thumb over his shoulder.

"Thanks again for stopping."

He smiled, taking a couple of backward steps before turning and striding to the car. Before getting in, he turned to the watching Tamara. "It was a pleasure," he said, rather awkwardly. For a moment, he hesitated, and Tamara found herself wondering where he was going which was strange because she didn't know him at all, so why should she care.

"Enjoy your thing," she called after him.

He stopped, part way into the car, looking back at her as if he was about to speak. He didn't. Instead, he shot her a brief smile before getting in and shutting the door. The car gently pulled away, David waving casually out of the window, and Tamara felt a little disappointed she hadn't engaged with him further. After all, any man who could freely admit he knew less about cars than a woman he'd never met was a rare find indeed.

Incredibly, the mobile phone in her hand beeped with a voicemail message notification. She glanced at the screen where she could see the slightest network coverage was visible.

"Miracles can happen," she told herself, looking down the road as David's car disappeared around the bend.

CHAPTER EIGHT

TOM JANSSEN WALKED into the ops room with Eric a half step behind. DS Cassie Knight was powering up the computer on her desk and greeted them as they entered.

"You cost me a day out on the water," she said, shifting some paperwork from her desk to clear space to work.

"Sorry about that," Tom said.

"That's okay. I wasn't keen anyway. It's Lauren who has the water wings in our house. Growing up on the coast I should imagine. Quite frankly, I'd rather keep the old terra firma under my feet."

Eric looked at her quizzically. "Isn't Newcastle on the coast?"

"Aye, but it's a proper city, you know? The sea is for looking at, maybe a bit of surfing if you're on a hen do or something, but you won't find me or my family out on the water with sails and the like."

"Shame," Tom said. "You're missing out. There's nothing quite like it."

"Nothing quite like drowning either," Cassie said absently. "No, a shower or, at a push, a bath is about as far as I'll go."

"What's wrong with having a bath?" Eric asked.

Cassie sipped from her takeaway coffee cup. "What's wrong with spending a half hour lying in your own filth? Nothing, I guess. If that's your thing."

"Well, sorry to ruin your plans," Tom said with feeling, "but we have a missing seven-year-old girl to find, and her mother's been murdered."

Cassie shook her head. "That's cold. Kill the mother and take the child? Are we working on the assumption the girl's been abducted?"

Tom shook his head. "No assumptions. From my reading of the scene, the victim, Scarlett, wasn't able or willing to put up a fight. Fiona reckons she was asphyxiated but with no indications of a ligature or even bare hands marking the skin, her best guess is the use of a pillow or similar to smother her."

"Didn't fight back?" Cassie asked, surprised. "Maybe she was already unconscious. Once their life is under threat, I've come across times when even the most timid and tiny people have fought like demons to stay alive." She inclined her head to one side. "Not that it did 'em much good like, you know?"

"I think you're on the money, Cass," Tom said. "Scenes of crime are working it and once they've catalogued everything then we'll have Scarlett transferred to pathology. The tox screen should help determine if she was out of it when she was killed."

"What if the killer used GHB?" Cassie looked up at Tom. "Do we have a time of death because date-rape drugs disappear from the system pretty quick."

"Sometime between midnight and two in the morning, so we should get an answer on that."

Tom glanced up as Tamara entered behind them. She was still dressed in her leggings and hoodie.

Cassie raised her eyebrows at the DCI. "I know it's dress-down on weekends, Boss, but..."

Tamara pointedly examined her detective sergeant.

"I've had one hell of a morning, Cassandra, and it may very well be getting warmer, but you are still on thin ice. Trust me."

Cassie lifted her coffee cup once more, hiding her smile. "I'd find a new yoga teacher if I was you. It's supposed to be cathartic and relaxing."

Tamara glanced sideways at her and the look was enough to stop Cassie in her tracks and she slowly swivelled her chair around to face her own desk, breaking the eye contact.

"Problems?" Tom asked, barely above a whisper.

"No. It's all good, don't worry." Tamara ran a hand through her hair. She really wanted to take a shower now. "Can you bring me up to speed?"

"Sure. We have a twenty-seven-year-old murder victim, single mother, lived locally with her daughter. The latter has special needs, limited mobility and linguistic skills, and hasn't been seen since late last night when the babysitter left."

"Okay," Tamara said. "Are we in an abduction scenario here?"

"Quite likely, but we haven't been able to establish a motive yet," Tom told her.

"We've already spoken with the daily carer who visits the house along with the babysitter – a friend and neighbour – and also met with the victim's father."

"Already?"

Tom sighed. "Hunstanton's a small town. The babysitter called him once word was going around."

Tamara rolled her eyes. "Terrific. How is he coping?"

"About as well as you might expect."

"That bad?"

"Yes. I've assigned Kerry Palmer as family liaison for the duration. I figured that would be okay."

Tamara agreed. "Good call. Main focus has to be to find the daughter?"

"Absolutely. After I couldn't get hold of you earlier, I spoke to the Chief Super and he agreed to cancel all rest days over the weekend and put as many bodies into the town as possible knocking on doors. We've got extra numbers coming from King's Lynn to support us along with anyone spare from along the coast."

"Great. Where are you with that?"

"Hunstanton-based uniform are already knocking on doors, but I think we need someone out there on point for CID, relaying anything useful back to us," Tom said, gesturing to get Cassie's attention. "I had you down for that, Cass. When the reinforcements arrive, we can widen the door to door and have teams picking through the street looking for any sign of which way Maggie went or who might have taken her."

"No problem, I'm on it," Cassie replied.

"Good," Tamara said. "Any chance this is a self-solver?"

Nine times out of ten, a murderer was often found to already be in the victim's sphere, be they a family member, spouse – present or former – friend or acquaintance. If so, then this case would likely be wrapped up within a couple of days.

"We have people to explore, certainly," Tom said. "Scarlett, the victim, was most likely out on a date last night. She had a text message come through while I was standing over her body, thanking her for last night, whatever that referred to. The number wasn't stored in her address book."

"Met someone that night?"

"Maybe, but the babysitter was of the opinion she was heading out on a date."

"Maybe the date was awful and she hooked up with someone else?"

"Well, we know she arrived home just after ten o'clock, alone, and in a fit state. She was content by all accounts. There was no reason to think she'd had a bad night. It would have taken some doing to go out with one guy—"

"Or girl," Cassie said, piping up without looking up from her desk.

"*Or girl*, yes, thank you DS Knight," Tom said.

"You're welcome," Cassie said quietly.

"But to then ditch the date and pick up someone else and be home around ten. That would take some doing."

Tamara nodded her agreement. "Okay, get onto the service providers and find out who that number belongs to and have a technician assigned to get into her mobile just in case some jobsworth at her service operator starts quoting data protection or other such nonsense."

"The request is already in," Tom said. "I raised it myself."

"What about the child's father? Is there an angle there?"

"Apparently, he is a waste of space, criminal record around drugs, both taking and supplying. Eric's pulling his file as we speak. Although he's not involved in Maggie's life nor her mother's, according to Scarlett's father."

"Perhaps he's had a change of heart?" Tamara said. "The father? What's he like?"

"Decent, caring... in something of a state of shock," Tom said. "Unsurprisingly. The carer and the babysitter say he is very involved in their lives, attentive. He raised Scarlett as a single parent after her mother died at around the age his granddaughter is now. I got as much as I could out of him earlier, but we can talk to him again later. Once he's home and in his own surroundings, we might get more out of him."

"Agreed. Has Kerry taken him back there?"

Tom nodded.

"So, if she was out on a date with your mystery texter, can we assume she wasn't seeing anyone regular?"

Tom grimaced. "According to the father, she had no time for dating—"

"Parents are always the last to know. My mum still thinks I used to visit the library two evenings a week when I was fifteen."

Tom smiled. "I do not want to know what you were up to instead."

"No, it would damage the view you have of me," she said, returning the smile. "Can I take it you've been given an alternative reality? One the father is unaware of."

"Yes. She's been knocking around with a guy called Jon Young."

"Do we know him?"

Tom indicated Eric. "Old school friend of our detective constable's, I believe."

Eric approached them. "*Friend* would be pushing it, but we were at school together. He was a bit of an... well, he had a high opinion of himself, that's for sure. Cocky... arrogant. Always thought he was something special. Still does too, I reckon."

"You and he are still in touch?" Tamara asked.

Eric was pensive. "No, not exactly."

"Then, what exactly?"

"I see him about from time to time. He's still lording it over people, but we're not at school anymore. He had the street cred back then, one of the cool kids; popular, funny, the girls loved him and for the life of me I still can't understand why."

Cassie coughed. "Yeah, why don't high-school girls like short guys who are interested in history and trees?" She shook her head, tipping her cup in Eric's direction. "It's a mystery, Eric. It really is."

He sneered at her which only sought to broaden the half-smile on her face into a grin.

"The bad boys always win at high school, Eric," Cassie said. "They have danger about them. They're guys their mothers and fathers wouldn't want them dating... although the mothers will understand why. Of course, by now they either married their own bad boy, who rapidly went from interesting to fat and irritating within a decade, or they're divorced... and she's subsequently realised the error of her ways and found herself a short guy with a stable job." She tilted her head towards Eric, smiling. "Maybe even one who talks to trees."

Eric shook his head. "There's nothing wrong with wanting to save the environment for future generations."

"Quite right, Eric... and there's nothing sexier, believe me," Cassie said, wagging a pointed finger in his direction. "All joking aside, the point is that bad boys are fun, exciting. But by the time they hit their mid to late twenties, believe me, the novelty has worn off and most of those girls you went to school with wouldn't touch them with a ten-foot barge pole. And most will regret they ever did."

Tamara cleared her throat. "Fascinating as this little insight into teenage relationships is, Eric, what can you tell us about this Jon Young now?"

"Not a lot, to be honest," Eric said. "I see him around, but I try to avoid him. That's not hard because he usually steers well clear of me as well, before and since I joined the police."

"Does he have a record?"

"Petty stuff... he was nicked for joy riding back in the day. He must have been seventeen. As I recall, he got probation and a community service order for that one. Prior to that he was a ringleader in a shoplift-to-order scheme he had going on with a couple of his friends; noting down what people wanted and then they went round the shops lifting it all. That was cautions all round. The parents were onto the school about it," Eric said, smiling at the memory. "As if the teachers had the ability to stop that sort of thing. Jonny's dad was a local estate agent back then, considered himself pretty special. Apparently, he was down at the station hammering his fist on the counter demanding to see his son. I can't imagine where Jonny got his sense of entitlement from."

"And now? What's he been up to?" Tamara asked.

Eric leafed through his notes. "Four years ago, he was arrested and subsequently cautioned for a breach of the peace; a domestic that spilled out into the street. A drink driving conviction from two years ago, his second in four years; banned from driving for twelve months with a further six penalty points added when he got it back... but aside from that, nothing. I'm not surprised. He was always a bit heavy-handed around school and college, quick temper and not afraid to lash out first and sort out the consequences after. I can also tell you he was a couple of streets away from Scarlett's place this morning. I saw him myself when Becca and I came out of the chemist with George. He looked like he'd been on an all-nighter with his mates."

"Is everything okay," Tamara asked, "with Becca and George?"

"Yes, more or less," Eric said. "That's a point, I said I'd check in with Becca and see how they're getting on." He looked at the clock. "I said I'd do that an hour ago."

There was a tinge of fear in his voice.

"Once the briefing is through, make the call, Eric. Family comes first." Tamara thought hard. "Mr Young sounds like a charmer. And he's been knocking around with Scarlett?"

Tom nodded. "According to Chris Lester, husband to Scarlett's friend, Joanne, yes. Definitely worth a conversation with him as soon as we can, but I don't see how the abduction angle plays into it. What reason would he have to take Maggie?"

Tamara frowned. "Let's have a word with him and take it from there. Eric, you were looking into Maggie's father?"

"Yes," Eric said, turning back a page in his notebook. "Anthony Slater, goes by Tony. He is well known to us. Scarlett's father, Alan, was bang on with his memory. Tony was sent to prison for possession with intent to supply. He was quite the player locally in the distribution of Class B drugs; notably cannabis, mephedrone and amphetamines. Remember that spell when the rave cultures of the nineties had a bit of a revival? Events were popping up in barns or fields in the middle of nowhere, off the back of a bit of social media?"

Tamara shook her head. "Might not have spread to the West Midlands."

Tom recalled. "It was a thing around here for a while, supposedly an urban underground music spreading out of London; largely a handful of individuals making it look grass roots in order to make a few quid. It wasn't popular with locals or landowners. I think they were trying to spark a new Glastonbury type of event. Didn't last."

"Well," Eric continues, "Tony Slater was in and around those events. He had quite an operation going on and the judge cited him as a major player in the industry in his sentencing comments."

"How long did he get?"

"Seven years but he only served four," Eric said. "Reading between the lines, he offered up a few names in exchange for mitigation. He's been out for eighteen months, so plenty of time for him to come across Scarlett again."

"Is he living locally again?" Tamara asked.

"Yes. I have his address here," Eric said, waving his notebook in the air. "I've left a message for his probation officer, but she hasn't got back to me yet."

"Are you comfortable speaking with Jon Young, Eric?"

He shrugged. "Why shouldn't I be?"

His answer was spiky, and Tom saw the DCI was taken aback.

"No reason, Eric. I'm thinking your previous relationship with him might be useful. If I speak to him, he may put his guard up whereas with you, he could be more forthcoming."

"Yes, yes of course," Eric said.

"But you're not going alone—"

"I'll go with him," Cassie said. "I know you want me coordinating the search, but I can go with Eric and he can drop me off afterwards." She looked at Eric. "He lives in town, doesn't he?"

Eric nodded. Tamara glanced at Tom, and he agreed.

"Right, the two of you head off," Tamara said. "Tom, can you—"

"Speak to Scarlett's ex, the father and gauge his reaction. If we don't get some traction on finding Maggie," Tom asked, "at what point do we use the media?"

Tamara grimaced. "I hate using the cameras in that way… often it leads to inaccurate leads and every jilted lover with a grudge calls in to point the finger at their ex. It could do more harm than good."

Tom sighed. She had a point. "But…"

"This evening," she said, her reluctance obvious. "If we haven't got a concrete lead on her by five o'clock, we'll use the media. Fair enough?"

He inclined his head. "Fair enough."

CHAPTER NINE

Traffic in and around the town centre was building. Despite the wind coming in off the sea, the sun had brought the shoppers out and Hunstanton was gearing up for the coming season. Eric brought the car to a stop, leaning over into the passenger seat to see out of the passenger window and up to the flat occupied by Jonny Young.

"It's flat Fourteen B," he said, pointing up at the top floor of the imposing stone semi-detached building. In its heyday, these two properties would have been owned by wealthy local merchants or businessmen but now the buildings were far too large to be used by the average local family, four stories plus a fifth in the basement, and with very little garden space. That was common with Victorian properties in Hunstanton, built on narrow plots but spanning multiple floors. Parking was also precious, and these two buildings had enough space for two, maybe three cars at a push down the side.

At some point, an entrepreneur had purchased both townhouses and split them into flats. The buildings had lost their grandeur over the years falling into the most basic level of repair, far from their original glory. No doubt the landlord was making a pretty penny and would one day cash in on the capital asset. That day might not be far off bearing in mind the rise in property prices over the previous ten to fifteen years as the north Norfolk coast continued its resurgence.

"Thank you, Eric," Cassie said, looking down at Eric whose head could easily be described as encroaching into her personal space. "And I can probably tell you what you had for breakfast this morning by the state of what's stored between your teeth."

He looked at her blankly. "Say again?"

She gently placed two hands on his shoulders and eased him back to the driver's side of the car.

"I can smell your toothpaste, Detective Constable."

"Ah... too close?"

"Definitely."

"Sorry."

"Come on," Cassie said, popping the door open.

"We can't leave the car here," Eric protested. "It's on double yellows."

Cassie was on the pavement by now, adjusting her coat. She looked back at him. "Eric, we're the police. We can park where we like whilst on official police business."

"But—"

"I'll see you up there, then," she said, closing the door.

Eric muttered a curse under his breath and got out, locking the car and hurrying after Cassie. He caught her up at the foot of the steps up to the front door. The basement flat had metal grilles on the windows to deter burglars, but Cassie couldn't help but think they might be there to keep the occupants in.

"Fourteen, you said, right?"

"B," Eric said.

Cassie pressed the intercom and the buzzer sounded. She

waited less than a second before giving it three more blasts in quick succession.

"In a hurry?" Eric asked.

"I see no harm in riling him up a little, do you?" For added measure, she hit the buzzer again, holding the button in for an inordinate amount of time, released it and repeated the action twice more. "It really is a terrible sound."

The intercom crackled.

"All right! Bloody hell, someone better be dying out there!"

"Good morning, Mr Young," Cassie said in a cheerful tone. "We're from Norfolk Police. May we come up and speak with you please?"

The intercom was still active, but Jonny said nothing for a moment, then he pressed something and the door clicked allowing them to enter.

"Amazing," Eric said.

"What is?"

"You can be quite nice to people when you want to be."

"Aye, well, they sent me on a course for it and everything," she said leading the way inside.

The shared lobby was empty, dark and had a strong aroma of damp hanging in the air. The bright sunshine barely penetrated the gloomy interior, giving the impression it was an overcast day, and the tiled floor was grubby. It couldn't have been cleaned in months, if not years. Cassie looked around, stepping forward and glancing up the stairwell to the floors above.

"Geez... I've forced entry into derelict squats that were in better condition than this place."

A door opened somewhere above them, the sound echoing through the building.

"Door's open!"

They exchanged a glance and Cassie offered Eric to go first with an open hand.

"You heard the gentleman; the door's open."

Eric huffed and set off up the stairs, each tread shrieking under his weight.

"So, you and this Jon go back a way then?" Cassie asked, lowering her voice, as they wound their way up.

"Yeah. Can't stand the bloke though, to be honest. Never did get on with him at school."

"Well, don't let it cloud your judgement when we speak to him."

"I won't," Eric said but Cassie wasn't convinced.

"You're doing the talking, remember."

Eric didn't reply but she was sure he'd heard her. Jonny Young's place was on the top floor, a small apartment tucked into the eaves of the vast building. Reaching the landing, they saw his door was ajar and Eric knocked gently as he pushed it open.

"Hello!" he called.

"Yeah, you can keep the noise down. I'm right here," Jonny said, standing in the doorway to his kitchen and watching them enter. Cassie saw his gaze linger on Eric, looking him up and down. "Shoulda known it'd be you. Honestly, you still can't take a joke or what, Eric?"

"Hey Jonny," Eric said.

Cassie noted a hesitancy in his tone. Eric was far more assertive these days, but he was sounding like the Eric of old, or at least last year when she first transferred from Newcastle.

"No, it's nothing to do with this morning," Eric said. Then he stammered. "Well... not about this morning when I saw you... you know—"

"Bloody hell, spit it out will you," Jonny said. "I got things to do today you know."

Cassie looked past him into the kitchen. It was a right state. It looked like her student accommodation at university, a shared house with three other girls, all of whom didn't care much for clearing up after themselves. But they'd been teenagers. This guy was a grown man.

Jonny walked across the narrow corridor linking all the rooms of his flat and into another, beckoning them to follow. Cassie's nose wrinkled as they entered. Foil takeaway cartons lay on the floor next to the sofa and from the lingering smell there were fish and chip papers somewhere too. Jonny sank down onto the sofa, a dark brown two-seater that must be hiding a wealth of stains from the human eye.

"Mind if I let some light in?" Cassie asked, crossing the room to the solitary window and adjusting the blind. Sunlight streamed in and Jonny shielded his eyes with the back of his hand, swearing under his breath.

"Yeah, I do actually! I was sleeping before you woke me up and—"

Cassie turned on him, taking in his appearance in natural light. His pupils were dilated and very obvious despite his raised hand before his face. She exchanged a knowing look with Eric. There was no way he'd be sleeping anytime soon.

"We need to speak to you about your relationship with Scarlett Turnbull, Jonny."

"Scarlett?" He looked surprised, then shrugged. "What about her?"

"The two of you are in a relationship, right?"

"Off and on, yeah. What of it?" Jonny looked between Eric and Cassie, his raised hand turning a pointed finger that he prodded at both of them in turn. "Whatever she's said, it's a bloody lie."

Cassie noted the grazes on the knuckles of his right hand, judging them to be fresh.

"What did you do to your hand, Mr Young?" she asked.

He glanced at the back of his hand and dropped it into his lap, covering the wounds with his other hand.

"Fell over..." he said quietly, "bit too much to drink and that. You know how it is?"

She nodded, crossing to position herself on the other side of Jonny, putting him between the two of them. "Hmm..."

"Look... what's this all about?" he asked.

"You tell us, Jonny," Eric said. "What do you think Scarlett might be lying about?"

He scoffed. "Ah... come on, Eric! You know what women are like when you get into an argument... they push buttons, wind you up..." he leaned forward in earnest. "She'll be exaggerating... as usual."

"You get a bit heavy-handed when you're wound up, do you, Jonny?" Cassie asked, leaning towards him, close enough to smell the alcohol of the previous night's session seeping from his pores. "Do you like roughing up all women, or just the single mums with vulnerable children?"

Jonny leaned away from Cassie, holding his hands up in supplication. "Look... things got heated... but I swear there's nothing for you lot to get involved in. I mean, it's done... and we've spoken since." He looked at Eric, Cassie standing upright and backing a step away. "It's all sorted. She'll withdraw whatever it is she said, I'm certain. Just go and see her—"

"Jonny, Scarlett was found at her place this morning—"

"Found? What do you mean found?"

"She's dead, Jonny," Eric said. "Scarlett is dead."

His mouth fell open. He didn't blink but he did look to Cassie for confirmation.

"It's true, Mr Young. What's more is, she's been murdered."

His eyes narrowed and he tried to swallow but his throat was too dry, and he strained. "Now look... I didn't do it!"

"We didn't say you did," Cassie replied. "But it's nice to know you're trying to put yourself in the clear before asking about what happened to your girlfriend—"

"She's *hardly* my girlfriend... we just knock about sometimes—"

"How do you *knock about* with someone like Scarlett? It's not as if she's footloose and fancy free, is it?" Cassie countered. "Speaking of which, how do you get on with Maggie?"

"M–Maggie...? I... okay, I guess," he said flustered. "I mean, she doesn't say a lot and... what am I supposed to say to her?" He was fraught. "What do you think I've done for crying out loud?"

"When did you last see Scarlett?" Eric asked.

Jonny sank back into the sofa, shaking his head in disbelief, frowning. "The day before yesterday... I think."

Cassie perched herself on the arm of the sofa next to him, smiling warmly. "You'll need to do better than *I think*."

"All right, yeah, definitely the day before yesterday. I had to go and see her to make up for..." he sighed, looking away.

"Make up for what, Jonny?" Eric asked, picturing the bruises on Scarlett's arms. "For assaulting her?"

"Oh, man! I didn't assault her..." he threw his hands in the air, "it was an argument that got out of hand. That's all. It happens all the time. Let's keep it in proportion!"

"That's funny. It doesn't happen in my house," Cassie said, looking at Eric. "What about yours, DC Collet? Do you feel the need to get a bit fighty when you fall out with your loved ones?"

Eric shook his head.

Jonny laughed but it was a sound without genuine humour. "No, of course not. Little Eric over here would rather get a hammering than stand up for himself, wouldn't you, Eric?"

Jonny Young had passed from defence into attack in a matter of moments. Cassie couldn't help but wonder if that was how he managed an argument as well, notably with Scarlett, and possibly yesterday.

"So," Cassie said, forcing him to make eye contact with her, "tell us about the argument... and the extent of the fisticuffs. And don't think to leave any details out because *we are really paying attention* and you'll be caught out, which will only make us lean on you more."

"Bloody hell, what is wrong with you people?" Jonny said.

"We don't like bullies, Mr Young," Cassie said, pursing her lips. "And I think you're a bully."

Jonny held her gaze for the shortest possible time, he was sweating, looking away and down at his feet.

"What was it?" Cassie persisted. "She wanted out and you couldn't bear it?"

He laughed again, only this time it was genuine. "You don't know the half of it. She didn't want out, I did!"

Cassie was surprised by the intensity of his reply. She looked around the room. "But she was desperate to keep... all of this in her life?"

Jonny didn't appreciate the sarcasm. "Yeah, well, beggars can't be choosers, can they, and you'd be surprised what some people want."

Cassie didn't doubt it. "I often am. So, tell me gorgeous, what was it she saw in you?"

Jonny glared at her. "I told you, we were off and on. Mostly off as far as I was concerned. Particularly recently. Look, she was fun... sometimes, but that's as far as it went you know?"

"Why?" Eric asked. "Why recently?"

Jonny waved the question away. "Scarlett's been weird lately... talking about the future and... what are my plans. All kind of girly stuff, you know?"

"Girly stuff?" Cassie asked.

"Yeah. Planning, ambition... commitment."

"And in your world, these are only themes for women?"

"No, of course not," Jonny sighed, "but it is what it is. I just want things to stay as they are. That's all."

"And Scarlett?" she asked.

"Wanted more..."

"From you?" Cassie asked, trying not to smile.

"Yes," Jonny sneered. "From me. You'd be lucky to have me, but you wouldn't get close love."

"Gutted," she said with a wistful smile and sighed theatrically. "If only I could change. So, you're telling us you roughed Scarlett up because... she wanted more commitment from you?"

"Yeah. That's about right."

Cassie turned to Eric. "That's a tough sell."

"Well, it's the damn truth!" Jonny said, despairing. "But I'll tell you what I told her, I'm not looking to be a dad anytime soon and definitely not to..."

"To what?" Eric asked.

Jonny shook his head.

"To Maggie?" Eric said, failing to mask his disapproval.

"Look, she's a great kid... you know, for what she is and that, but honestly, can you see me looking after her? I mean, really?"

"No, certainly not," Cassie said. "I'm struggling to believe Scarlett thought you had it in you either, to be honest."

"No need to get personal, love."

He looked at Eric, splaying his hands wide.

"Seeing as none of us are standing on ceremony, Eric, is

there anything else you need because I really want to get my head down."

Cassie snorted. "We've just told you your girlfriend has been murdered and you want to go and get some sleep?"

"It is what it is, love. And I've told you, she's not my girl-friend. I got to admit, it's a strange way of getting free from someone but it's the way it is."

"That's cold, Mr Young," Cassie said. "Heartless." She meant every word.

Jonny looked at Eric again, and in turn, Eric looked at Cassie. Jonny smiled. "Ah, I get it." He waved a hand between them. "She's your boss, isn't she?"

Eric looked away, his cheeks and neck flushing.

"Of course. There's no way chicken Collet could come around here on his own." He placed his hands on his knees and smiled up at Cassie. "I'd watch your back with *Politically Correct Eric* here," he said, thumbing his hand at Eric. "Always more likely to run than stand his ground in my experience."

"I think I'll trust my judgement over yours, Mr Young."

Jonny sat upright, sucking air through his teeth. "Like I said, Scarlett and me were pretty much done. It's a shame, we had good times, but what can I do about it? The last time I saw her, we parted ways and we were done. Over. Finished. I don't wish harm on her, and I didn't do anything to her and I'm annoyed you're bothering me on a Saturday when I haven't been to sleep since Thursday night. So, if there's nothing else, I'd really like the two of you to piss off, love."

Cassie took a deep breath, leaning into his space, keen for him to know she wasn't intimidated by his attitude.

"We want a list of the people you spent last night with, *love*, and then we're going to speak to them and make sure they can account for your whereabouts. And believe me, if you're lying to us," she tapped him on the forehead with her index finger, "we're going to come back here and *Politically Correct Eric* is going to kick your door in and bounce you down the stairs and into a police cell. Do you understand?"

He smiled at her, seeming to enjoy the confrontation.

"Always happy to help the boys, and girls, in blue," he said in a whisper. "But instead of hassling me, you should probably be trying to find that weirdo she's managed to pick up."

Cassie moved back. "What weirdo?"

He grinned. "Yeah, you think you're hot on the detail and you haven't got a clue, have you? Scarlett has a side line... pretty lucrative as it turns out. I was well sceptical, but she proved me wrong."

"What side line?" Eric asked.

"Social media stuff... videos, trying on clothes and that," he said, resting his hands in his lap. "She uploads them to the internet and people watch them... she gets ad money based on the number of views or subscribers or something. I don't know, but it was easy money. She made the videos to upload at home." Eric and Cassie exchanged glances. Jonny laughed. "No, it's nothing dodgy... I mean it's not porn or anything. She'd just try on outfits... do make-up tutorials... whatever she thought people would be interested in watching. She's been blown away by the response of her videos. I know I was."

"And she picked up a fan?" Cassie asked.

"Oh, she had thousands of subscribers. If you knew Scarlett, you'd know why. She's really likeable... when she's in a good mood anyway. But this one guy starting commenting on her posts, and I mean *all of them*. Then he started contacting her across all her channels you know? It was downright creepy. I'd have given him a slap if I came across him, that's for sure."

"And what makes you think he's local?"

"Did I say he was?"

"Well, if he was a threat to her, then he'd have to be, wouldn't he?"

Jonny inclined his head. "Something he wrote one day made Scarlett think he might be around somewhere close or, at least, have some local knowledge. That's all."

"Was she concerned?" Eric asked.

Jonny thought about it, looking serious and then meeting Eric's eye. He nodded. "Yeah, I think she was. Concerned enough to have me fit a couple of extra bolts to her front and back doors."

CHAPTER TEN

TOM RANG the doorbell and stepped back, glancing through the window to his right. The front room was empty and it didn't look like anyone was home. However, movement came from the other side of the door and a young woman opened it. She had a broad smile as the door swung back, only for it to fade into surprise when she looked up at Tom. He stood a foot taller than her and clearly she'd been expecting someone else.

"Hello," she said. "Can I help you?"

Tom brandished his warrant card.

"DI Janssen from Norfolk Police," he said, looking past her and into the house. The hallway was cluttered with what one might expect to find in the home of a young family, children's toys, a push chair and he spotted a laundry basket, full to the brim, at the foot of the stairs. "I'm looking for Tony Slater. Does he still live here?"

"Yes, of course. I'm Olivia, Tony's girlfriend," she said, glancing over her shoulder. "He's in the kitchen." She called to him. "Tony!"

"Tell him I'll be right there... I'm just looking for my phone."

"It's okay, it's not Charlie."

There was a brief pause and then a man emerged from the kitchen at the rear of the property, looking curiously towards them.

"Well, who is it then?" he asked as he entered the hallway, approaching them and warily eyeing Tom up and down.

Olivia smiled awkwardly at Tom. He returned her smile and looked past her towards the approaching man.

"Tony Slater?" he asked.

"Yes." He looked at Tom with a half-smile. "Who's asking?"

Tom had the feeling Tony knew who he was; once someone passes through the system, they, and you, have a knack for smelling one another out. Tom assessed him. He was naturally tanned with a Mediterranean appearance, dark hair that was swept back from his forehead and lightly styled with some product that gave his hair a gentle sheen. He wore finely-manicured stubble on his face and a small, studded earring in his left ear lobe. He was around five foot nine and athletic, dressed in light brown combat trousers and a loose-fitting Henley shirt. Tattoos protruded from beneath the shirt, spreading onto the back of his hands. If he was expecting a visit from the police, then he was incredibly calm. Although, it was fair to say he was experienced and would likely not be fazed by the unexpected knock on the door. He could easily be faking it.

"Tom Janssen," he said to Tony, showing his identification once more. "Detective Inspector, Norfolk Police. I need to speak to you about Scarlett Turnbull."

At mention of her name, his face dropped, and he shifted his weight between his feet, nervously touching the end of his nose with the back of hand and averting his eyes from Tom's.

"Who's Scarlett?" Olivia asked, surprised, looking between the detectives and her partner.

"Ah... a blast from the past, babe, that's all," Tony said, smiling artificially and placing his hands gently on her shoulders and steering her away from the door. "Don't forget you said you would call your mum back." He looked at his watch. "And she wanted to head out with your dad, remember." She lingered for a moment, but Tony wasn't going to speak until she left them. Reluctantly, she nodded and stepped away. Tony watched her go and turned to Tom, lowering his voice, glancing back to make sure Olivia was indeed out of earshot. "I've not had anything to do with Scarlett in years..." he shrugged "so, what are you doing here?"

"When did you last see her?"

"Scarlett?"

Tom nodded.

He sighed, shaking his head and turning the corners of his mouth down. "I don't know... honestly," he said, "I've no reason to see her."

"Take a guess."

Tony scoffed. "All right, a year, maybe eighteen months ago. But, even then, I only bumped into her in the high street." He laughed. "And I didn't exactly get a warm welcome."

"The two of you didn't get on?"

Tony thrust his hands into his pockets, leaning on the door frame. "We did once... but that was a long, long time ago."

"Prior to your going to prison."

Tony sniffed, his expression darkening. "Yeah. She broke it off with me while I was inside. I mean, we'd split a few times before that... we had something of a... volatile relationship."

"Volatile?"

"Yeah. Toxic might be a better description."

"I understand you were both using at that time," Tom said. "Is that correct?"

Tony drew himself upright, coming away from the door and adopting a defensive stance. He looked sternly at Tom.

"What's all this about? You're talking about things that went on a lifetime ago, mate."

"My officers were called to Scarlett's home early this morning," Tom said. "Her body was discovered there."

"Her... her body?" Tony said, his mouth falling open. "S–Scarlett's... she's dead?"

"Yes. It hasn't been released to the public yet, but we believe she was likely murdered."

"I–I... don't believe it," he said, his shoulders sagging as he took in the news.

"And what's more, we are still trying to ascertain the whereabouts of her daughter, Maggie. Your daughter."

Tony's head snapped up and he found Tom staring at him intently.

"Maggie's missing?"

"Yes, she is. And that's why I'm here, Mr Slater. I have to ask you; do you know the whereabouts of your daughter?"

Tony stood open-mouthed, folding his arms across his chest.

"Mr Slater? Do you have any idea where we can find your daughter?"

Momentarily, he shook his head, his brow furrowing. "N–No, no... I'm sorry, I have no idea where she might be. I'd be the last to know, I'm sure about that."

"How much contact do you have with your daughter?"

He drew in a sharp breath, exhaling swiftly. "None at all. Absolutely none," he said, the latter barely audible above a whisper. "Scarlett hasn't wanted me in her life for years. Even before I went to prison, she should have got shot of me. Me being sent down made it easier for her for certain."

"So, it was her choice and not yours?"

Tony coughed, an awkward involuntary sound more related to the discomfort he was feeling at the question, Tom imagined, rather than any ailment.

"It was all such a long time ago," Tony said, pensive. "And at first, yeah, I saw it as a blessing to not be saddled with…" he seemed pained by his choice of words "… Maggie is full on, you know? It's not something you can pick up and put down. You have to be fully committed to be… involved."

"Or you just have to be a parent," Tom said, keeping his tone and facial expression neutral. Tony didn't care for the comment.

"Really? So says the man who has probably never had to cope with a disabled child. Is that right? Or do you have any real insight into what it takes? Because I'll tell you this, I agonised over whether I should or shouldn't be involved regardless of what Scarlett felt. In the end, I reckoned she was better off without me."

"Who, Scarlett or Maggie?"

"Both!"

"Raising a child takes love, Mr Slater. Everything else is secondary—"

He laughed. "You coppers are all the same. You see everything in black and white! Look at that guy over there, criminal… junkie… look how he abandons his kid so he can live a selfish life of crime. Is that what's running through your head right now? I'd put money on it that it's exactly what you're thinking."

Tom had to admit, it was. Not that he'd ever say so.

Tony's nose wrinkled and he appeared dejected. "No matter what you do in life, once convicted, you're only ever remembered for what you did." Bitterly shaking his head, he raised it and stared into Tom's eyes. "I've got nothing to do with whatever has happened to Scarlett... *nothing at all* and I swear to you, I don't know where Maggie is. If I did, I'd tell you." He put his hands out wide to either side of him. "I've no reason to lie to you. No reason at all."

"How was Scarlett when you last saw her?"

"Like what... a year or so ago? How the hell would I know? Angry at me, for sure. Not that I can blame her when you think what I was like back then."

"You've changed?" Tom asked.

He nodded. "Life can change if you're prepared to make the effort. Prison taught me that."

"Rehabilitation in action?"

Tony laughed. "Hardly."

Tom looked at him inquisitively.

"I met a guy inside... a blue-collar criminal. Not one like me at all, but we had a shared character trait. Selfishness. I watched him tackle it head on and win too. He made me see there was another path to walk and he guided me onto it." He was gauging Tom's reaction. Seeing as he didn't dismiss him, Tony continued. "The greatest tool for redemption is time, and I had a lot of that to get through... although, I accept, I don't think they had a prison sentence in mind when whoever it was said that."

"No, I doubt they did," Tom agreed. "And now you're a changed man? You sound like you've found your faith."

"I try my best, Inspector, I really do."

"Can you tell me where you were last night from around nine o'clock through into the early hours?"

Tony held Tom's eye. "Sure. I was here with Olivia."

Olivia appeared at the end of the hall, her head cocked as she listened in. Tony smiled at her before turning back to Tom.

"I've done some terrible things in my life, Inspector, truly terrible, and I wasn't a decent man. You couldn't trust me as far as you could throw me." He cast an eye over Tom. "Although, I imagine you could throw me pretty far, as it happens." Olivia sidled up to him and he raised his arm, cupping her around the shoulder and drawing her into him. He kissed her affectionately on the top of the head. "But I am different now. I have a new life," he said, looking down at Olivia smiling up at him. "I used to blame the drugs for the things I did and before that, I blamed my parents... life, society, but it's none of that. It's all on me. I have to live with the man I was, but it will not define the man I am or will be in the future. It's a second chance for me here." He squeezed Olivia tighter, and her smile broadened. "And I'm taking it."

"And what of your past, your responsibilities?" Tom asked.

"You mean Maggie?" Tony asked. Tom noted the absence of a reaction from Olivia.

"Yes, what of your daughter?"

"I would do anything to help you, Inspector. She is my flesh and blood, even though I have no connection, no bond, with her at all. When you speak to me about her – about Maggie – it doesn't feel like she's a part of me. I know that sounds terrible, but it's as if she's a part of a different life. That Tony is dead now and any relationship he had with Scarlett, and Maggie for that matter, died with him. If I knew where she was, believe me, I would tell you."

"But you don't."

He shook his head. "No, I don't. Look, if it were me, I'd be asking her father, Alan."

"We have spoken with Alan—"

"Then you'll know how entwined they are as a family."

"I gather he is incredibly supportive," Tom said.

"Yeah… supportive. Now you're just talking semantics."

Tom was intrigued. "What do you mean by that?"

"One person's support is another's control, wouldn't you say?"

"You think Alan Turnbull exerts control over his daughter, presumably in a negative sense?"

Tony grinned. "Yeah, I'd say so. If you're looking for someone close to Scarlett who will probably know more than he lets on, then I'd be talking to Alan."

"That's quite an accusation you're making."

Tony exhaled deeply. "Well, it is what it is. You asked and I'm telling you. What you do with that information is on you, not me."

A horn sounded outside and Tony looked past Tom as a minibus pulled up to the kerbside.

"That's Charlie," Olivia said.

Tom looked round. The minibus was stencilled with St. Martha's Church along the side. A round-faced man, sporting a huge smile, got out of the driver's side and waved to them enthusiastically. Both Tony and Olivia waved back.

"Come on, Tony, get a move on. Everyone will be waiting on us!"

"Well, if you weren't running late, as usual, then they wouldn't be waiting, would they?" Tony turned to Tom. "May I go?" he asked, tipping his head towards the minibus. "We're taking a group to the bowling green on Cliff Parade. It's a last-minute thing; making the most of the sunshine."

"You do this a lot?" Tom asked.

Tony smiled. "I told you, I'm making a new life… and I'm making a difference." He gestured to the waiting Charlie, standing on the pavement with his hands on his hips. "May I?"

Tom smiled. "Yes, of course. Thank you for your time."

"Look, I know I'm not involved in her life, but if I can help find Maggie, I'll do it. I swear to you."

Tom nodded.

"And will you keep me posted on what happens with her?" Tony glanced nervously at Olivia. "I won't lie and claim I have any real connection with her, emotionally or any other way beyond that of human caring... because I don't... but she is still my daughter."

"Of course," Tom said, conflicted as to what Tony Slater really felt towards her. In one breath he disowned her but now, he seemed unsure of his stance.

Olivia and Tom stepped out of the house while Tony grabbed a jacket from a hook beside the door and slipped his mobile phone into his pocket, kissed Olivia and hurried outside. He slapped the waiting Charlie on the shoulder and the two men got into the minibus.

Tom watched as they drove away, Olivia and Tony exchanging a wave. Tony's eyes met Tom's for a brief moment and Tom studied his expression without drawing any conclusion as to what it conveyed. Tony Slater wasn't quite what he'd been expecting.

Olivia smiled at Tom, turning back to the house.

"May I ask you something, Olivia?"

She hesitated before turning to face him. The sun was in her eyes, and she shielded them with the flat of her hand, still squinting. "Yes, what is it?"

"You asked who Scarlett was?"

"Yes. So?"

"And yet you weren't surprised when Tony spoke of Maggie."

She was pensive, expressionless, or trying to be so.

"I just found it... curious."

She looked away in the direction the minibus had taken. It

was long gone. After a moment of silence, she bit her lower lip and shrugged.

"Tony is very quiet about his past," she said. "I don't know why he wants to keep much of it from me. Perhaps he worries I'll no longer see him for the man he is if he did?" She faced Tom. "He told me he had a child, Inspector. A daughter whom he doesn't know, see or play any involvement in her life. He didn't say so, but I know he feels guilty about that, shame for not being the man he should be... should have been. However, I think you can only be the person you are and not the person everyone else, society, says you should be. It takes real courage to accept who and what you are and to live with it. Wouldn't you say so?"

Tom thought about it. "Unless who or what you are shatters any illusion of a moral compass." He held her gaze. "In that case, you would need to alter who you are or be removed from shared society."

"You can lock people up, Inspector Janssen, but the toughest of prisons are in your own mind." She tapped her the side of her head for emphasis. "Believe me, that's where the battle for morality is won or lost. For what it's worth, I think you should trust what Tony says."

"Which part?"

"About wanting to build himself a new life. To start afresh and to make a difference, a positive difference."

"How did the two of you meet, if you don't mind my asking?"

"At church," she said, smiling at a memory. "Tony was open with where he had been – in prison – and that he was looking to make amends; to become a part of the community. He called it sinning, but I never did. He's a good man. A man who made poor life choices, certainly, and had to hit rock bottom before he could even begin to find his way back up."

"And you believe he is doing that?"

"Oh yes, I do," she said, nodding enthusiastically. "He works so hard. You must appreciate how difficult it is for someone with a past like his, a criminal record for stealing and selling drugs, to find regular work. Tony doesn't complain. He doesn't vent about people looking at him with distrust, or subtly taking their valuables with them when they leave him in a room alone. He knows the mountain he has to climb and he *is willing* to do it. Hard work. Honest work. Work that pays barely enough to raise a family and yet he still does not complain."

She put a flat palm on her stomach and looked down. Tom hadn't noticed before because Olivia was wearing a loose-fitting dress. He was far from an expert on these matters, but he understood.

"How far along are you?"

"Three months," she said, smiling. "We couldn't be happier."

"Congratulations," Tom said. Her smile widened. "One thing I need to clarify. Perhaps you can help. Where was Tony last night?"

"That's easy. He was here with me."

"Right," Tom said. "All evening and all night? He didn't go out at all?"

Her smile faded and she glanced away momentarily. It soon returned as she looked directly at him.

"All night," she said firmly. "He didn't leave my sight."

"You're sure?"

She hesitated momentarily before confirming with a curt nod.

"That's good to know, thank you," Tom said.

"Did someone do something?" she asked.

"Excuse me."

"To this Scarlett woman? Did someone... hurt her?"

Tom nodded. "Yes, I'm afraid so." Olivia wasn't present when Tom explained what had happened to Scarlett. "She was murdered in her home late last night and I think she knew her killer."

Olivia held his gaze, the answer hitting her hard. "And you think...? No," she said, shaking her head. "Tony couldn't do that. He wouldn't be capable."

"I've been in this job a long time, Olivia, and I've learned one thing above all else. Everyone is capable. If the right buttons are pressed, if suitable conditions arise, then everyone has it in them to do the very worst of things."

She stared at Tom and he thought her eyes glazed over before she blinked furiously, touching the corner of her eye with the back of her hand, making out as if something had blown into it on the breeze.

"Not my Tony, Inspector. Not the Tony I know."

"I understand."

"You shouldn't think too badly of him, Inspector Janssen. I reckon that might be why he's buried his past so deeply. He wants to be judged on the man he is and not the man he was. That Tony is dead to this world, I truly believe that."

Tom allowed the words to sink in and made to leave.

"Thank you for your time," he said, walking back to his car still unsure of what to make of Tony Slater.

CHAPTER ELEVEN

Tamara Greave's mobile beeped on the desk in front of her. She considered reading the message but thought better of it, bearing in mind she was on a call with the Chief Superintendent.

"I don't think I need to tell you how this looks, Tamara," he said, gravely. "When people are worried about the safety of their children, then questions are asked. I need to see movement on this matter. Where are you with finding this little girl?"

"We have teams going house to house, sir," Tamara said, spotting Tom entering ops in the background. Eric looked up from his desk and pointed him towards her. Tamara gestured for him to join her. "I've also put checkpoints on the main routes in and out of Hunstanton. We're checking cars and asking locals if they've seen her, however..."

"However?" he asked.

"Well, the timeline we're working to suggests Scarlett was murdered late last night and I think we can determine with a high degree of certainty that her daughter, Maggie, was taken at that time or shortly afterwards."

"So, the checkpoints are too late. Is that your implication?"

Tom hovered at the doorway and she beckoned him inside.

"I believe that is a reasonable assumption, sir, yes."

"What about the search teams?"

"Combing the area for any indication of her passing through, sir."

There was a moment of silence on the line where she could hear his breathing.

"Sir?" she asked.

"Yes... I'm thinking. Could the girl have run away from the scene... be hiding somewhere?"

"Not in our opinion, or that of her assistance carer or family, sir. Maggie was in need of round-the-clock care and couldn't move under her own steam. Someone must have removed her from the house at some point during the night."

"I see. Next steps then, Tamara?"

She looked at Tom. "I think it's time to utilise the media, sir. We can get Maggie's picture out on the television, describe her needs. She..." Tamara hesitated, finding the words unfortunate but apt, "would stand out to people."

"Right. I'll notify the press team. When do you want to run with the press conference?"

"Six o'clock?" she asked.

"Certainly. I'll make myself available."

"I can take the lead if you'd prefer not to come in, sir?"

"No, no, no. I'll rearrange my plans."

"Okay, sir. Thanks very much."

She put down the phone, taking a deep breath.

"Pressure from above?" Tom asked.

"Unsurprising, all things considered." Tamara ran a hand through her hair. The Chief Super may well take the lead in the press conference, but she'd be alongside him. She'd have to get home and take a shower, change and be back for the media rounds. "The town is gearing up for the season and the last thing anyone wants to see is negative talk in the area."

"Yeah," Tom said quietly, "murderers are bad for business."

"Unless you're a pathologist," Tamara said, picking up her mobile phone. The text message was from her father. She'd read it later. "Speaking of which, Scarlett's body has been transferred into Dr Paxton's care. He's away this weekend but is cutting his trip short and coming back to carry out the autopsy."

"Good of him," Tom said.

"I don't think I gave him much of an option, to be fair."

Tom smiled. "Which means no autopsy findings until... what, Monday at the earliest?"

"I should say so." Tamara stretched out her arms. It'd already been one heck of a day, far from the relaxing Saturday she'd planned. "How did you get on with Scarlett's ex?"

Tom's brow creased. "Curious character."

Tamara was intrigued. "In what way, curious?"

"Well, had I spoken to him under any other circumstances then I'd have thought he was the model example of how the system can work. Past criminality, sent to prison for drug-related offences... to all intents and purposes, he should become a career criminal, habitually reoffending and keeping the likes of you and me in employment through to drawing our pension."

"Now I'm curious," she said, sitting forward, elbows on the desk and pitching a tent with her fingers.

"By all accounts he's cleaned himself up. He's found faith, set up home with a new partner who is his greatest advocate, holds down a job and volunteers in the community as part of his congregation." He looked at Tamara. "You see, a model example of how things are supposed to work."

"You have reservations though, don't you?"

He laughed. It was a cynical sound. "Maybe I've been doing this job too long." He shook his head. "He's just too good to be true. And, in our job, when something is too good to be true, then—"

"Nick 'em," Tamara said.

"Yes, that's almost what I was going to say."

Tamara concentrated. "Can we place him with Scarlett?"

Tom shook his head. "He claims not to have seen either Scarlett or Maggie for a year or more. In a town of Hunstanton's size, I find that difficult to believe, but it's what he says. However, motive is lacking for him. I didn't sense any animosity towards Scarlett for their past relationship, or for his lack of involvement in his daughter's life."

"Not a family guy, huh?"

Tom cocked his head. "I wouldn't say that. Olivia, his current partner, is pregnant and they seem happy about it."

"A new baby who isn't so challenging as a child with special needs is a very different proposition though, isn't it?"

"I dare say it would be, yes. And we shouldn't rule out the extra baggage that'd be in tow of having to deal with an ex. Especially if neither party wants it."

"Uninterested in his daughter, do you think, or more like he couldn't face the drama?"

Tom thought about it. "I got the impression the answer was yes to both at different points in the conversation. He asked to be kept abreast of developments."

"And how did he take the news of Scarlett's murder?"

"Very calmly," Tom said.

"There seems to be a lot of it about," Eric said from the door, rapping his knuckles on the frame. Tamara beckoned him inside. "Cassie and I met with Jonny Young, Scarlett's supposed boyfriend. He denies they are still an item and distanced himself from any regular relationship with Scarlett. He claimed they were well and truly over."

"I know you saw him this morning, Eric," Tamara said, "but can we place him in the area last night?"

"He's given us a list of names who, he says, will vouch for him being with them last night," Eric said. "I still have to speak to them, but Jonny seemed quite comfortable that they'd back him up."

"You know him from old," Tamara said. "Do you recognise any of the names on the list he gave you?"

Eric took out his notebook, flicking to the right page and scanning the list.

"A couple of them, yes, but not all."

"Get round them and confirm his alibi and while you're at it, see if you can confirm or refute Jonny's version of events regarding the status of his relationship with Scarlett."

Eric nodded. "Will do." He lingered for a moment. Tamara realised he had more.

"Go on, Eric."

"Jonny talked about Scarlett earning money through social media, uploading videos and so on." Eric turned the page in his notebook. "I've done a bit of digging and he's not wrong. Scarlett had over a hundred thousand subscribers to her channel and she pumped out four or five videos a week."

Tamara sat back. "What is the nature of the content?"

Eric shrugged. "All sorts; clothing try-ons, yoga sessions, advice on hair care and make-up. A real mixture. She has thousands of views recorded against each upload."

"And that's how they get paid, isn't it? On the number of views."

"I think it's more about the advertising that is shown but I imagine that's comparable to the number of views. The point is, she was earning good money. I cross checked with her bank account and she takes home more in a month than I do." Eric smiled weakly. "Although, I am drastically underpaid."

That brought a smile to Tamara's face. "But never under-valued or underappreciated, DC Collet."

Eric flushed. "Jonny also claimed she'd picked up a follower who was a little too familiar. I've been going through the comments and there is one guy who keeps commenting time and time again. It's downright creepy."

"Do we have a name for him?"

Eric shook his head. "No, just a cartoon avatar and a name, *fallen_angel*."

"Catchy," Tamara said. "Aren't fallen angels prostitutes?"

"That's one description, yes, but also harks back to the old Christian traditions about angels being cast out of heaven and it's also military code for a downed UFO," Eric said excitedly. He looked between the two senior officers, both watching his excited reaction with bemusement. "Not... that this guy is an alien or anything... I was just saying..." He cleared his throat. "Anyway, I'm in touch with the host website's customer support. They're going to have someone call me back. I think what I was asking for was above the pay grade of who I spoke to. Jonny reckoned that Scarlett thought this guy was a local. It's worth a look."

"Agreed, Eric," Tamara said. "Give them an hour and if you haven't heard back feel free to contact them and remind them this is a murder and a child abduction case we're working on."

"I will."

"If he does turn out to be local, you're not to go and speak with him alone. Do you understand?"

Eric nodded vehemently. "I'll grab Cassie when she's done with the search teams. Further to that, I've been going through Scarlett's social media. She's quite active. At first, I wondered where she would find the time, what with running around after her daughter, to hospital and so on, but then I got to thinking. If she's stuck at home a lot, and can't go anywhere, then she's likely to be very active, isn't she?"

"True, that follows," she said. "Anything interesting?"

"Not directly related to her murder, I don't think, but if she had few friends, which is the impression I had, then she's more likely to have virtual friends. Makes sense, right?"

"Virtual friends?" Tom asked. "I don't follow."

Eric explained. "No, I don't mean literally virtual friends. I just mean she's likely to be closer to the friends she has in the virtual world. After all, on the internet, you can be whoever you want to be, can't you? It's part of the appeal."

"That makes sense, Eric. Keep going with it and see if you can find any patterns, close contacts, that sort of thing. It's even better if she was involved with anyone locally."

"She's in loads of groups locally, they're *liked* in her profile."

"Start running them down, Eric. Good work."

He smiled. "Worthy of a pay rise?"

Tamara looked at him, her expression fixed. Sheepishly, Eric backed out of the room and returned to his desk.

Tamara looked at Tom. "He'll go further than I used to think, you know?"

"If he can stay the course," Tom said.

"Problems?"

Tom pursed his lips. "I think the job is playing havoc with his family life."

"Ah... I see. That'll explain earlier. It's a shame. Anything I need to be aware of?"

"Not as far as I know, but I'll keep you posted."

"How about yours?" she asked.

"Fine."

She frowned. "Fine? That's it?"

Tom smiled. "Yes, well what can I say? When we're both not chasing around after Saffy or Alice is at the hospital working, she's helping her mum. We operate on autopilot a lot these days."

"How is her mum?"

"Her latest bout of chemo is hitting her hard and her body's response hasn't been as positive as the doctors had hoped for this time around, but we'll see. The prognosis hasn't changed, so we're all still hopeful. What else can we do?"

"Give Alice my love, won't you?"

"Yes, of course," Tom said. "Thinking about this press conference you're going to give later, I think it'd be a good idea for me to inform Alan, Scarlett's father. At least he'll be able to brace himself for what's coming. The press will be camped outside his house—"

"We can ask them to give the family space."

"A missing little girl? The red tops will hoover it up."

She knew he was right. They'd be after every angle they could find, not least the incompetent police force should they run out of by-lines within a couple of days.

"Perhaps we could suggest moving him to another address. Do you think he'd go for it?"

Tom wasn't sure. "I'll raise it, see if he has anywhere else to go but as I understood him earlier, Scarlett and Maggie are all that he has left."

"The poor man," she said. "He's being put through the wringer at the moment. Let's see if we can find his granddaughter. You'll go to his house now?"

"I will," Tom said, standing up. "There's something that Tony Slater said that concerns me."

"What's that?"

"He pretty much accused Alan Turnbull of coercive control

over Scarlett." Tom frowned. "Having spent a bit of time this morning with Alan, I know there is no love lost between the two of them, but…"

"I know you're conflicted on Tony Slater but how did you find him in that moment?"

Tom considered his answer. "Credible."

"In that case, feel Alan out on the issue… but tread lightly. His daughter has been murdered and Maggie is still missing, so I don't want any blow back suggesting we treated him shabbily."

"I understand. I've had word that Scarlett's body has been removed from the house. We still need to have the next of kin officially identify her. I might set that up for this evening and then Dr Paxton can have a straight run at it when he arrives tomorrow."

"Makes sense. Have Kerry bring Mr Turnbull in as soon as you've had a chance to set it up."

Tom resumed his walk to the door. He looked back. "You'll be taking a shower, I presume?"

"I intend to go home and change, yes. That will also include a shower. Why?"

Tom gestured to the window behind her desk. "You might want to let a bit of fresh air in."

He left, leaving Tamara puzzled. Still dressed in her yoga clothes, she sniffed. "As diplomatic as ever, Tom, thank you," she said under her breath. Picking up her mobile phone, she called her father.

"Hi Tammy, I just wanted to let you know your baby is all tucked up back in the garage."

"Great, Dad. Thanks for sorting that out."

"No problem. The chap who brought her back says he thinks you've holed your radiator."

"Did he?" Tamara muttered a silent curse.

"Yes. He was worried your husband would be annoyed at giving him another job to do—"

"Well, I hope you told him to—"

"Yes, yes, yes, Tamara, I put him in his place."

"Good! I also managed to figure out what was wrong—"

"And I told him that as well," her father said, chuckling. "Although maybe you could find yourself a husband and then he can come and collect you from the roadside when your beautiful classic breaks down in future."

She felt bad then, but only for a moment. "Did you have plans?"

"No, nothing short of keeping your mum from interfering in your life."

"Ugh... what's she up to?"

Her father laughed. "Not for me to say, dear."

"I won't like it though, will I?"

"Doubt it. Tamara?"

His tone piqued her curiosity. He seldom used her given name, not unless she was in trouble as a child, or he was having a serious moment.

"What is it, Dad?"

"I know your mum does go on about it, but maybe you could give it some thought."

"Give what thought?"

"Well, I'm not getting any younger and neither is your mum."

"And?"

He paused, the silence hanging between them. "And no one wants to be alone, do they? It's not much of a life—"

"Dad. You're right, Mum does go on about it... far too much and it may have escaped your attention, but I haven't been alone for months now. If it's not you and mum, it's your blasted cat—"

"Cats."

Tamara sighed. "Has she got another one?"

"Yes, the protection league called."

"Dad, they don't call you. You call them."

"Ah, right. Well, your mum called and—"

"Yes, I get it. We have more cats." She put a hand across her eyes, drawing it down her face. "Dad, I need another favour. Can you come and pick me up? I need a shower before I'm on TV later."

"You're going to be on the telly?" Her father was clearly excited at the prospect.

"Yes, but not in a good way. Can you come and get me?"

"I'll be there in fifteen minutes, darling."

CHAPTER TWELVE

ERIC KNOCKED on the door again, only this time he did so with more gusto. He glanced sideways at Cassie who took a step away from the porch and peered through the front window.

"Any sign he's home?"

"No, I can't see anyone," she said, cupping her hand against the glass to offset the glare of the reflection. The sun was setting, the cloudless sky offering them a perfect view of the orange glow sitting low in the sky across The Wash. The temperature was already rapidly dropping. It was likely to freeze overnight.

"It's a state in there though." She looked at Eric. "You know this guy, don't you?"

"Richard? Yeah, he was one of the *in crowd* at school."

"Along with Jonny Young?"

"Yep."

Eric failed to mask his disgust.

"Are you finding it hard?" she asked, watching him intently.

"How do you mean?"

"Dealing with these guys you went to school with?" she

asked. "If the way Jonny spoke to you this morning is anything to go by, then—"

"Just leave it would you?" Eric asked, irritated.

"Okay, sorry," Cassie said. "Only asking."

"Yeah, well don't. All right?"

Cassie held up a hand by way of apology, coming to stand next to Eric. She hammered her fist on the door. "We've got better things to be doing," she said, just as a key turned in the lock and the door cracked open, revealing two bleary eyes staring out at them.

"What?"

"Richard Wenn?" Cassie asked, brandishing her warrant card.

"Oh, bloody hell," he said, lowering his eyes to the ground, closing the door and releasing the security chain. He opened it again, glancing from Cassie to Eric. He recognised the detective constable, breaking into a smile that seemed genuine.

"Eric... how are you mate? Long time, no see."

"Hi, Ricky," Eric said. "Can we come in?"

Richard Wenn looked back into the gloomy house, scratching absently at the back of his head. His hair was unkempt, and he hadn't shaved today. He was sporting a pair of loose jeans and a white T-shirt and had nothing on his feet. He yawned, stifling it with the back of his hand.

"Did we wake you?" Cassie asked as the occupant welcomed them into his home with an open hand, moving the door and stepping to one side.

"As a matter of fact, you did, yes."

Cassie cast an eye over him as she entered. She could smell alcohol and cigarettes on him, but it was a stale smell, most likely from the previous night. Once they were both inside, Richard closed the door and pointed them towards the rear.

"You'll have to excuse the mess. I wasn't expecting company."

Cassie went first with Eric bringing up the rear. The living room was as she expected to find it, a tip. Bachelor pads were little more than student digs around here. She threw open the curtains and what was left of the day's light came in. Richard sank into a large armchair with lots of arm padding, reaching for his packet of cigarettes and a lighter, he offered Eric a smoke.

He declined. "No thanks."

"Oh right, you never did smoke, did you?"

"Not my thing," Eric said, looking around.

"Please," Richard said, gesturing for them to sit down and exhaling the first drag of his cigarette and grimacing. "What are you doing here?"

"We've come to ask you about last night, Mr Wenn," Cassie said.

He laughed. "Please, Richard... Ricky," he pointed at Eric, "or anything similar. If you say Mr Wenn I look around for my dad." He yawned again. "And I really don't want to see him here."

"You don't get on?" Cassie asked, sitting down on the sofa opposite. Eric chose to remain standing.

"Nah, not a lot. Too alike," he said, sucking in another drag. "That's what my mum says, anyway. Now, you were asking about last night? Who's done what?"

Cassie inclined her head. "Who says anyone has done anything?"

"Because you're in my living room," Richard said. "At an ungodly hour."

Eric frowned. "It's just gone six o'clock."

"And I went to bed at ten this morning," he said, splaying his hands wide. "Not that I slept much."

"Don't put so much of that up your nose, then you'll sleep better," Cassie said, pointing at the glass-topped side table next to his chair.

Richard looked to his right. There was a credit card, a zip-lock plastic bag, empty, but the plastic was cloudy, and a white powdery residue was visible on the glass. He quickly flicked out his hand, wiping it across the surface before shooting a worried look which morphed into a sheepish smile at Cassie.

"Oops," he said, grimacing. "My bad and all that." He rubbed at the end of his nose, sniffing. "Is that why you're here?"

"No, it's not," Cassie said. "We've got more going at the moment."

"Great," he said. "Thanks. I think."

He was less sure of himself now though, his eyes nervously flicking between the seated Cassie and the standing Eric.

"Apart from causing insomnia, it also makes you para-noid," Cassie said.

"Yeah, so I hear." He looked at her in earnest. "What did you say you wanted to ask me?"

"Last night. You were out with Jonny Young, weren't you?"

"Jonny?" he asked, narrowing his eyes, trying to work out what information they were after. He reached for an ashtray before sitting back with it in his lap and tapping the end of the cigarette into it. "Let me think now…" He looked at the ceil-ing, thoughtfully. "Jonny was there—"

"He told us you were with him all evening."

"Ah… must be right then. Yeah, actually, I was with him all night. Until I copped off with this lass. Then I came home with her after."

"And when was that?"

Richard screwed his face up in thought. "Three, three-thirty... something like that. When the pubs closed we all went on to this guy's house in Hunstanton for a bit of an impromptu party. It was pretty good."

"Whose house was that?"

"Couldn't say," Richard stated, shaking his head. "Not sure I could find it. It was off Lincoln Square... north side. Nice gaff, though."

Cassie looked out into the hall as if she could see through walls. "And your lady friend, or gentleman, let's not be sexist, is still here and can confirm that?"

"No. She's gone. When I woke up this afternoon, she'd already left," Richard said. "Sorry."

"And what's her name?" Eric asked.

"Sorry, Eric. I never caught it. You know how it is?"

Eric pursed his lips. "No, no I don't."

"Ah... no, you wouldn't. It never was your style."

Cassie gauged Eric's reaction. There wasn't one. His expression was stern.

"You were with Jonny all evening until you left the party?" Cassie asked.

"Yes," he said, nodding. "Right the way through. We were on a bit of a crawl. Started in the afternoon and went from there."

"He never left your sight, all night... pubs, streets, the party? With you."

Richard frowned. "I... I'm pretty sure about it. I mean, I wasn't joined at the hip or anything."

"So, there were times when he wasn't around?"

Richard dismissed the question. "Look, he was always there when we were getting rounds in, going between pubs... he would have gone to the toilet and stuff, wouldn't he? I mean, we all do. So..." he shrugged, "why on earth do you care anyway? What do you think he's done?"

"Murdered his girlfriend." Cassie fixed him with a stare. Eric stood to one side, unflinching, despite Cassie's blunt answer.

Richard smiled, thinking it was a joke. When the two of them remained silent, the smile faded.

"You're serious."

"Deadly," Cassie said. "So, if I was you, I would ensure you think very carefully about your answer because being an accessory to murder does not go down well in criminal courts."

"N–Now look here," Richard said, lifting a shaky hand and pointing at Cassie. "No one ever said anything about a murder..."

"When?" she asked.

"What?"

"*No one said anything about a murder,*" Cassie repeated. "When didn't they say it?"

He exhaled, lowering his head and grimacing, running a hand through his hair. He muttered a quiet curse.

"Richard? Has Jonny Young been in touch with you today?" Cassie asked.

Richard lifted his head, biting his lower lip as he exchanged a look with Eric. Angling his head towards his shoulder, he screwed his face up. "I might've had a text or something."

"Okay, let's try this again, shall we? Can you account for Jonny's whereabouts all of last night?"

He met her eye. He was pained. Stubbing out his half-smoked cigarette, he sank back in his seat and looked up at the ceiling.

"There are no answers in the Artex, Richard," Cassie said.

Slowly closing his eyes, he took another breath before looking across at Cassie.

"He ducked out for a bit, last night."

"Where did he go?"

He shook his head. "I don't know." Cassie didn't believe him, her expression obvious. Richard grew defensive. "I swear, *I don't know*. He was with us, laughing and joking around, and then... he spotted something and said he had to go and check something out."

"Check what out?" Eric asked.

Richard stared at Eric, exaggerating an eyes wide expression. "I don't know! Are you a bit deaf, these days?"

"How long would you say he was absent for?"

He shrugged. "I don't know... ten, twenty minutes, maybe more. I didn't keep count, you know? I was on it with the others and there was that—"

"Lass, yes, you said," Cassie replied. "Maybe you can tell us what Jonny was like when he came back? I'm presuming he did actually come back."

"Yes, yes of course."

"So?"

Richard was reticent. "He... was different." He frowned. "Not as lively, I'd say. I guessed the fresh air had sobered him up a bit, but he soon got back into the swing of it."

"Different, how?"

"I don't know."

"Do try, Richard, please," Cassie said. "Was he subdued, angry, preoccupied... the English language is rich and varied with adjectives. Maybe try and use some, yes?"

Looking up at Eric, Richard pointed a finger casually at Cassie. "She's ferocious! Is she like this all the time?"

"Worse," Eric said, flatly. "I'd answer the question, if I was you."

Richard sighed. "Definitely preoccupied or distracted. I asked him if he was all right and he said, yes. He was a bit snappy about it though. I got him a drink and he saw it off in one."

"And then?"

"And then nothing. He went to the bar and got another round in... and that was that."

"Where did you think he went?"

Richard hesitated and then shook his head. The pause was momentary but enough for Cassie to seize upon.

"What is it, Richard? It's in your best interests to tell us, and it might be in your friend's as well."

"Ah, man," he shook his head. "I can't see how it has anything to do with—"

"Let us be the judge of that." Cassie was forceful, but she knew if she pushed too hard it might see him clam up. "Please."

"Okay," he said, sitting forward and bringing his hands together. "It was Mark. Jonny saw Mark."

"Who's Mark?" Cassie asked.

Eric spoke. "Mark, Jonny's brother?"

"Yeah, Jonny's little brother," Richard said, confirming with a nod. "He walked by the window and Jonny took off to speak to him. Like I say, I'm sure it's not related."

"Then why didn't you mention it?" Cassie asked.

"Don't know, really." He shrugged. "Jonny just seemed surprised... no, not surprised. It was more like he was bothered seeing him."

Eric looked confused. "Why would seeing Mark bother him?"

Richard splayed his hands wide apologetically. "I don't know. Which, I think I've already said a number of times."

"They spoke to one another?" Cassie asked.

"Couldn't say. Mark was past the pub before Jonny got outside. He walked after him. I didn't see what was said or anything."

"But that was the only time you can recall Jonny leaving the group? You're certain of that?"

Richard's expression was a picture of concentration. Eventually, he bobbed his head. "Yeah. Absolutely sure."

"And, just to be clear, Jon Young called you today and asked you not to mention this?"

"Yeah," he said, reluctantly. "Well, he texted me, but yeah."

"Can we see the message?" Eric asked.

"Nope, sorry. Deleted it."

"Did he ask you to do that too?"

"Yep," he said with a firm nod.

"Any chance you could not tell him that you told us?" Cassie asked.

Richard nodded. "Yeah... no, absolutely not. I'll call him as soon as you leave, probably."

Cassie rolled her eyes.

"Well, at least I'm being honest with you," Richard said, his smile returning. "And that has to count for something, right? Mind you, I'll have to tell him I told you about his seeing Mark, so... I don't know. I'll figure it out."

"Have a good evening, Mr Wenn." She pointed at the remnants of his cocaine use. "Next time I speak to you, if there is a next time, make sure you're a bit more careful. I'm sure your own bed is a damn sight more comfortable than the one we'll keep down at the station for you. It's fully tiled, but the mattress is thin, covered in plastic and pretty much smells of piss most of the time."

He smiled weakly, acknowledging the warning. "Understood."

Cassie signalled for Eric to leave, then she stopped. "One

more question, Richard. What time was it that Jonny ducked out?"

"Um... early evening... eight-thirty-ish, I reckon. Could be a bit before or after, to be fair. The pub wasn't too busy, so I think it was around then."

"Thank you," Cassie said, pointing Eric to the door. "Don't get up, Mr Wenn. We'll see ourselves out."

Once the front door clicked on the latch, Cassie fell into step alongside Eric.

"What do you know about Mark?"

"Mark Young?" Eric asked. "Nothing recent. Jonny's little brother, but they were like chalk and cheese growing up. Mark was a bit weird. Something of an anxious kid, you know? He always wanted to do the right thing, was polite and helpful to anyone who asked but had a propensity to go off on one. I never saw him attack anyone; it wasn't like that. Like I said, complete opposite to his big brother."

"What's the age difference between them?"

"Three years, give or take. Mark was three years below us at school, that's for sure. Nice lad. I often wondered how the two could have the same parents, grow up in the same house and attend the same school and yet have such completely different personalities. Strange how it goes sometimes, isn't it?"

They walked in silence for a while, heading back to the car. When they reached it, Cassie leant on the roof, looking over at Eric whose fingers were poised on the door handle for her to unlock it. She bounced the keys in her palm.

"Tell me this, Eric. When we're asking about Jonny's whereabouts in relation to Scarlett's murder... why does Jonny ask his mate to keep it from us that he spoke to his younger sibling?"

Eric stared at her, pensive. Then he shook his head. "I can't think of a reason."

"No, nor can I, Eric," she said, unlocking the car. They both got in. She glanced sideways at him while he was putting on his seatbelt. "But it certainly makes me want to ask the question."

Eric clicked the belt into place. "One thing for sure is that if Ricky – sorry, Richard – is right on his timing, then it couldn't be Jonny who killed Scarlett. She was alive when she came home at ten o'clock according to the babysitter."

Cassie inclined her head in agreement. "I still want an answer to the question."

"Of whom? Jonny or Mark?"

"Oh, Mark… definitely Mark."

CHAPTER THIRTEEN

THE DOOR at the far end of the corridor opened and PC Kerry Palmer led Alan Turnbull through it, holding it open as he shuffled past her. To Tom, Alan looked much older than he had done when they'd first met that day. Unsurprising, he guessed, seeing as the man most likely spent the hours since discovering the fate of his daughter churning over the *what ifs* and *maybes* that could have changed the course of events. It was only natural.

Tom greeted him with a handshake. Alan looked tired, the weight of the world reflected in his eyes which looked sore. Tom ushered him to the seating area of the waiting room where Alan tentatively perched himself on the edge of the nearest chair, looking up at Tom, dejected and miserable.

"Please tell me you're out looking for my granddaughter?" he asked. He looked back along the corridor to where he'd entered. "It's getting dark out there... and cold. She doesn't do well in the cold, Inspector."

Tom had spoken to him via Kerry's police-issue mobile phone, avoiding using the land-line number at Alan's house because it had been unplugged. As it turned out, the media were quick off the mark and keen to speak to him to enhance their coverage of events for the weekend news.

"Yes, of course, Mr Turnbull—"

"Alan, please," he said quietly.

"Do you remember we discussed how we are responding over the telephone? We have teams scouring—"

"Yes, yes you did." Alan looked up at Tom and away again, confused. Then he nodded. "The search teams are out and…"

"We are going house to house and interviewing everyone living near to her, as well as speaking with all of Scarlett's connections in the area."

"Well, that shouldn't take long," Alan said. Tom encouraged him to continue with his eyes. "Well, Scarlett doesn't – didn't – have many friends."

Tom sat down opposite him, keen to keep the formality at a minimum. Under the circumstances, Alan Turnbull was managing, but Tom observed it was a thin veneer and imagined he could break down at any moment. Ideally, he wanted to carry out the official identification and have him spirited back to his familiar surroundings as soon as possible, but the search wasn't progressing as they'd hoped. There was no sign of Maggie and no witnesses to give them a steer in the investigation.

It was more than likely Maggie had left the house in the dead of night when everyone nearby was sleeping. As it stood on the first evening following her disappearance, all they had to work with was Scarlett's social circle along with her online activities. Not that he felt he could explain this to Alan. The man needed something to hold on to, something to hope for. That was Maggie's safe return. Tom wasn't going to take that away from him. However, he needed help.

"Alan, I know this is incredibly difficult for you but, of all people, you are the one who has spent the most time in your daughter's home and I was hoping..." Alan glanced up at him, fearful, "...that you could let me know if there is anything out of place."

"I–I can go to her house?"

Tom held up a hand apologetically. "No, I'm sorry, that's not possible." He gently placed a flat palm on a folder lying on the chair beside him. "I have some photographs and I was hopeful, either prior to or after you've made the identification this evening, that we could have a look at them. Just to see if anything jumps out at you."

Alan Turnbull's gaze drifted to the folder, his expression was at best pensive and at worst horrified.

"There are no images of your daughter contained in the folder, Alan," Tom said, as reassuringly as he could. "It is more the objects in the room; is anything missing, has anything been moved. That type of thing."

Alan took a deep breath, fixing Tom with a curious gaze. "Forgive me, but that seems... strange. You know someone was in the house, clearly."

"Yes, that is true," Tom said. "However, we don't know why someone would be in the house and identifying a motive could lead us to Maggie."

Alan cocked his head. "I don't understand."

"Well," Tom said, putting his palms together in front of him as if in prayer, "we are trying to figure out if Scarlett knew her attacker and therefore allowed them into the house voluntarily or whether this was the act of a stranger, who forced their way in. You see, we don't have any signs of a forced entry. In fact, we believe the front door was left on the latch. Does that strike you as unusual?"

"Oh yes, it does. Very much so." Alan's forehead furrowed. "Scarlett was very security conscious. I drilled that into her from a young age... I had to, what with being a single parent and working the hours I did to make ends meet. Scarlett wound up on her own after school most days and she had to be careful." Shaking his head, he exhaled. "I'm very surprised to hear that indeed."

"Okay, that's very helpful. We can go over the rest now or—"

"After, if you don't mind," Alan said, staring at the door to the viewing chapel of rest, perhaps picturing his daughter lying in situ beyond it. "I... I would like to see my daughter now, if that is at all possible?"

His voice sounded hollow, distant. He was preparing himself for the worst experience a parent could imagine having to go through. Tom nodded, looking up at Kerry Palmer.

"If you could give Kerry and me a moment, we will just check that they are ready for you."

"Yes, of course. Thank you."

Tom held the door open and Kerry entered first, Tom closing the door behind them with a brief glance at Alan, sitting quietly, hands clasped together in his lap, staring straight ahead.

"You've been with him all day, Kerry. What do you make of him?"

Kerry considered her answer. "He's evidently in shock. I haven't had much out of him. He hasn't eaten at all, which is unsurprising I suppose." She looked glum. "It's a lot to process, but I think he is coping, just about."

"That was my take as well. Do you think he'll be up to looking through photos of the scene? I don't like to do it when everything is so raw, but we don't have much choice. We're not getting anywhere and time is—"

"I think he'll want to do it, sir," Kerry said in earnest.

"Those two girls are his entire life. You should see how many photos he has of them in albums at his home. He was showing me them this afternoon. The pride he has in his daughter, and Maggie in particular, is lovely. They are all so close. It's heart breaking."

"I know it's difficult, but remember your training," Tom said. "As a human being we all want to reach out and help someone who is drowning but," he placed a gentle hand on her forearm, "you have to keep one foot on the riverbank, or you'll get carried away on the same current."

"I understand," Kerry said. "I'll stay focussed. I promise." She shuddered.

"Someone walking over your grave, PC Palmer?"

She shook her head. "No, I'm freezing to my core, that's all. It's all the sitting around." She immediately backtracked. "I'm not complaining, honestly." She lowered her voice, fearful of being overheard. "I think Mr Turnbull, Alan, is struggling. Reading between the lines, I think he supports Scarlett and Maggie as much as he can, both emotionally and financially. Much to his own detriment."

"Meaning?"

"I wasn't spying, but I saw a final demand red letter bill in his kitchen. I'm not sure who it was from... and his house... it's so cold in there. I suggested he turned the thermostat up earlier and he flat out refused. Do you know he has an indoor coat and an outdoor one? He wears the indoor one to keep warm around the house so that he doesn't spend money on heating but the outdoor is thicker, otherwise he wouldn't feel the benefit when he does venture out."

Tom sighed. "Times are hard for many these days."

"But heating your home is the bare minimum, isn't it?"

"Yes, it is. Maybe, when you get a chance, have a look and see if there is anything we can do for him; take advice from the energy companies or maybe speak to the council, get him some help from somewhere if possible."

"I'll see what I can come up with, sir," Kerry said, smiling. "I'm really worried about what will happen to him once we're not with him. It'd be nice to make a positive difference to his life."

Scarlett was lying in the centre of the room, her body covered in a sheet. The mortuary assistant entered, greeting Tom and smiling at Kerry.

"Is the next of kin ready?" he asked.

Tom went to the door, opening it and looking across the corridor at Alan. His head snapped up, his expression pale and fearful.

"We are ready for you now, Alan. If you're ready?"

He nodded, gathering himself and slowly standing up. He seemed to do so with some trouble. He saw Tom notice.

"Comes with age, Inspector Janssen. You'll see."

Tom smiled weakly, holding the door open for a hesitant father who passed by him, pausing momentarily in the doorway as he caught sight of his daughter's body, albeit shrouded from view. He glanced sideways at Tom before dipping his head in thanks and entered.

Both Tom and Kerry maintained a respectful distance as Alan Turnbull came to stand alongside his daughter. The assistant waited for Alan to make eye contact and then slowly drew the sheet away from Scarlett's face, folding it neatly back at the upper chest line before stepping back. Scarlett was still dressed in the clothing she'd been found in, the vintage high-necked red dress. She looked like she was sleeping peacefully.

Alan Turnbull stared at his daughter, unmoving. From his right, Tom looked on. This part of the job never got any easier. He allowed the man a bit of time, giving him the opportunity to confirm her identity, which wasn't forthcoming, before asking the question.

"Alan. Is this your daughter Scarlett?"

He nodded, his voice cracking as he spoke. "Y–Yes… this is Scarlett."

At the mention of her name, his head bowed, and he began to cry. It was a pitiful, wretched sound and for a moment Tom feared he was about to collapse to the floor, preparing himself to step forward and break the old man's fall. However, Alan steadied himself, regaining his composure although still weeping freely. He reached out a shaking hand to her face and Tom had to intervene.

"I'm sorry, Alan," he said, putting his own arm in between them to form a physical barrier. He couldn't be permitted to touch the body. It was a sad reality that Scarlett's body was now evidence in a murder investigation and until such time as an autopsy could be performed, contamination of any possible trace evidence had to be avoided.

Alan Turnbull didn't take his eyes from Scarlett, his hand still outstretched in such a way as if he was stroking her cheek.

"My daughter…" he whispered, crying openly. "My little girl."

Tom saw Kerry's head bow in the corner of his eye, and she raised a hand to cover part of her face. He felt the same emotions within himself, witnessing such grief would touch even the coldest of hearts.

Alan struggled for breath, then swallowed hard, clenched fists by his side. Loudly drawing breath, his eyes still trained on Scarlett, the worst moment seemed to have passed.

"It is a common phrase heard, Inspector Janssen," he said, audible only due to the lack of ambient noise in the room, "that a parent shouldn't have to bury their child. That is not the plan in the cycle of nature."

"No. I agree it's not supposed to play out that way."

Alan turned to face Tom, his eyes burning brightly with anger. "And I sure as hell can't bury my granddaughter as well." The anger diminished before subsiding to be replaced by hopelessness. He looked weary beyond his years.

"We are doing everything in our power to make sure you won't have to, Alan. I give you my word."

Alan Turnbull met Tom's eye, assessing his words. Apparently satisfied, he broke eye contact.

"I appreciate your sincerity, Inspector. I truly do."

With one last lingering look at his daughter, he silently mouthed the words *I love you* and closed his eyes. Opening them, he looked at Tom and then Kerry. "Whatever help I can give you, I will."

Tom led him from the room and back into the waiting area, their footsteps echoing on the polished floor. Tom offered Alan a hand to sit down but he waved the offer away.

"Thank you, but I'll manage."

"Arthritis?"

Alan smiled. "Arthritis was all I had to cope with a decade ago... and how I long for those days!"

"Are you sure you're up to this?" Tom asked, concerned that seeing his daughter may have been too much for him, or at least, he may be too emotionally charged to go through the photos.

"No, I'll be fine," he said, looking up at Tom. "I promise. If I didn't feel up to it, I would say so."

Tom saw no need to press further, crossing the room and lifting a low table, bringing it back and placing it down in front of Alan. From the folder he had brought with him, he began to take out the carefully selected photographs taken at the scene and laid them out on the table before Alan.

"I just want you to comment on anything that looks odd to

you, out of place. Perhaps something is there you've never seen before. Any detail at all, no matter how insignificant you might believe it to be."

Alan's eyes darted from picture to picture, his hand hovering tentatively above the table.

"May I?"

"Yes, of course," Tom said.

Alan took his glasses from his coat pocket, putting them on and scooping up the first couple of pictures, angling them to get a better view. The lighting in the waiting area wasn't great with drawn blinds down over the few windows present in order to shield the occupants from anyone passing by outside.

Kerry found the cords to the blinds, opening them up to allow what little light there was left from daytime to stream in. Luckily, they were on the west-facing side of the building and the setting sun cast an orange glow upon them.

Alan moved through the images. On the fourth, he murmured something but when pressed by Tom, he dismissed it.

"Nothing unusual that I can see," Alan said, putting another photo down and picking up the next.

"Take as much time as you need," Tom said.

Alan was onto the photos taken in Scarlett's bedroom now, Tom having screened out any containing his daughter. He stopped, focussing on one image and allowing the other to drop to the table. He stared at it. Tom was curious.

"What is it, Alan?"

"I had no idea..." he said quietly. Before Tom could ask again, he turned the photo towards Tom, his expression splitting a half-smile which widened as he pointed to something with his forefinger. "The book."

Tom leaned over to get a better look. It was a shot of the

bedside table. All that was visible was the lamp, which was on, and a tatty old paperback.

"What about the book?" he asked.

Alan lifted his glasses to rest on top of his head, cupping his mouth and chin with his free hand.

"I had no idea she'd kept it." He broke away from examining the photo, indicating the book to Tom. "We are Lions," he said, smiling. "We read this to Scarlett when she was but a child... couldn't have been much older than Maggie is now. Well, I'll be..." he shook his head, the smile fading. "I haven't seen this book for nigh on twenty years."

Tom couldn't see the relevance to the case, but it was a genuinely fond memory for Alan, so he saw no need to curtail it.

"What is it about?"

"Oh... it's an old folk tale about two brothers," Alan said, looking at Tom and then Kerry. "One brother is very popular, quite the dashing young man, intelligent and charismatic, as well as an enviable athlete. Everyone holds him in high esteem whereas his younger brother is the opposite." He held up a pointed finger. "Not that he couldn't be all of those things, but he is different, introverted and physically weak." He laughed. "The writing covers a lot of ground regarding humanity... love and how to confront and overcome adversity. Overall, how to live a life would be an apt description."

"You used to read it to Scarlett?" Tom asked.

"Not only me, but also her mother, Margaret. That is who Maggie is named after... her grandmother, my late wife." His expression became vacant and he stared forward, reliving a distant memory perhaps. He shook it off. "Anyway, sorry for the trip down memory lane, it's just I haven't thought about that story in a long, long time."

He placed the photo down and resumed his examination,

but it was to no avail. Having looked at the remainder and then picked up some that he had previously viewed, he shook his head apologetically.

"I'm terribly sorry, but I see nothing... untoward or out of place here."

Tom thought, in this scenario, he would be more disappointed than he appeared, but he couldn't fault his attempts to find something. Maybe nothing untoward, apart from the deceased and her missing daughter, was there to see after all.

"That's quite all right, Alan," Tom said. "It was something of a long shot."

"I'm sorry."

"No need to apologise." Tom gathered the photographs together and made to put them back in the folder. Alan's attention seemed fixated on the photo still on the top of the pile, the one with the book. He noted Tom's attention, looking away and pursing his lips.

"Is there anything else I can do?" he asked.

Tom closed the folder, lying it on the chair beside him.

"I did want to speak to you about something," Tom said.

"Anything, Inspector. Anything at all, if it helps?"

"Well, I met with Tony Slater earlier today."

At mention of Scarlett's ex-partner, Alan's demeanour darkened somewhat but he remained resolute.

"I see. And what did that reprobate have to say for himself?"

"That he hadn't had contact with either Scarlett or Maggie in over a year at least."

Alan shifted uncomfortably in his seat.

"Good. Did I tell you my opinion of the man this morning?"

Tom nodded. "You were... forthright in your opinion of him and conveyed that clearly."

"Forthright?" he said, scoffing. "Then I didn't do him enough of a disservice."

"He said a number of things, even raising the point that he felt you exerted a great deal of influence over Scarlett," Tom said, watching closely for any reaction. Alan was unfazed, staring intently at Tom. "He even suggested it was unhealthy."

Alan slowly nodded. "Did he indeed?"

"Yes. How would you describe your relationship with your daughter?"

He drew a deep breath, his upper lip twitching. He was angry and trying very hard to contain himself. Closing his eyes, he concentrated, evidently choosing his words carefully.

"My daughter, Scarlett, was a troubled teenager, Inspector. I hold myself personally responsible for that." He sighed, shaking his head. "You see, I was a terrible parent... not uncaring or absent by intention, but I wasn't around as I should have been. I was a single parent, losing Margaret when Scarlett was still very young as we did scuppered things. It took me a very long time to come to terms with my loss. Hell, I struggled just to put my socks on in the morning and heaven knows what Scarlett was feeling."

"It must have been hard for you."

"Hard? What do you know about such loss?"

Tom inclined his head. "I lost my own father at an early age, not as early as Scarlett by all accounts, but I can understand the pain."

"Then you do know," Alan said. "And yet I couldn't process my own pain, let alone recognise my daughter's. She kept her feelings from me, arguably not wishing to burden me more than I was already. But I mistook her silence for an ability to move on, to forget." He shook his head. "She hadn't forgotten... and I should have been there to help her." Shrugging, he looked to the ceiling. "But I couldn't set myself right, let alone her. I told myself I was doing a grand job, and I was to an extent... ultimately though, I failed."

"You are being too hard on yourself," Kerry said.

Alan glanced sideways at her, smiling appreciatively. "You are very kind, PC Palmer, but I must face up to my failings. I told myself that keeping things just as the two of us against the world I was devoting all that I had to offer to my daughter, when what she needed was the affection of a mother." He laughed, a dry, humourless sound. "Or the affection of a father who was able to feel. Not a robotic parent," he said, waving his hands theatrically in the air, "who was going through the motions, enacting the playbook he thought was required."

He fell silent, mulling over his words. Tom watched him.

"So, how do you respond to Tony's comments?" Tom asked.

Alan Turnbull drew himself upright, meeting Tom's gaze with a hard stare.

"Well, I couldn't have had that much control, or I wouldn't have allowed him anywhere near her, would I?"

It was a strong argument.

"You refute the accusation?"

"I do, in the strongest possible manner, Inspector," he said, bitterly. His tone softened. "I made mistakes, certainly. By closing off her emotional recourse, she sought to numb herself to the world through the use of recreational drugs, alcohol and... promiscuity. But, if she hadn't done so, if she hadn't had those experiences – even taking up with the likes of Tony Slater – we wouldn't have had Maggie and Scarlett wouldn't have grown into the daughter she became. One I am tremendously proud of, I might add."

Tom accepted his candour, recognising the passion with

which he spoke about Scarlett. Personally, he was the same with Saffy.

"Tell me, how did Scarlett manage financially?"

Alan smiled. "Scarlett could be frugal, if need be, but it was always a struggle." He rocked his head from side to side. "I help out where I can, and I know the welfare are supportive where Maggie is concerned. As much as they can be, at any rate. Why do you ask?"

"I was wondering if you knew of any extra ways in which she brought in money, beyond what you've just said?"

Tom waited for an answer, deliberately choosing to keep the question open and vague. Alan thought hard and then shook his head.

"No, I'm sorry. What are you getting at?"

"Just routine," Tom said flatly. "What about friends? I know we touched on them this morning and you just said she didn't have many, but I was wondering if you might have thought about any particular acquaintances or confidants that she may have had?"

Alan splayed his hands wide, apologetically. "No, none that I can think of. I'm sorry. Like I said, I don't think she had many close friends. If she did, then she didn't speak to me about them."

"Okay, Alan. Thank you for going through all of this. I know it can't be easy." Tom gestured to Kerry. "PC Palmer will take you home now."

Alan held Tom's eye, then broke off and smiled at Kerry, heaving himself out of his chair with a groan.

"Thank you. You're very kind."

"I'll be in touch with any developments as soon as I have them," Tom said. "And do feel free to have Kerry check in with me if you have any fresh thoughts or concerns regarding progress."

Alan smiled appreciatively and shuffled off with Kerry beside him. She looked over her shoulder at Tom and he gave her a subtle thumbs up. She smiled and checked in with her charge as they walked. Opening the folder, Tom took out the photograph that had caught Alan's eye. Looking at it, he thought about Saffy and how he would take it in turns with Alice to read with the little girl every night. Putting the photo away, he took out his mobile and called home.

CHAPTER FOURTEEN

ALICE PICKED up almost immediately and Tom could hear trepidation in her tone.

"Is everything all right?" he asked.

"Yes, we are fine," she said. He heard her move through the house and the familiar squeak of a hinge on the interconnecting door from dining area to living room. Cartoons were on in the background. "Saffy's watching the telly."

"Who is it?" he heard Saffy ask.

"It's Tom, darling."

"Hi, Tom!" she shouted.

He heard the phone beep and the television got louder now he was on speaker.

"Hi, Saffy. Are you being a good girl for Mummy?"

"No!"

He laughed and the speaker was switched off, Alice walking back into the kitchen.

"Don't believe her, she's a delight. Although we've had to cry off in going over to see Mum."

"Why?" he asked, surprised. It wasn't like Alice to miss a planned visit, especially now while her mother was ill.

"Saffy has been coughing this morning and she has an elevated temperature. Only a touch over thirty-eight, but with Mum—"

"You can't take the risk."

"Yeah, exactly. We did a video call through the laptop."

"How is she. Your mum?"

Alice brightened. "Well, I think. This is one of her better days I reckon. She looks tired but she's positive and that's a good sign. When she's really down in the dumps everything is a disaster, isn't it?" A brief silence followed and she changed the subject. "I saw Tamara on the TV just now. Is that what you're working on today, this little girl who's missing?"

"Yes," he said. "Her carer found her mum in the house this morning and there's no sign of her. I'm really starting to worry now. We haven't found hide or hair of her. Hence Tamara and the Chief Super giving the press conference."

"That's awful, Tom. Just awful. That little girl, she's—"

"Pretty much Saffy's age, yes, I know."

"Oh Tom, can you imagine what it would feel like if…"

He inhaled heavily, his chest tightening. "Yes, acutely. That's why I called, to keep one foot grounded, you know?"

"Of course. There but for the grace of God and all that."

"Yep," he said. His phone beeped to notify him of an incoming call. It was Eric. "Listen, I have to take another call."

"Of course," she said. "Do you know when you might be home?"

"No, I've no idea. It depends on the success of the search teams and countless other things. I'll call you later though."

"Okay, thanks. Remember, we'll be waiting here when you get home."

"Give Saffy a hug and a kiss from me, would you?"

"If I can get anywhere near the little madam, then I will do!"

Tom laughed and switched to Eric's call.

"Eric, where are we?"

"I chased up the customer support team and was escalated further up the chain," he said excitedly. "Finally got to someone with authority."

"And?"

"This creepy guy who's been messaging Scarlett; our *fallen angel* is none other than William Slegg."

"Less catchy as a social media handle."

"His registered address is at one of the caravan parks between Beeston and West Runton."

"A caravan park at this time of year is a secluded location."

"That's my thinking too," Eric said, "but it is supposition. I've no reason to think he is involved."

"Do we know him?"

"He doesn't have any criminal convictions, but he was arrested and questioned after reports of a strange man loitering outside a primary school three years ago. No charges were ever brought though."

"That's a concern, Eric. Have you run it past the DCI?"

"No, she's still doing media stuff downstairs. I've got something else as well."

"Go on."

"You remember I said Scarlett was really active on her social media? Well, there is one person in particular that she communicated with quite a bit. The social media name is *tea-drinker*, but it didn't take much to uncover her real name; Jenny Bovis. She lives in Hunstanton. She and Scarlett interacted most days and more than just sharing jokes and humorous pictures of cats and stuff. She seems closer than anyone else to Scarlett, so—"

"Have you spoken to Cassie?"

"Yes, uniform have the search going well but she feels a lot like a fifth wheel down there."

"Okay, stick to the original plan, pick her up and the two of you go and sound out this Slegg character. If there's any indication that he has Maggie or if you feel any threat at all, I want you to call in the cavalry."

"Got it."

"I mean it, Eric," Tom said sternly. "I don't want you trying to be a hero—"

"Can you tell that to Cassie?" Eric said. "Something tells me she won't hold back for anything."

Eric was right. Cassie could be hot-headed, and he found himself questioning himself. He shook it off. Cassie Knight was a competent detective sergeant and he had absolute faith in her.

"I'm sure the two of you will manage. Can you send me an address for Jenny Bovis? I'll go there and then we can meet up afterwards for a debrief."

"If this Slegg guy gives me the jitters, can I bring him in?"

"If you have any inkling he's involved in this, arrest him and turn his place over. We're looking for a missing child. Every other concern is secondary."

TOM PARKED the car in Southend car park. The evening was cool and he was grateful for the light breeze coming off the water a hundred yards away beyond the Waterside Bar. The amusement arcades on Le Strange Terrace and behind him alongside the leisure centre played their music loudly, the machines projecting the noise of slot machines and arcade games to lure in passing trade. The flickering mix of neon and strobe lights cast odd shadows around him.

Looking up at the flats, the two floors above the ground floor retail units, he knew Jenny Bovis lived on this side overlooking the car park. The flats on the other side of the building overlooked the bandstand, the green and the old pier which was little more than another amusement arcade now; the pier having burned down and fallen into the sea many years ago. Those flats had balconies and rarely changed hands, such was the nature of the views of the sea.

Tom mounted the stairs, casting an eye over those few who were out on the promenade, some walking their dogs, others jogging, all illuminated by the line of lights strung between the Victorian-style lampposts.

Light emanated from a window of the flat registered to Jenny Bovis. Eric sent through a brief with the key information he'd dug up on the woman and Tom had read it in the car. The electoral roll had her as the sole occupant. She was divorced and two children were listed as dependents. They were both in their late teens and possibly no longer lived with her. She also had no criminal record.

He rang the doorbell and moved to the side of the walkway to allow a neighbour to pass with her pushchair, a sleeping child strapped into the seat. She thanked him. He smiled and the door opened. A redheaded woman looked him up and down before looking to Tom's left and right. She seemed surprised. He took her in. She was in her late forties, according to his information, but she looked far older. Her hair was cut short on the back and sides, shaped into a large quiff, and dyed either purple or blue, Tom couldn't tell in this light. The close-cut sides of her head were dark brown but greying. She was dressed in jogging bottoms, furry rabbit slippers and a vest, from which tattoos sprang in every direction. She had a subtle nose ring and sported thick-framed glasses.

"Can I help you?" she asked.

"I'm looking for Jenny Bovis," Tom said.

She eyed him suspiciously. "That's me. Who are you?"

He took out his warrant card. "DI Janssen. I need to speak—"

"About Scarlett," she said, sniffing. "I've been expecting you. You'd better come in."

She went back into the flat, leaving the door open and Tom followed, closing it behind him. The flat was small, the entrance hallway narrow, and as he passed through he saw there were four rooms off it; a small kitchen, a bedroom and a bathroom. The last was the living room, with one small window overlooking the car park below. The television was on and Jenny muted it after finding the remote down the side of the sofa, where she'd been sitting.

A small dog lifted its head from a soft bed in the corner of the room, examining the newcomer but didn't see fit to come over and investigate further, merely put its head down and went back to sleep.

"I hope you don't mind dogs?" she said.

Tom shook his head, looking at the creature. It wasn't a breed he recognised, but it was one of the yappy ones that he found irritating. He was pleased it didn't get up.

"You said you were expecting me."

Jenny offered him a seat and sat back down herself. Tom pulled out a chair from under the small dining table and sat down.

Jenny shrugged. "After I heard this lunchtime," she tilted her head towards the television, "about what happened to Scarlett."

Her name had only been put out in the evening press conference. Jenny must have guessed what he was thinking.

"It's a small place, Inspector. Word travels fast around here."

That was true.

"You and Scarlett are friends?" he asked.

"Yes," she said, her eyes glassy. "I had a lot of time for Scarlett... and her little one. Lovely little thing, Maggie. Have you any idea where she is yet? I saw your colleagues on the telly talking about her."

"We are working on it, I assure you. How did you become friends?"

"Neither of us can get out and about like we used to, Inspector. That's the beauty of social media; you don't have to leave home to be there." She smiled. It was a kindly smile. "We just seemed to hit it off. I was always active in the community, used to be at any rate and Scarlett was looking to find people locally to chat too. It went from there really."

"The reason I'm here," he said, casually looking around, "is that I'm trying to find out more about Scarlett. About what makes her tick. Her father has been helpful—"

"But she keeps a lot from him."

Tom pursed his lips, not wishing to lead her. "So we understand. Why was that do you think?"

"Oh, they're close in many, many ways. Pretty inseparable much of the time. I'd love to have had that closeness with either of my parents," she said, smiling wryly. "But I didn't. They were both useless."

"What about Alan?"

"Lovely man," she said. "Not that I know a great deal about him. I've never met him, it's just from what Scarlett tells me and she speaks really highly of him. No, the reason she held back was much the same as any child does; you don't want your parents knowing everything, do you?"

"Was she up to anything illegal—"

"Illegal? Scarlett?" She shook her head. "Heavens no. Scarlett was on the level. It's more about... the personal things in life. You don't want to discuss all of that with your parents... and definitely not with your dad!"

"Boyfriends?"

"After a fashion... recreational pastimes and all that."

"You mean drugs?"

Jenny sighed. "I guess it doesn't matter now, but yeah, that sort of thing."

"We were under the impression she'd moved past all that."

Jenny raised her eyebrows. "And she had, but... recently... she'd been doing some stuff. Everyone finds a way to cope, don't they?"

Tom wondered what stresses Scarlett had been under recently that hadn't been present in her life prior.

"What was going on with her?" Tom asked.

She scratched absently at the side of her head, grimacing. "Combination of things, I think. I know little Maggie has been difficult recently, more ill than normal and I don't know whether Scarlett picked some of the bugs up or something, but she's not been herself."

"In what way, not herself?"

Jenny's brow creased. "Just... unwell. She can't have been sleeping. She looked a mess last time I saw her, very down."

"When was this?"

She thought about it. "Earlier in the week I reckon. Monday or Tuesday. It's hard to tell as most days are the same."

"What do you do, if you don't mind my asking?"

"Ah... well, I'm on the sick," she said, apologetically. "I used to work as a seamstress, bridal-wear was my speciality but that seems like an age ago now." She caught him looking at her and smiled. "I know it's hard to believe, and I don't look it, but intricate stuff was my forte."

Tom smiled. "I wasn't thinking anything of the sort."

She laughed. "Well, you'd be the first ever not to make a snap judgement!"

"Doesn't pay to do that in my job," he said honestly. "Was Scarlett having any difficulties in her relationships?"

"You're talking about that muppet, Jonny, she's been knocking around with?"

Tom didn't reply, merely waited for her answer.

She shook her head. "He might be quite nice to look at but, boy, what a waste of space he is. I told her she could do better than him."

"What did he make of Scarlett's side line?"

Jenny grimaced. "At first, I think he was indifferent but when she was filming clothing content, he wasn't so keen. I know she never used to tell him about all the compliments she'd get." She shook her head. "Doesn't bear thinking about. I reckon he was quite jealous and possessive."

"We understand there might be someone else in the picture as well. Someone she may have set up a date with or met last night. Did she mention that to you at all?"

Jenny held Tom's gaze, sucking her lower lip. She was reluctant to answer which intrigued him.

"She did mention someone, didn't she?" Tom asked. "Who was it?"

"I don't know," she said flatly. Tom was unconvinced but didn't get a chance to press her. "I genuinely don't know, Inspector, honest I don't, but... she did say someone was making a play for her." She confirmed her own description with a nod. "Yes, that was how she said it; someone was making a play for her. Someone unexpected."

"An interesting turn of phrase," Tom said. Jenny looked at him, curious. "*Met* someone, been *introduced* or been *asked out* are arguably more conventional descriptive phrases. That someone was making a play for her... sounds either old-fashioned or that it was someone she already knew. Wouldn't you say?"

Jenny thought on it, then slowly nodded. "Yes, I think you might be right, now that you mention it."

"Any idea who it could be, any inkling at all?"

"No, as I said, I don't. Funnily enough, she was very coy about it... which probably means you're right. She was completely comfortable with it though, happy – no, not happy – amused... but I didn't know why or whether she was going to follow it up."

"She never said if she was going to take it further?"

"Exactly." She shook her head. "I told her to be careful." Jenny was matter of fact, jabbing a finger in the air before her. "That Jonny Young... is a bad egg, I tell you, just as I told her. He might blow hot and cold, but he liked the control he had over Scarlett, and he wouldn't take kindly to competition, I'm certain of it. Not that he'd go after the bloke; hell no, he'd take it out on Scarlett as usual."

"I have the impression he could be heavy-handed."

"Oh, yes. He certainly can. Especially if he had a drink in him. But as to who this mystery fella was, I can't help you. Not that I didn't ask, but Scarlett just smiled when I did. It was like she was a bit embarrassed by the attention." She shrugged. "I might be way off the mark, but that was what I thought." She held up a hand. "Please don't quote me on that."

Tom nodded. "Can you shed any light on Scarlett's online activities?"

Jenny searched Tom's expression, pensive. "You're talking about the video uploads, aren't you?"

"I am, yes. You're aware of them?"

"Of course! I encouraged her to do it. She even ran some ideas past me before doing them."

Tom hadn't expected that response, and it must have shown.

"Don't be a prude, Inspector. This is the twenty-first century and it's not like she was doing pornography, soft or hard. It was all tasteful stuff, mostly, that girls and young women would watch." She frowned. "Did pick up the odd nutter in the comments, but that's just men for you!"

Tom raised his eyebrows.

"Present company excepted, obviously," Jenny said. "But seriously, why ever shouldn't she? Scarlett is a pretty girl... not classically beautiful, but attractive, and her personality was so warm and giving. You can't fake that stuff. People respond to her. It was great and she earned a few extra quid for her and Maggie."

"Is this one of the things her father wouldn't know about?"

"Absolutely! He would never approve of such things, but he didn't have a computer, not even a smart phone, so she figured she'd be safe."

"And the content she made?"

"Like I said, nothing risqué... apart from maybe the swimsuit and summer wear she'd try on. Most of it was hair and make-up, outfit combinations. That sort of thing. In this day and age, girls and young women need help to look their best as their peers are not exactly forgiving when they get it wrong. It was harmless. Although, I told her she could likely make a few quid if she did the whole adult thing. Scarlett was an everyday girl, but one who'd lived a little. If you know what I mean?"

"There is one particular lead we are following," Tom said, careful not to give too much away, "and he may have been—"

"The creepy comment guy?" Jenny said. "Yeah, that freaked her out a bit. He used to send her pictures of himself... you know the type, unsolicited pictures." She shuddered. "Urgh... puts you right off. Scarlett started seeing him places, or at least she thought she was seeing him places. I told her it was paranoia. I mean, it's the internet... and she never said who or where she lived and all that, so what would be the odds of him showing up here. I told her not to worry."

"And she stopped?" Tom asked. "Worrying?"

"Yes, I think so," Jenny said. "She said she'd put some extra locks on the house but after a week or so, the feeling passed and I'm not even sure she used them after a bit. I know she didn't feel comfortable about living in Fort Knox."

"We haven't found recording equipment in the house. Do you know what she made her videos with?"

Jenny exhaled, concentrating hard. "She had a camera... a decent one that recorded video as well as stills. And she got a tripod. She wasn't making Hollywood films though. It was all pretty amateur stuff. There's a market for the natural content and Scarlett was a natural. Bless her." She was silent for a moment. She looked at Tom. "I can't believe she's gone... and Maggie? Who would take such a sweet innocent thing?"

"Yes, it is distressing," Tom said. "But we are doing everything we can to find Maggie. Did Scarlett ever speak to you about Maggie, her father or her relationship with anyone else? I'm thinking specifically regarding Maggie now."

She shook her head. "No, not really. The father was out of the picture as far as I know. I don't think he wanted to be involved and I know Scarlett was a bit frustrated about that."

Tom was surprised. "She said so?"

Jenny nodded. "Yes, her words exactly. Apparently, he used to be a total loser, but he turned over a new leaf... and Scarlett, well, she wanted to give him another chance. With her," she added swiftly, "with Maggie, not Scarlett."

"Right, and what did he make of that?"

"I don't know. I asked, but she brushed me off and so I didn't push it. After all, it's none of my business, is it?"

"I suppose not," Tom said, processing the information. "When was this, do you recall?"

"Oh, yes, easily. It was last month when she mentioned it to me, so it's recent."

Tony Slater was many things; a drug addict, a dealer and now, he was a liar.

Tom glanced sideways out into the hall. "I'm sorry for the question I am about to ask, Jenny, because you've been very helpful, but I'm afraid I have to—"

"Anything, if it helps?"

"I would like to have a look around your flat."

She locked eyes with him, momentarily confused before she realised. "You're looking for Maggie, aren't you?"

Tom was expressionless. "Yes. Yes, I am."

Jenny held his gaze for a moment.

"I could request a warrant but—"

"There's no need," she said, "please, do what you have to do. Just don't judge the state of my bedroom. I'm the only one who's been there in years."

Tom thanked her and explored the flat. It took a matter of moments. There was no sign of Maggie. Coming back into the living room, he found Jenny still sitting on the sofa, her legs tucked up beside her, leaning on the arm with one hand supporting her head. Her other hand had a tissue rolled up in it. She'd been crying. She'd switched the channel on the television and was watching another local news bulletin commenting on Scarlett's murder and the missing child. On the screen was a photograph of a proud, smiling mother with her arm around her daughter. The sound was still muted.

She looked at Tom, fearful. "You must find her, Inspector. You have to."

CHAPTER FIFTEEN

THE CARAVAN PARK was one of three perched on the cliff edge between the Beeston Bump and West Runton. Their destination was the smallest and lay between the two larger, more established, holiday encampments. The Norfolk Coast Path wound its way past them, a route for hikers and tourists to take in the sea views, beaches and mixed Norfolk landscape. The county was well known for being flat but there were also hills, which many people appeared not to realise. The famous Beeston Bump, formed by glacial movements thousands of years previously, used to have a twin which had long since been reclaimed by the sea, much as this area of the coast would in due course.

Eric slowed the car at the entrance, looking for signs to direct them to the correct caravan. Unlike most sites, this one was very small and apparently less well organised. Cassie was also looking but the sun had set and there was scant illumination to guide them beyond irregularly spaced lamps at the side of the roads.

"We're not going to have to knock on every caravan, are we?" Cassie asked.

"Might come to that," Eric said, looking around. Most of the caravans were not lit and therefore unlikely to be occupied. There were a few with lights on, the sunshine having brought people to their coastal retreat for the weekend.

Someone knocked on the driver's window, startling both of them.

"Sheesh," Cassie said. "Scared the daylights out of me."

Eric wound the window down and a rugged face leaned in, glancing between the two occupants.

"Can I help you?" he asked.

"Yes, thank you," Eric said. "We're here to see a friend of ours... William Slegg. We're not sure which caravan is his."

"Billy, huh?"

Eric nodded. "Yes, Billy."

The man focussed on Eric, chewing something absently on one side of his mouth.

"You don't look like Billy's usual sort."

Cassie leaned forward to see past Eric and smiled. "And what sort of people usually visit Billy?"

The man shrugged noncommittally. "I don't know... weird sort, I guess. You ain't weird, are you?"

Cassie glanced at Eric and back to the man. "Well, I'm not, but my friend here would fit in perfectly."

Eric rolled his eyes and the man grinned, showing cigarette stained and blackened teeth. He coughed, a grating, hacking sound, covering his mouth with the back of his hand.

Cassie raised her voice. "Have you seen Billy have any visitors today... or have anyone staying with him do you know?"

"Nope, can't say as I know. I'm the caretaker of this site..." He looked around, off into the darkness of the caravans, "and not much happens here without me seeing it."

"Right," Cassie said. "So, you live here, on the site I mean?"

"Nope. I live down the way in Sheringham. Keeps himself to himself does Billy. Haven't seen his mother around anytime recently either come to think of it."

"Does she come often?" Eric asked.

"Nope, can't say she does."

Cassie looked at Eric, almost imperceptibly passing judgement on the usefulness of this exchange with a shake of the head.

The caretaker pointed to where the track split about thirty yards away with one route heading off to the left.

"Old mother Slegg's caravan is down the left fork there," he said. "The last one before you reach the sea and it'll be the first one into it."

He stood upright, turned and walked away into the darkness without another word.

"Thank you!" Eric called after him. The man waved a hand in the air but didn't look round. "Interesting character."

"Yes," Cassie said, "and if he describes Billy and his mates as weird, then we must be about to meet a right humdinger!"

Eric put the car in gear, looking sideways. Cassie glanced at him.

"What?" she asked.

"You don't think I'm weird, do you?"

She smiled apologetically, slapping the side of his thigh with the back of her hand. "It takes one to know one, Eric, and I wouldn't change you for the world. Now," she pointed to the road ahead, "onward to Billy's. You never know, we might be about to solve this case and bring Maggie back to her granddad."

Eric sighed, moving off. "I don't know whether I want to find her here or not."

The site only housed fifteen to twenty pitches. No doubt there were more available to people who arrive in motor homes or with tents once the season properly got underway, but at this time there were only the static homes there. They were all of a uniform size, some with decking built out around them, ranging from a three-by-three metre square, facing the sea, to the full wraparound deck adding almost a third of living space to that of the interior.

Only two of the other caravans showed movement inside as they passed, and no one paid the arrivals heed. The last caravan stood out from the others. There was no decking or outside adornments and even with only the car headlights to illuminate it, they could see it was in a poor state of repair. The cliff edge was frighteningly close to the caravan, the headlight beams disappearing into the inky blackness of the night where the grass and sandy soil beneath fell away to the beach below. Eric parked the car and the two of them got out.

The rumbling waves striking the cliff below carried to them on the breeze. Eric walked a short distance ahead just to see how close the edge was, exaggerating a shaking of his head to signify it was too close for his liking.

"A couple of big storms this year and this place will be seaborne," he said, looking at the caravan and indicating it with his thumb.

Cassie raised her eyebrows. "Rather him than me. Shall we?" she asked, gesturing with an open palm to Eric and he approached the door. One light was on in the main living area, denoted by the number of windows and the size of the main window which, during the day, would have a lovely view of the sea and the coast stretching away.

Eric rapped his knuckles on the door. It was thin plastic and felt insecure. They waited but there was no movement within. Cassie stepped back and looked at the windows. The caravan was elevated so she couldn't see inside, and venetian blinds were dropped across all of them in any event. Eric knocked again, harder this time.

"Mr Slegg. Police!"

Cassie saw the blinds in one window move, separated fractionally by two fingers, just wide enough to allow someone to see out but not in. The fingers slipped back inside. Still, no one came to the door. Eric looked at Cassie, exasperated. She stepped forward and hammered on the door with a balled fist.

"Open the bloody door, Billy, or my colleague will kick it in!"

Eric frowned at her, lowering his voice. "I'll bounce off this thing... it's so thin, I'll—"

The lock moved and the door creaked open on old hinges. A narrow-faced, apprehensive man peered out at them, eyes wide.

"Let me see your identification, please," he said quietly, his eyes darting between them.

Eric obliged, taking out his warrant card and holding it out. The man reached for it but Eric withdrew his hand, so his wallet was out of his grasp.

"Detective Constable Collet," he said, indicating Cassie beside him. "This is Detective Sergeant Knight. We're looking for William Slegg."

The man flinched at mention of the name, his upper lip noticeably twitching.

"Billy. My name's Billy," he said, nervously rubbing at the end of his nose with the back of his hand. "Only my mum calls me William, and you're not her." He looked at Cassie. "And neither are you."

"I'm sure I'm as pleased about that as you are, Billy," she said, smiling. "May we come inside?"

Billy Slegg looked over his shoulder, rolling his lips together, thinking about it.

"Come on, Billy," Cassie said. "You're letting all the heat out."

He relented, nodding curtly and stepping back. Eric caught the door, threatening to fly back against the side of the caravan, and he allowed Cassie to enter first before following. Inside the caravan was a tip. Every surface in the kitchen area was full of dirty crockery, plates, bowls, cups and glasses. The washing-up bowl in the sink was full and virtually overflowing with cold water that had been sitting for some time based on the oily residue visible floating on the surface.

The booth housing the dining table fared little better. The seats were piled high with clothing, all thrown randomly and not folded or stacked. It was unclear whether this was clean or set aside for laundry. The dining table itself had several cardboard boxes stacked upon it, the contents of which were unknown. At the far end was a wraparound corner sofa facing a small television. Magazines and leaflets littered the floor and seating. Billy Slegg sat down in the one part of the sofa available to use for actually sitting on, lifting his feet and sitting cross legged. To his left was a side table and upon it was a laptop, the fans whirring away trying to keep the machine cool. Eric's eyes drifted to the screen and Billy noticed, quickly closing the lid. Behind where he was sitting, a large piece of radio equipment was on a window sill. It looked like a piece of kit from an old war movie, old school and imposing. Billy reached around and turned a dial which clicked to signify it was now off.

Billy stared at them warily. "What do you want here?"

Eric and Cassie exchanged a look. That was an odd question. Eric assessed him. Billy Slegg was easily in his forties, possibly even older but it was hard to tell. He wore his sandy-brown hair to collar length, but he couldn't spend much time caring for it because it looked lank and greasy. His complexion was dark but not tanned, what with the time of year, and he sported wrinkling and cracking around the eyes, denoting he was probably closer to his fifties than Eric first thought. His hair, thinning on top and receding from his forehead, made his narrow features look elongated and out of proportion. This, coupled with many weeks' worth of wispy beard growth, Billy Slegg had the appearance of a Taliban fighter, minus the *shalwar kameez.*

"We're here to speak to you about Scarlett Turnbull, Billy," Cassie said, her eyes trailing around the caravan. Eric followed her gaze, breaking off and settling on an old poster stuck to the wall with Blu Tack. It was hanging away from the wall now, pulling away under its weight, much as he'd found with his old movie posters on his bedroom wall growing up. The picture was of a saucer-shaped craft passing over trees. It was a famous shot given a new lease of life when used on set in a popular television show Eric remembered his mum watching when he was young. The caption read *I want to believe.*

"Scarlett? Never heard of her," Billy said, ignoring Cassie and focussing on Eric. Eric pointed to the poster.

"Do you?"

Billy looked at the picture.

"Do you believe?" Eric asked.

"Of course!" Billy said, scoffing. "The evidence is quite frankly overwhelming at this point…" he eyed Eric. "You're a detective. You tell me there's no evidence." He asked the question softly, as if he was daring Eric to deny the existence of UFOs.

"I want to," Eric said quietly, earning him a stark look of

despair from Cassie. Billy hadn't noticed. He smiled at Eric, raising his eyebrows, the smile broadening to a grin.

"Of course, you do. It's the only thing that makes any sense, right? They've been here for years, centuries even. They walk among us."

"Who are they?" Cassie said, folding her arms across her chest and leaning her back against the kitchen counter, but first checking she wouldn't wipe something onto her coat in doing so.

Billy sneered at her. "You don't want the answer to that."

"I don't?" Cassie asked, smiling.

"You can't handle the answer," Billy said, turning back to Eric. "Can she?"

Eric exhaled. "Probably not, no."

Now it was Cassie who scoffed. "Well, I'm a bit busy with human scum at the moment to be worrying about little green men as well—"

"Grey."

"Excuse me?"

"Little *grey* men," Billy said, knowingly. "They're not green and never have been. They are grey. So are the Nordics, but they blend in better because they're more like us... although much taller, which is where their name is derived from."

"Because?" Cassie asked, trying to keep a straight face.

"Because..." Billy leaned towards her, "...they look Scandinavian... You get it? They're tall, blond-haired and muscular." He tapped the side of his head with his forefinger. "Helps them blend in."

"For what purpose?" Cassie asked.

Billy's eyes gleamed, the corners of his mouth shaping a slight smile. "So, they can study us."

Cassie frowned, then clapped her hands together and turned to Eric. "Right, you," she said pointing her hands, still clasped together, at Eric, "continue to speak to this gentleman, and I am going to have a look around."

Without asking, she walked towards the rear of the caravan where the bedrooms and bathroom would be.

"Hey! You can't search my place without permission... don't you need a warrant!" Billy said, putting his palms down and lifting himself off the sofa so he could see over the kitchen counter. He looked at Eric. "You need a warrant, right? You have no rights here." Looking to where Cassie was last seen, he called, "I am a free man!"

Cassie's response came swiftly. "Eric, explain to Mr Slegg how the earthling police officers can carry out a search if we believe a crime is underway, without the need of a warrant."

Billy looked at Eric, confused. "Is that true?"

"Yes, it is Mr Slegg."

He sank back into the sofa, perplexed. "I never knew that. Really? I mean, really?" He shook his head. "This country is such a police state."

"It's hardly a police state, Mr Slegg. We're looking for a missing child."

Billy pouted. "And... you think she might be here?"

"No one said it was a girl, Mr Slegg," Eric said, coming to stand before him. Billy looked concerned. "So, how would you know it was a girl we are looking for?"

Billy grimaced, then met Eric's eye with a hopeful expression. "Would you believe a fifty-fifty guess?"

"You were detained once—"

"That was a long time ago and... and I hadn't done anything wrong."

"Loitering outside a primary school," Eric said. "It's not a good look."

"It was a misunderstanding," Billy said. "The parents were

paranoid, that's all. You can't walk down the street in this country anymore."

Cassie bounded back into the room. "Where did you think you were when a load of little kids in uniform came out, Billy, a singles' bar?"

Eric looked up inquiringly and she shook her head.

"No sign of her."

"No sign of who?" Billy asked.

Cassie turned on him. "Right, time is of the essence here, Billy. We are looking for a seven-year-old girl who was abducted overnight."

"Not by me, she wasn't," Billy said. "Although," he looked skyward.

"Don't start with that again or I'll..." Cassie let the threat tail away. Eric knew the last thing she wanted to do was arrest this man and have to listen to him talking. Billy was hanging on Cassie's words, waiting for her to finish. She let out a frustrated sigh. "You've been harassing Scarlett Turnbull—"

"I have not!" he protested. "Scarlett's my friend."

"Do you usually send sexually provocative comments to your friends, Mr Slegg?" Eric asked.

He looked offended. "She liked my comments... she said so."

Eric took out his pocketbook, examining his notes. "Double figure number of comments..." Eric looked at him, gauging the reaction, "daily, for the last two months with increasing frequency. Care to explain?"

Billy flushed, sheepish. "Just trying to be nice, that's all."

Eric continued, "Only for the comments to dry up in the last week, trickling down to one or two a day earlier this week and nothing Friday or today."

He looked awkward, shifting uncomfortably in his seat.

"Not a crime to move on."

"No, but following her around is," Cassie said. "Was that meant to be complimentary?"

Billy glared at her. "I didn't *follow her around*. I just wanted to say hello..." his eyes flitted between them "I thought she might like to go for a cup of coffee or something." He shrugged. "Not that I drink coffee... it gives you cancer."

"Thanks for the tip," Cassie said. "Any others, while you're at it?"

"Avoid the radon."

"Excuse me?"

"Radon gas," Billy said, raising a hand, extending his forefinger and making a loop in the air that saw him point down at the floor. "Coming up from the earth's core... poisoning you from within."

"Again... thanks," she said, frowning. "I think."

Eric cleared his throat. "You scared her, Mr Slegg. You scared Scarlett so much that she had extra security fitted at her home."

Billy shook his head, genuinely horrified. "No, no... I wouldn't want that, ever. I–I... think she's really nice, that's all. Her and her daughter—"

"You know of her daughter," Eric said, alarmed.

Billy's upper lip began twitching. Eric guessed it was a tell-tale sign he gave off that he was under stress. Billy waved both hands in the air, dismissing the idea he'd done anything wrong.

"I didn't follow them or anything," he protested. "It's all online... look." He reached for his laptop, setting it down before him on his crossed legs and lifting the screen. His fingers operated at speed, and he brought up a page, turning the screen to face them. "See, you can find anything online."

He'd brought up a web page detailing where Scarlett lived,

who was recorded at the address and how long they'd lived there. It must have been scraped from the electoral roll.

"It's all freedom of information stuff," Billy said. "And you can back trace an IP address easily enough. If you know how, at any rate."

Cassie looked at Eric. She saw it as plausible; he could tell.

"And as for not commenting as much... she hasn't been putting out as much content recently," Billy argued. "She was very regular but the past month or two she hasn't and I'm not going to keep commenting on videos I've already seen." He laughed, genuinely amused. "I mean, that'd be mad!"

Cassie exchanged a look with Eric, raising her eyebrows, but didn't comment.

"You have a good internet connection out here?" Eric asked.

Billy pointed up. "Dish on the roof... satellite comms."

Cassie was incredulous. "How on earth do you have your own satellite... oh, forget it!"

"My dad was a telecoms engineer, and he kept his money for a rainy day," Billy said, smiling. "My family, we've always been ahead of the curve. I tell you, when the cataclysm comes, my place will be the one with the lights still on."

"Cataclysm?" Cassie asked, and then dismissed her own question. "No, don't answer. I'm done with this. Billy, have you seen or spoken to Scarlett in the last forty-eight hours?"

"No, I haven't. Why?"

She ignored his question, asking pointedly, "Did you arrange a date with Scarlett last night?"

"No," he said, flushing red and clearly surprised to be asked such a question. "Why?"

"I actually believe you, Billy," Cassie said, turning to Eric. "Come on, we're wasting our time here, and," she glanced around, "I'm worried I'm going to catch something if we stick around much longer."

"Catch something?" Billy asked.

"Yes," she threw her hands in the air in exasperation, "rabies... or something. Eric, let's go."

Eric agreed and the two of them made for the door.

"Thanks for your time, Billy," Cassie said, looking back as she reached the door. "Sorry to interrupt... whatever it is you're doing this evening."

"Listening," he said, smiling.

"Listening to what?" Eric asked, immediately regretting asking and noting Cassie shooting him a dark look.

Billy pointed up with his right hand and reached for a set of headphones, lying on the sofa next to him, with his left. "Sounds from up there. Cosmic interference, alien radio waves, desperate cosmonauts... all sorts."

Cassie bit. "Desperate cosmonauts?"

"Oh yes," Billy said enthusiastically. "You know, in the early sixties during the Vostok Space Programme, a capsule carrying three cosmonauts returning to earth screwed up their calculations and instead of performing re-entry, the capsule skipped off the atmosphere and they were catapulted out into deep space... ham radio hacks of the day, people just like me, listened to their *increasingly* frantic Morse Code SOS signals for an hour or two until," wide-eyed, he slowly passed a flat palm through the air in front of and away from him, "silence."

Cassie smiled at Eric. "I had to ask, didn't I?" She looked at Billy. "Maybe the little green men could have picked them up?"

Billy wagged a finger at her. "Again, they are not—"

"Not green, yeah, I got you," she said. "Eric, *let's go.*"

Once outside, Eric closed the door behind them and they

walked to the car. The wind was picking up and it was colder now, the temperature dropping quickly. Cassie shivered.

"Fascinating, isn't it?" Eric said reaching the car.

Cassie grasped the passenger door handle, staring hard at Eric. "How a grown man can get to that age and be so delusional that he probably can't tie his own shoelaces without first donning a tinfoil hat?"

Eric smiled. "Yeah, I guess so. I can't see murder and abduction being his thing, though, can you?"

She shook her head. "Harmless in that sense. I still don't get the primary school thing. That was odd."

"Years ago, though," Eric said, "and nothing since. Maybe he was telling the truth and it was a misunderstanding."

"Yes, possibly. He is an oddball and if I saw him hanging around near a school, I'd probably give his collar a feel too."

"You'd drag him into the bushes and give him a kicking, Cass," Eric said, grinning.

"Thinking about it," Cassie said, "he might be harmless, but it'd be bloody frightening if you had to share the Christmas holidays with him though, huh?"

"True," Eric said, unlocking the car.

Cassie took out her mobile, hitting a speed dial. The call was answered quickly.

"Tom, it's Cassie. I'm afraid it's a bust here; William Slegg is a no go. He's as soppy as a box of frogs," she said, glancing at Eric as she got in the car beside him and pulled the door to, "but he's not our man. There's no sign of Maggie having been here. If this guy is capable of murder and abduction, then you can paint me pink and fly me like a kite."

CHAPTER SIXTEEN

Tamara looked around the incident room. Phones were ringing and every time an officer ended a call, another would come through. It had been like this since they'd delivered the press conference which went out live on the local BBC news channel. Such was the way with media these days, every newspaper had run with the conference footage on their own websites and social media platforms, just as they'd wanted, and information was flooding in.

"Excellent result, so far, wouldn't you say, Tamara?"

She turned to see the barrel-chested figure of Chief Superintendent Watts bounding up to her. His cheeks were glowing more than usual. He must have just finished a cup of hot tea or coffee,

"Yes, sir. I just hope…" she left the comment unfinished.

"Hope what?"

She couldn't shrug the thought off, which was difficult because this whole media circus was the chief's idea. "That the information coming in is of sufficient quality to… justify the level of resource applied to it." She read his expression, the warm smile rapidly fading. "Sir," she added.

"Some of the biggest cases in history were solved through sifting data, Tamara. You know that." He waved a hand through the air indicating the incident team, hard at work. "Somewhere in all this might be that one piece of information that unlocks this entire case—"

"As long as we are not buried under the weight of information and manage to find it in time," she said, flatly, failing to restrain her scepticism. "There is a little girl's life that may be in the balance and—"

"Indeed, which is the very reason we need to move quickly and involve the local community in finding her."

His tone was such that she knew not to labour the point. At any rate, it was done now. They had a difference of opinion, but her own disquiet around this approach was less so than Tom's. It was a good job she was having this conversation instead of him. Although, that said, Tom was the sort to keep his personal feelings better hidden than she ever did. Sometimes she wondered if being outspoken was a blessing or a curse.

"I hope you're right, sir."

"I am, absolutely," he said, puffing out his chest as if that were necessary. The man was a peacock, always had been in the time she'd worked under his command, albeit a peacock with slightly scabby feathers these days.

"My only concern is that if the lead we are looking for doesn't come in here, then we are wasting what precious time we have to locate Maggie."

"Have faith, DCI Greave," Watts said. "Have faith."

Her mobile rang and she excused herself, finding a quiet corner of the room to take the call. The number was withheld, and she answered coolly.

"Tamara Greave."

"Hi, Tammy!"

"Why are you blocking your number to me, Dad?"

"Oh, that's your mother's idea. She says if you know who's calling you don't tend to answer unless you want to."

That was true, but largely only when her mum called.

"Dad, what's up?"

"Nothing Tammy, nothing at all. We watched your television programme earlier—"

"Press conference, not television programme."

"Yes, yes, I know. Your mother and I thought you came over very well."

"You look tired," Francesca could be heard saying in the background.

Tamara ignored the comment. "Listen, it's a bit manic here, Dad. Can I call you—"

"Oh yes, I'm sure you have a lot to do what with finding that little girl and all. That's terrible, it really is. I just wanted to let you know."

"Let me know what?" she asked, acknowledging the Chief Superintendent gesticulating at her with some urgency for her to join him on the other side of the room. She waved and gave him a thumbs up before turning her back and lowering her voice even though no one could overhear her. "What is it, Dad? I really am busy here."

"I had a call from David, asking after you. Lovely chap."

Tamara was confused. Should the name mean something to her?

"Who?"

"David. He called me this evening to check you got home all right after the Healey broke down this morning."

Now she remembered, her good Samaritan. "Ah, right. How... did he—"

"Get your number? I thought that, but you called me from his phone, remember?"

"Yes, of course. Well, that was nice of him." She turned to see her boss watching her impatiently. "Dad, I really have to go—"

"He said he'd give you a bell."

"What?" she asked, focussed now. "You gave him my mobile number?"

"Well, yes. I did. Is there something wrong—"

"A total stranger?"

"He's not a total stranger, he's David."

She sighed. "Never mind, Dad. It's okay."

"A–All right, dear. If you're sure?" He sounded uncertain, fearful he'd done something wrong which, of course in her eyes, he had. "Will you be home late?"

"I don't know, I really don't," she said. "I might pop back for something to eat but," she looked at her watch, "maybe not."

Hanging up, she crossed the room to stand alongside the Chief Superintendent who was on the shoulder of a call handler. The receiver went down and the constable turned to face them both.

"We have a sighting," Watts said.

"Of Maggie?" Tamara asked, feeling a pang of excitement and hope.

"Possibly," the constable said. "A woman who lives two streets away from the Turnbulls saw a man carrying a sleeping child, at least he thought she was sleeping, along her street just before midnight. A neighbour's dog was barking at him as they passed which drew her attention just as she was closing the curtains in her bedroom. She thought it a bit strange, the girl being in her bedclothes and a dressing gown and clutching a teddy of some kind. She went to bed as usual. Now, she's wondering if this was the killer."

"Credible?" she asked.

The constable nodded. "Sounded so, yes. The age of the child matches more or less. The briefing you gave told us Maggie isn't a large child for her age."

Tamara exchanged a glance with Watts who was hanging on her every word to see what she was going to do. The notion flashed through her mind that her boss had little operational experience of a case like this and was waiting on her response. If the child was clutching a cuddly toy, then she was still alive when she left the house. This was great news.

"We need to get out to her and take a statement. We'll need to get a sketch artist over there as soon as possible to give us an image or representation, clothing, facial features... as much as we can and then pass that out to the press. If he was on foot that far from the house, it suggests he wasn't driving."

"Which means he, and therefore Maggie, might well be in close proximity to the Turnbulls' home," Watts said.

"That's it in a nutshell, sir." She smiled at him. "Looks like your call may have paid off after all."

Watts beamed at her. "Go and find this little girl, DCI Greave."

Tamara was about to excuse herself, planning on joining Tom and the rest of the team upstairs in the ops room. She knew they'd been running down leads and was keen to learn what they had and have this latest lead investigated as soon as possible. She was pleased they'd got a break in the case as up until now they'd been hitting dead ends with nothing concrete to follow up on.

"Before you go, Tamara," Watts said, falling into step alongside her. "I have to run something past you."

She stopped, turning to face him. "Sir?"

"As you are well aware, there's quite a lot of disquiet around this matter already—"

"It's been less than twenty-four hours, sir," she said.

"These things take time unless there is a family member at the heart of the abduction and, even then, it can still take days to locate an abducted child."

Watts held up his hand to silence her. She didn't appreciate the gesture.

"I hear what you are saying, DCI Greave." The use of her title and surname reminded her of being chastised by her mother when she was young. "But we are not used to these matters occurring on our shores, so to speak. Perhaps, with your experience in the cities, it is different. I consulted with the assistant chief constable this afternoon and in his opinion, of which I am in agreement, we should bring in some extra help in this particular case—"

"Absolutely, sir. We can certainly use greater manpower."

"Undoubtedly," he said, averting his eyes from her gaze. Clearly there was more afoot. "However, we thought a proper *understanding* of this individual might help unravel his mind-set, complex as it may be."

"You've lost me," she said, wishing he'd just spit it out.

"We're bringing in an expert... a psychologist, someone who can really break down what it is going on in this individual's mind."

"A criminologist? Someone qualified in the mindset of child abductors?" she asked.

"Well... one shrink is as good as another, as my old father used to say," Watts said, flashing her a smile. Tamara looked at him blankly. Someone else to get under her feet. "You'll make her welcome, won't you?"

Suddenly aware she was looking at him agape, she nodded slowly. "Yes, sir. Of course, I will."

"Excellent, Tamara," he said, clapping her gently on the upper arm and then retracting his hand as if he'd either made a social faux pas or, which was more likely based on the equality seminar all senior officers attended earlier in the week, concerned he'd committed a sexual harassment offence. He looked awkward, embarrassed. "Excellent," he repeated.

Watts walked away and Tamara exhaled heavily, resuming her course to the ops room. Climbing the stairs, her mobile rang and she saw the number was withheld. Taking a deep breath, she answered, shouldering the doors open at the top of the stairwell and entering the corridor to CID.

"You really don't need to hide your call, Dad, what is it now?"

"Tamara?"

She hesitated at the entrance to ops. The voice was familiar, but she couldn't place it.

"Yes, who's this?"

"I–It's David White. We met earlier today."

"Erm…"

"At the side of the road. You'd broken down."

She smiled. "Yes, of course. David. I'm sorry, I thought you were someone else."

"Evidently. Is your father a bit annoying?"

She laughed nervously. "Yes, but not quite as bad as his wife."

"Oh dear… anyway, I hope you don't mind me calling you like this?"

She did but was too polite to say so. Glancing through the glass insert to the door, she could see Tom was inside briefing Eric and Cassie. He saw her there and waved. She returned it.

"Tamara?"

"Yes, sorry, I'm here," she said. "I'm just a little distracted. Work. You know how it is?"

"Must be long days for you at the weekend, teaching classes," he said.

"Teaching?" Tamara asked, turning her back on the room,

then remembering he thought she was a fitness instructor. "Ah... well, it's all go." Changing the subject, she searched her memory for what he did for a living but wasn't sure she'd ever asked. "How was your... um... thing?"

"Very good, yes. Just made it in time," he said.

"Good." Keen to crack on, she sought to end the small talk. "Listen, thanks for your help today, it was kind of you to stop. Very kind."

"You're welcome."

"And, thanks for the call, I appreciate it, but I—"

"Oh yes, sorry, I won't keep you. As it happens, the event I attended today has led to a little more work and I'm staying on until Monday, maybe longer. I was just wondering, seeing as neither of us are married or anything," she recalled that exchange earlier, "that... um... you might care to join me for dinner... or a drink or... something. What do you think?"

Tamara, caught unawares, hesitated and then smiled. She could sense his nerves jangling, his face reddening at the other end of the line. She leaned against the wall, flattered to be asked. It wasn't what she'd been expecting.

"Well..." she said, uncertain.

"I know it's out of the blue and you don't know me from Adam, but we could meet somewhere neutral, anywhere, on your terms. I have no idea where, mind you. This really isn't my part of the country."

Tamara thought about it, biting her bottom lip. Her instinct was to say no, but it'd been a while since anyone had made the effort, not least her.

"Can we talk about cars?" she asked playfully.

"Erm... sure, yes. We can... i–if you like one-sided conversations," he said, laughing.

She grinned. "We don't have to talk about cars."

"So, is that a yes?" he asked, hopeful.

"A tentative yes, but I am very—"

"Busy with work. You did say. Tomorrow evening maybe? I'll be working during the day and I don't know when I'll finish."

"Me neither, but okay," she said, "tomorrow evening sounds good, but with the caveat that I may need to cancel at short notice. It depends on—"

"Work, yes, I understand. And whether you have a change of heart between now and then, perhaps even as you park your car outside the restaurant?"

"Quite possible," she said. "It has been known. Are you okay with accepting that level of risk?"

"I'll take my chances, Tamara."

"Good. I'll text you the place… but I'll need your mobile number. It came up blocked."

"Yes, your father told me I'd have to hide it, or you were unlikely to answer."

"Did he now?" she asked, amused. "Remind me not to spend much on him for his birthday this year, would you?"

"Don't be too hard on him. He seems like a lovely man," she did not disagree, "and I will remind you, provided you show up for our date, that is. I'll look forward to seeing you tomorrow."

"Yes, so will I," she said, smiling and hanging up. Within moments she received a text message from David with a smiling emoji. "I really will," she said to herself before striding into ops.

CHAPTER SEVENTEEN

"ANYTHING COMING IN ON THE PHONES?" Tom asked as Tamara entered the op's room.

"We have a sighting from last night," she said. All three of them turned to her expectantly and she sought to keep their hopes in check. "It's not confirmed as Maggie, but a man was seen carrying a girl fitting her description a couple of streets over from Scarlett's home on Victoria Avenue." She tilted her head to one side. "It's in the right area and fits our time frame. The witness described the little girl as being asleep and we've no reason to doubt that."

Cassie's hand shot up. "I'll go and speak to her."

"Good," Tamara said. "I was planning to ask. We're bringing in a sketch artist. I want something visual to hand out to the media. Seeing as they're here, we may as well utilise the coverage. And, coincidentally, if we can give them something fresh to run with then we have every chance of keeping the narrative on side."

"You sound concerned," Tom said.

"I am. I want finding Maggie to be the focus of this story

rather than the press looking to keep interest in the story alive through other means."

Apart from Eric, they'd all been involved in other cases and witnessed both the positive and negative side of press attention. They were only in the first day of the investigation but if no developments could be seen, then the focus could shift onto the family of the victim, their associates or neighbours and ultimately onto the investigation team itself. Chief Superintendent Watts was already trying to get out in front, that was what Tamara was certain the appointment of a psychologist was all about; not only to assist but to be seen to be doing everything possible to find the little girl. It was hard to escape the thought that perception was at the forefront of her superior's actions and not what was best for the investigation.

She looked at the information board, updated with a lot of information since she'd last had a chance to read it. She pointed at the picture of William Slegg. Cassie answered.

"A proper fruitcake," she said, "but he's not who we're looking for."

"A dangerous fruitcake?" Tamara asked.

Cassie shook her head, tapping the biro in her hand against her desk. "No, can't see it." She glanced sideways at Eric. "You?"

"No. I agree. He's odd but not a murderer," Eric said.

Tom pointed to a flow chart depicting Scarlett's connections, friends, family and associates. "I've spoken with Jenny Bovis, a good friend of Scarlett's, separate from her family or social circle. Scarlett was open with her about her sideline earning money through the internet, ran things past her, and to some extent I think she was her closest confidant."

"Anything coming out of that conversation?" Tamara asked, her curiosity piqued.

"Background is all," Tom said, despondent. "Scarlett kept that side of her life secret from her father and from her boyfriend. Jenny doesn't hold Jon Young in high regard at all."

"No one does," Eric said under his breath. Tamara ignored the comment.

"Does this Jenny know who Scarlett may have been meeting on Friday night?"

Tom shook his head. "No, Scarlett told her someone was into her but wouldn't elaborate on it. *Coy*, is the description she cited."

"So even her closest friend was in the dark. That is curious. Presumably, he, or she, was well known to the social circle. Do you agree?"

Tom thought about it, nodding his agreement. "That would follow, yes."

The phone on Eric's desk rang, the detective constable turning away to answer it, holding the receiver close to his ear and speaking in hushed tones.

Tamara felt a stab of pain at the back of her head. Her shoulders were tense and she closed her eyes, rolling her head to try and ease the tension. Although they couldn't rule anything out, she had the feeling the answer to the question of Maggie's disappearance, along with the murder of her mother, was closer to home rather than as a result of someone passing through, a chance meeting with a ruthless stranger.

Focussing on the information boards, she examined the crime scene. Other than the presence of Scarlett's body, there was no indication of violence which further supported her theory that whoever had been in the house was welcomed and likely known to the occupier. Sadly, that didn't bring them any closer to identifying the culprit.

"Okay, bye," Eric said, putting the phone down.

Tamara glanced his way. He was staring into space.

"Everything all right, Eric?"

He didn't look round let alone acknowledge the question.

"Eric?"

He shook his head, turning to face her. "Sorry, what?"

"Is everything okay?" Tamara asked softly. There was something in his expression, a sadness in the eyes she'd not seen in him in the past that was becoming ever more common these days.

He hesitated and then nodded.

"Anything we need to know about?"

"No," he said, shaking his head. "It… was a personal call."

He broke eye contact, reaching for his notebook and pen before crossing his legs and resting the notebook on his leg. He looked pale, more so than usual. He cupped his mouth and chin with his free hand. Looking up, he met her eye and shrugged.

"It's all good, honestly."

Tamara didn't believe him and by the look on Cassie's face, she didn't either, but it wasn't her place to say, so she returned to the briefing.

"Okay, Cassie, you're going to go and speak to this witness. With a bit of luck, she will be able to give us a good description and if she got a view of his face, maybe we can bring her in and have her go through the books of known local sex offenders. I'm still inclined to think it's someone in Scarlett's circle, but it'd be good to run through this. Speaking of which, Eric, can you go through the register and see if there's been any unusual activity from any of those we know about? Any breaches of restrictions, complaints regarding unannounced visits to offspring or the like?"

"Yes, I can do that," Eric said, making a note.

"If you need to pop home, Eric, you—"

"No, it's fine. I'm happy here."

He didn't look up from his writing, dismissing the offer with a shake of the head.

"Tom," Tamara continued, "I think someone should give the father an update. I know Kerry is with him, but she's not in the loop as much as we are."

"No problem. I can stop in."

Tamara checked her watch. The evening was pushing on and they only had the one solid lead. The strength of which was yet to be determined.

"Make sure you call in at home, too, while you're at it, Tom."

He looked at her quizzically and she took him aside.

"I can see how today has affected you."

"I'm fine," he countered.

"I know, but Maggie is pretty close to the same age as Saffy and I can see it in your eyes," she said. He looked away. "There's no harm in calling home for half an hour after you've visited Alan Turnbull." She winked. "We can manage without you for that long. Have something to eat while you're there, I'm sure you've not found time all day."

"No, that's true but I'm not hungry."

"Fair enough, but go home, say hi to Alice and give Saffy a big hug. It'll do you good."

Tom glanced at the clock. "She'll be asleep," he said before holding up a hand by way of acceptance, "but I will. You're right, it'd be good to step away for a moment."

"Do you mind if I tag along?" Eric asked, joining them and overhearing the last of the conversation. "I'd like to see how Alan is getting on. I spent some time with him this morning. I know you asked me to look into—"

"It's okay, Eric. Yes, by all means. We all need to breathe in this case."

186 J M DALGLIESH

Eric was grateful. Tom tapped him on the arm. "We'll leave in a couple of minutes."

Eric left them and Tamara lowered her voice. "Keep an eye on him, would you? Something's going on there."

Tom followed her gaze to Eric who was gathering his wallet and mobile from his desk.

"You think there's a problem?" Tom asked.

"Maybe, but he's unlikely to share."

Tom nodded. "He must get that from you," he said, smiling and leaving her side and heading into his office. He returned moments later with a jacket and a book in his other hand. Tamara eyed it.

"Light reading material to distract you?"

For a moment, Tom looked confused and then he lifted the book up so she could see it.

"It's the book Scarlett was reading."

"Significance?"

He turned the corners of his mouth down and shrugged. "Probably none, but something Alan said made me wonder."

"Which was?"

"That they used to read it together when Scarlett was a similar age to Maggie, after her mother died." He thumbed through the early pages. "I don't know why it's stuck with me but is it an odd coincidence that she's now reading it at the time of her own death?"

Tamara thought about it. "Have you read any of it?"

"No, not yet. Still, it can't hurt." Tom caught Eric's attention. "Come on then young man, let's head off." Turning to Tamara, he shot her a quick smile. "I'll be back soon."

"Take your time. If anything important comes up I'll call you."

CHAPTER EIGHTEEN

ALAN TURNBULL'S home was a bungalow on the outskirts of Hunstanton overlooking the lighthouse at the end of Cliff Parade. Tom was pleased not to find a media scrum encamped outside the property but as he pulled the car into the kerb, a figure did leap out of a hatchback parked on the other side of the road. The local journalists and the television media were not as hard-nosed as their counterparts in the national tabloids, and Tom was certain if this story had broken at any other time of the week instead of a Saturday, they'd be all over it and all over Alan.

A woman approached him and Tom recognised her from one of the local East Anglian papers but he couldn't recall which one. She certainly clocked him though.

"DI Janssen?" she asked, knowing full well who he was.

"Good evening," Tom said, gesturing for Eric to head up to the front door.

"Are you here to brief Mr Turnbull on developments regarding his daughter's murder, or the whereabouts of his granddaughter, Maggie?"

She was asking politely, not brandishing a microphone or even a notepad.

"I'm afraid I can only refer you to the statements made at this evening's press conference," Tom said. "I'm sorry, but I'm sure you can understand."

She was disappointed, it was clear, but she smiled gratefully. Her body language shifted, less rigid and professional, more natural.

"This is such a terrible story to be covering," she said, thrusting her hands into her coat pockets to shield them from the cold night air. They were standing right on the coast, barely fifty yards from Hunstanton Cliffs. The wind was stronger than it had been in days, bringing much needed cloud cover in to keep the air temperatures up but the wind chill killed any benefit.

"Yes, it is," Tom said, stopping for a moment. "I thought, as a journalist, you'd be keen for such a big story to drop into your lap."

"Not at the expense of someone's life..." she glanced out into the dark expanse of the North Sea, "or for that of her daughter either. That's not why I got into this game, to be honest."

"Then why did you?"

She appeared thoughtful. "I like to tell stories... and report other people's. This is a lovely place to live most of the time. The community is quite special. Something like this risks all of that, makes us seem worse than we are." She looked glum. "Does that make any sense to you at all?"

He smiled reassuringly. "A little, yes."

"It sounded better in my head, I have to say."

Tom saw Kerry was talking to Eric on the doorstep and both looked out at Tom. He excused himself and walked up the drive. The journalist returned to the relative sanctuary of her car.

PC Kerry Palmer welcomed Tom inside, closing the door behind him. The bungalow was modest, clean and well presented. Kerry directed them through the house to the rear.

"Alan is in the dining room," she said.

"How is he?" Tom asked.

"It's a cliché... but he's bearing up. With what he's had to process today, I think he's doing remarkably well."

The house felt colder inside than out. Remembering what Kerry had told him earlier during the identification of Scarlett's body, he now understood what she'd meant. It was uncomfortably cold.

"Did you speak to Alan about the heating?" he asked.

Kerry nodded vigorously. "Absolutely, but he was steadfast..." she shook her head. "He won't have it at all; says the heating is too expensive and he'll have it on for an hour in the morning and again in the evening. Not that it's come on yet. I think he's lost track of time, to be honest. Understandable, I suppose."

Tom stopped in the doorway and observed Alan. He was sitting at the dining table, in an outdoor coat done up to his collar, multiple photo albums arrayed in a semicircle in front of him. He was slowly making his way through them, so focussed was he that he was unaware of Tom's presence. Every now and then, his gaze would linger on a particular page and examine something closer before moving on.

"He's been doing that for hours," Kerry whispered, standing beside Tom. "When he's done, he goes back to the beginning and starts over."

"We all find ways to cope," Tom said, easing himself into the room.

Alan turned as he came closer, surprised to see him.

"Oh, hello, Inspector Janssen," he said, forcing a half-smile. Indicating the photo albums around him, he gestured for Tom to take a seat beside him. "Come... come and see my beautiful family."

Tom pulled out a chair and sat down alongside. Alan immediately lifted an album and placed it down in front of him.

"This is Scarlett and my wife, Margaret," he said, pointing to a faded photograph where the colours, no doubt once vibrant, were now shrouded by the degradation of time and exposure to air. The image looked overlaid with a brown filter. The woman was the spitting image of Scarlett, wearing her hair long and with a blue and white polka dot headscarf tied around her to keep the hair away from her face. She wore large, brown circular sunglasses, likely the fashion of the day. In her arms was a little girl, Scarlett, and her mother was having to lean at an awkward angle to offset the weight of her daughter in her arms.

"How old would Scarlett have been there?" Tom asked.

Alan smiled. "Three, maybe four." He folded back the film holding the picture in place and looked at the rear where a date and location were handwritten. "Blackpool," he said, knowingly. "Scarlett would have been five when that was taken. Wow... I got that one wrong. It's funny what time does to the memory, isn't it, Inspector?"

"You only had the one child?" Tom asked, immediately regretting asking as he was unaware of their circumstances and didn't want to add to the man's grief.

"Yes, but not for the lack of trying," he said, solemnly. "It never happened for us again. Scarlett was the shining light... I dare say we'd have had a sibling or two if... had Margaret... well... you know?"

Alan had explained earlier that he'd been widowed when

Scarlett was a similar age to what Maggie was now, within three years of that photograph being taken. As if Tom had asked him to, Alan enthusiastically leafed through the assembled albums and triumphantly found what he was looking for buried beneath several others. He hefted up a wedding album and set it down before Tom, skipping through the first few pages until he found a photograph of himself and Margaret posing together for the camera, post ceremony, at their reception.

"I wouldn't fit in that suit anymore," he said, chuckling and pointing to his classic three-piece and patting his stomach. His finger traced the image, hovering over his wife who wore a big smile, her hair tied up and looking radiant in a red dress. "Isn't she beautiful?"

"Yes, very stylish," Tom said.

Alan held his finger over Margaret, gently stroking her cheek. He smiled warmly, bobbing his head. "Yes, she always was. We went for a low-key registry office ceremony," he said, glancing sideways at Tom. "Neither of us was particularly religious. I think that upset her mother, though, which was never our intention. Although, I did find faith after she passed... selfish really."

"Why was that selfish?"

Alan exhaled heavily. "Because I needed to believe that she was in a better place, not only for me but also for Scarlett. It's a terrible thing to have to explain to your daughter... well, anyway," he sighed, slowly closing the album and laying a flat palm on the front.

"How did you lose your wife, Alan? If you don't mind my asking?"

"No, not at all," Alan said glumly. Shortly after Scarlett was born, in fact on the way home from the hospital, we were involved in an accident." Alan looked at Tom forlornly. "We collided with another car; the driver was drunk even though it was barely after midday."

"I'm sorry to hear that."

"Yes, well, Scarlett was fine... and I suffered only cuts and bruises to go with my shock, whereas Margaret," he said, pausing and recalling the memory, "bless her, took the brunt of the impact. She recovered, of course," Alan said, splaying his hands wide, "but life was never quite the same again; restrictive movements, living with intense pain. Her condition deteriorated in the coming years and, in the end, her body..." he shrugged "just seemed to give up on her."

Tom didn't know what to say. He felt bad for bringing it up. "That must have been difficult for you both."

"Oh, it was, Inspector. Not that it affected how much I loved my wife or made me question our time together. She was still with me, and I would take that in any capacity in which it came."

"What about Scarlett?"

"Well, that was different. Scarlett has no memory of her mother being anything other than bed or chair bound, seeing her suffering like that was... normal." He chuckled, but it was a wry sound and devoid of genuine humour. "Normality in our family was different to most."

"Do you think being accustomed to her mother's condition will have helped Scarlett deal with Maggie's?"

"Oh, undoubtedly so!" he said. The conversation died and Alan slowly stroked the wedding album, finally tapping the cover with his index finger as if it was a sign of closure. "So, Inspector, I'm sure you didn't come over to join me on a trip down memory lane. You have news?"

"More of an update, really."

Alan glanced towards the door where Kerry and Eric stood

quietly, watching on. He tipped his head in Kerry's direction. "Your young WPC, do you still call them *WPCs*?"

"No, not for a long time now."

Alan laughed nervously. "I am sorry. I've always been a bit behind the times. Scarlett is always telling me – was – how I should join the twenty-first century... I feel like I'm still waiting to join the twentieth most of the time!"

"It doesn't matter, honestly," Tom said reassuringly.

"Well," Alan said, sitting up straight and inhaling deeply, "Kerry has been a godsend to me in the harshest of times."

Tom looked at Kerry and she blushed at the compliment.

"I'll put the kettle on, shall I?"

"Please, dear, thank you," Alan said. Kerry backed away and walked into the adjoining kitchen. Eric followed.

"That is good to hear, Alan," Tom said.

"She's a credit to you, she really is. Although..."

"Although?"

"Does go on a bit... These young people aren't as hardy as we used to be, you know?"

"I still consider myself young," Tom said, "and I like my creature comforts. I'm presuming you're talking about the heating?"

Alan flashed him a smile, but it was fleeting.

"Gas is expensive, Inspector. I appreciate her concern for my wellbeing."

"I think she sees you sitting in your coat and wants—"

"But I have an outdoor coat, Inspector. It is thicker than this one, so when I step out, I swap over and feel the benefit." He waved away any further questions on the matter. "Now, what brings you here?"

"I wanted to reassure you that we are following up several lines of inquiry but, what with the loss of light, we have suspended the search teams until daybreak."

Alan fixed him with a stare, putting his palms together and lifting them to his face, touching the tip of his nose.

"We have established a contact centre following the television appeal and people are calling in," Tom said. "We have every confidence in the team's progress."

Alan sat in silence for a moment, digesting the information. His eyes drifted to the book Tom had in his hand. He gestured to it. "Is that Scarlett's?"

Tom looked down at it. "Yes, it is. After you mentioned it to me earlier, I found it curious that she was reading it."

Alan smiled. "As did I, Inspector." He folded his arms, frowning. "That story is a few hundred years old... to think it still has relevance is a testament to the author, wouldn't you say so?"

"I'll have to take your word for it. I'm afraid I've not had time to get into it, bar the first couple of chapters, for obvious reasons."

"Ah, of course," Alan said, his eyes still focussed on the book in his hand. Tom noticed.

"Would you like me to return this to you, when the time comes?"

Alan waved it away. "No need. I've long since committed that particular story to memory, but I appreciate the offer."

"It will be available along with Scarlett's possessions once the investigation is over, just so you know."

A gust of wind caused the window to rattle in its frame and Alan's gaze drifted to it. The streetlights barely lit up the night sky, but he stared out as if he could see something beyond.

"When you hear the raven's call... it will be me singing to you," he said quietly.

Tom cocked his head, Alan dipped his. A wry smile

crossed his face and Alan reached over, patting Tom's forearm gently.

"Keep reading and you'll understand the reference, I promise," Alan said. His expression clouded and he looked pensive. "You're a parent, aren't you?"

Tom nodded.

"Then you'll understand how, as a parent, you look to your children to witness your hopes and dreams travelling beyond your own physical life."

"I do, yes. I've never thought about it like that, but..."

"They are our future. Our gift to the world when it is time for us to move on." Laying his hands on the table in front of him, he began stacking the albums into neat piles, only three high. "Tell me, how should a man feel about his own mortality when his gift to the world passes before him?"

There was nothing Tom could say to ease the weight of that thought. Not that he believed Alan was expecting an answer.

Alan stopped what he was doing and smiled apologetically. "Forgive me, Inspector. I can feel the well of despair drawing me to it."

"No apologies necessary," Tom said. "But don't give up hope, not while there is still a chance of us finding your Maggie."

"Hope is a dangerous vessel, Inspector. When dashed upon the rocks, one sinks very quickly."

———

IN THE KITCHEN, Eric was lost in thought. He noticed Kerry watching him intently. Feeling self-conscious, he frowned.

"What is it? What did I do?"

"Have you heard a word I've been saying?"

"Yes, of course," he said, indignant. Then his frown dissipated, and he shook his head. "No, sorry. I was miles away. What were you saying?"

"It doesn't matter. Are you all right, Eric?"

He looked away. "I'm hearing that a lot today."

"Probably because we care... and can see something isn't right. You can say, you know?"

He looked at her, his throat running dry, and he struggled to swallow, feeling his nose tingle and his eyes water. "I–I..." Fearful he was about to cry, he looked around for an escape but there was nowhere for him to go. He felt panic rising from within. Kerry stepped across and put a hand on his. The gentleness of her touch reassured him and looking at her face, she smiled at him warmly.

"What is it?" she asked.

"I–I'm not... coping, not at all—"

"It's a terrible case—"

"No, not that," Eric said, shaking his head. "I mean, yes, it's bad and all but... it's everything else... Becca... and George. I'm useless at it."

Kerry squeezed his hand, and he looked into her face. "Eric, you're a wonderful father, I'm sure of it."

He shook his head. "I'm not so sure. Becca doesn't think so."

"Well, she's just blooming well wrong, then! You tell her from me."

Eric sniffed hard, lifting his free hand to wipe the end of his nose. "I'm sorry, the last thing you need is me snotting on you."

"I'll live," she said.

Eric laughed nervously which only worked to free up more water to run from his nose and eyes. "Oh, I'm such a mess."

Kerry tore a piece of kitchen paper from a roll next to them

on the worktop and passed it to him. Eric didn't feel embarrassed, relieved more than anything else.

"What has she done to you?" Kerry asked.

Eric shrugged. "She's having a hard time of it… she's just
so stressed and gets so, so angry… like, all the time. I feel as if
I'm walking on eggshells everyday trying not to say or do the
wrong thing. No matter how hard I try I seem to be at fault.
It's so hard."

He realised Kerry was still holding his hand and she
reached up with the other, touching his cheek with her palm.
He saw compassion in her expression, was comforted by the
touch and felt the warmth of her breath on his face. They were
so close.

"Maybe it's not you who is at fault, Eric." She said,
stroking his cheek. "Have you considered that?"

Their eyes met and something unsaid passed between
them. Eric felt something, a flicker, a thrill, he couldn't process
it. She was so close. Movement behind saw the two of them
part abruptly as Tom entered the kitchen. Eric looked at him,
Kerry looking to the floor and turning away from them both.
Tom seemed to pause, looking between them.

"Everything okay?" he asked.

"Yeah, yeah," Eric said, quickly passing a hand across his
face and blinking away the threatened tears, averting his face
from Tom's gaze. Kerry cleared her throat, nodding her
agreement.

"Yes, fine." She glanced at Tom, he had a strange, knowing
look on his face. "Really…" she said. "It's all… um… good."

"All right then," Tom said, his tone indicating he knew
he'd walked in on something but likely he didn't know what.
Nor did Eric for that matter. Whatever feelings stirred within
him in that moment had passed and now he felt awkward
and a little guilty. Tom looked at Kerry and the tea she was

setting about making. "Skip the tea for us; we have to make a move."

"Right," she said, smiling and not looking at him but focussing on the task in hand. "Just for me and Alan then."

"What time are you planning on staying here until tonight, Kerry?" Tom asked.

"I hadn't thought," she said, stirring the teabag in one cup before doing the same in the next.

"Well, the phone lines will be kept open, but the search teams have broken off and won't go out again until daybreak. I suggest you get off home for some downtime and then return early tomorrow. Are you okay with that?"

"Yes, of course." She glanced briefly at Eric and away again. "There's no one waiting for me at home, though, so it doesn't matter."

Tom turned to Eric. "Come on, I'll drop you back at the station, or home, if you want to freshen up?"

Eric looked at Kerry, busily over-stirring the two cups. She must have felt his eyes on her because she looked over at him, pensive.

"No, the station will be fine," Eric said. "I've no need to be home."

"Are you sure? You don't want to be at the station all night."

Eric shook his head. "I'll only be in the way there." He caught Tom's inquisitive look. "It's fine, I'll call home from the station and make sure everything is all right."

"Okay. Let's be off."

Eric nodded and walked out of the kitchen. There was a pinch point in the kitchen, and he hesitated as he passed Kerry. She glanced sideways at him, smiling awkwardly and tucking her hair away from her face and behind her ear.

"See you, Kerry," he said stiffly, feeling self-conscious, his face warming.

"See you."

She didn't look up as he left and Eric came under Tom's watchful eye as he stepped past him and into the hall, but his boss didn't comment. How long was he standing there before they heard him and how much did he see? Was there anything to see? His thoughts were in turmoil. They left the house in silence, Eric striding purposefully towards the car. Tom didn't say anything at all, which he was thankful for. Perhaps he hadn't seen or heard anything. Eric hoped so.

CHAPTER NINETEEN

THE LIGHTS WERE STILL on when Tom pulled up in front of his home. It was approaching eleven o'clock and he had wondered whether Alice would wait up to see him or go to bed. Yawning as he unlocked the front door, he spied Russell, Saffy's terrier, pop his head up from his favoured sleeping position on the landing at the top of the stairs, look down on him and match his yawn with one of his own. The dog got up, stretched, and trotted down the stairs to greet him. Tom dropped to his haunches and Russell stood on his hind legs, resting his front paws on Tom's thighs, accepting a playful stroke and tousling of his ears.

Alice appeared from the living room.

"Hey," she said, smiling.

Tom righted himself and drew her to him, giving her a kiss and then hugging her tightly.

"Hey," he replied.

She leaned away from him, keeping her arms around his waist. "Rough day?"

He nodded. "As rough as they come."

She turned him and guided him towards the kitchen,

Russell in tow, leaping up at Tom's hand, tail wagging ten to the dozen.

"I've kept you some dinner. It'll reheat soon enough in the microwave."

"Thank you," Tom said, disengaging from her as she went to the fridge.

Tom took off his coat and hung it on the back of the breakfast bar stool, pulling it out and sitting down. Resting his elbows on the surface, he leaned forward and ran his hands through his hair and down the sides of his head, cupping them at the nape of his neck before stretching out.

He reached down and took Scarlett's paperback book from his coat pocket, setting it down in front of him. Alice clocked it as she removed cling film from a plate, placed an upturned bowl over the food and put it in the microwave.

"What do you have there?" she asked, programming the machine.

Tom frowned, picking the book up and holding it briefly so she could see the cover. He then flipped it to read the back page. "The victim, Scarlett, was reading this. Her father tells us it was a book they read together as a child."

"What's it about?"

"From what I can tell, having barely scratched the surface, it's about two brothers who unexpectedly pass away independent of one another and are reunited in the afterlife."

"Heaven?"

Tom shrugged. "I don't think so... more a fantasy type existence, having read the blurb, where they go on adventures, face great peril and battle greater evil."

"That sounds... cheery," Alice said. "Why have you got it?"

"I'm not sure, to be honest," he said, putting it down and

tapping it with his fingertips. "It just leapt out at me in a way that nothing else did."

"How is it going? The case I mean."

Exhaling heavily, he shook his head. "We're doing all the right things... have a lead Cassie is following up as we speak but, so far, nothing. We don't have any motive, not really. And as for locating the daughter..."

"Yes, I saw Tamara on the television alongside the Chief Superintendent appealing for information. Is that where the lead came from?"

He nodded, rubbing at his face to wake himself up a bit. "Yes. I wasn't too keen with relying on the locals to stimulate the investigation but if it comes off, then it's brilliant."

Suddenly, he felt tired, as if the trials of the day had sucked the energy out of him. The microwave sounded the alarm and Alice set a knife and fork down in front of him, picked up a tea towel and returned to the machine.

"Every time I think about Maggie, I can't help but picture Saffy in my mind," he said as she put the plate down in front of him, steam rising in wisps before him. "They're the same age, and I can't help but think what it would be like to lose her, my daughter, in that way."

Having not eaten since breakfast, the smell of the food made him feel ravenous, his mouth watering as he picked up the fork and ploughed it into the dish. Shepherd's pie, or cottage pie, he wasn't sure which and didn't care. It was one of Alice's best. Blowing on a mouthful of food, he stopped as he went to put it in his mouth. Alice was staring at him, a hand across her mouth, her eyes glazed.

"What is it?" he asked, uncertain.

"That's... the first time you've ever said that."

"Said what?"

"Called Saffy your daughter."

He lowered his fork, his brow furrowing. She was right. Taking a breath, he smiled at her. "That's how I see her. She is my daughter."

Alice came to him, placing her hand over his left, lying flat next to the plate. He turned it upright and they interlocked their fingers. She smiled at him, and he squeezed her hand.

"She is my daughter."

"But you've always been so careful to… I don't know," she said, looking to the ceiling for inspiration in selecting the right word, "to keep a distance."

He shook his head. "It's not that. Saffy had a father, and it wasn't my place to try and subvert his role, or to be a surrogate dad… and…"

"And?" she asked thoughtfully. "Adrian's death hit her hard, but it was you who was there for her, to pick her up when she needed it. Then, and every day since up until now. But you've always been reticent to be that person. That's fair to say, isn't it?"

"Yes, it is," he said, concentrating. "You see so many couples split and one, or both, partners bring someone new into the child's life. That's okay, but if they become attached to one another and then the *new parent* is replaced by another and another, then it has to affect the stability of the child, right? It has to."

Alice withdrew her hand from his. He thought he'd made a valid point but the expression on her face told him otherwise.

"So, reading between those lines, you've been doubting the longevity of our—"

"No! No, that's not it at all," Tom said, realising where she was going. He hopped off the stool and came around to her, encircling her waist with both arms and pulling her into him. She didn't resist. "Really, that's not what I was saying. I think... if I'm to be Saffy's father, then... then it should be more official, that's all."

Alice's eyes widened and then she raised one eyebrow sceptically. "Official?"

Tom winced. "Bad, bad choice of word."

Alice's nose wrinkled. "Very bad, Tom."

"Well, I'm a detective not a poet," he said, widening his eyes.

She laughed.

"Which is a good job, or we'd be destitute and sleeping on a park bench. So, what is the right word?"

He stepped back from her, taking her hands in his and holding them against his chest. "It's true, I have been thinking about things. About us, and where we go from here."

"This is a big step for you, Tom," Alice said, her smile broadening into a grin.

"Thank you very much for noticing," he said. "I can feel the ground disappearing beneath my feet with every passing second."

"You're tall, you can tread water for a while."

Now, he laughed.

"I think we should talk," he said.

"About *our future?*"

He nodded. "We've both skirted the conversation since that night... you remember—?"

"Oh, I remember," she said, nodding and pouting at the same time. "How could I forget the most awkward, ill-thought through marriage proposal of all time—"

"Yes, thanks again for mentioning that," he said, cringing at the memory. "But that was a long time ago—"

"Hmm... not all that long ago, Tomas," Alice said playfully, tilting her head to one side.

"Well, it *feels like* a long time ago."

Alice looked around at the patio doors, peering into the darkness beyond. Tom followed her line of sight, wondering what had garnered her attention.

"What is it?" he asked.

"Nothing," she said, raising a hand to his cheek and turning him to face her, "I was just wondering if an ex-wife was likely to walk in this time?"

He gently eased her away from him, Alice cackling as he tried to casually swipe a hand at her backside. Grabbing his shirt, she pulled him back towards her and threw her arms around his neck, smiling up at him and staring into his eyes. On tiptoes, she kissed his lips and he responded.

Alice withdrew and gently placed her forefinger on his mouth. "We should talk... but, first off, make sure you know what it is you want."

He kissed her finger, smiling. "I know what I want. I've known for some time."

Her eyes appeared to sparkle as they shared the moment. In that instant, something changed in their relationship. Perhaps everything.

"Dis–gusting!"

They looked to the door. Saffy was standing there, bleary eyed, her favourite cuddly toy tucked under one arm with both hands resting on her hips, striking the pose of an angry parent catching the children up after bedtime.

Tom and Alice separated, Tom lowering himself as the little girl shuffled across to him and scooping her up into his arms. "Hello, Munchkin."

Saffy wrapped her arms around him, hugging him tightly but, such was the size of his frame, she still felt delicate in his grip.

"I missed you," she said into his ear.

"I missed you more."

"No, you didn't," she said, leaning back and looking into his face. She yawned.

"Shall I take you back to bed?" he asked.

She nodded, placing her head down on his shoulder.

"What's that?"

Tom whirled to see what she was referencing, Saffy pointing at the book.

"That's a book I've borrowed. A father read it to his daughter when she was around your age, and now I think his daughter was reading it again now she's all grown up."

He chose to keep further details from her. She didn't need to know.

"Does she have a daughter?" Saffy asked.

"Who, the mother?"

Saffy nodded.

"Yes, she does," he said. "She's about your age too."

"Is she reading it to her daughter then?" Saffy asked. Tom stopped, his eyes darting between the book, Alice and Saffy. Was she? Was Scarlett reading it to Maggie, much as her father read it to her?

"I don't know," he said. "Perhaps."

"Will you read it with me?"

Tom momentarily considered the request. He saw no harm. "Yes, if you'd like?" She nodded enthusiastically. Tom carried her to the breakfast bar and picked up the book.

"But no reading tonight, young lady," Alice said, pointing at the clock. "It is way past your bedtime."

"Oww..." Saffy groaned.

"Come on, I'll take you up," Tom said.

"Will you lie with me?"

Tom glanced back at his dinner, rapidly going cold only a few feet away.

"Yes, of course I will."

"Yay!" Saffy said, hugging him once more. Alice smiled at him, mouthing the words, *I love you* as he walked by her with Saffy in his arms. He winked in reply.

Saffy's bedroom was in darkness and Tom eased the door open with his foot. Crossing to the bed, he gently lowered her down and she scampered across the bed and under the duvet. He flicked on her night light, propped a couple of pillows up against the headboard and lay down beside her. Saffy snuggled into him, closing her eyes and draping one arm across his waist.

"Can you read to me?" she asked.

"I'm not supposed to."

"I won't tell if you don't. Please."

No doubt she would drop off in a few minutes anyway, and so Tom opened the book and began reading quietly.

"I love you," Saffy whispered.

"I love you too, monkey," he said, pausing and kissing the top of her head.

CHAPTER TWENTY

TAMARA OPENED the door to the sound of football coming from the living room. She glanced in to see her father in his customary position, in an armchair, arms folded, snoring. Pulling the door to, blocking out much of the sound, she wandered through into the kitchen. Her mother was sitting at the dining table working on a crossword puzzle or a Sudoku. She didn't look up as Tamara entered, putting her bag down on the island and making a beeline for the fridge.

"We were beginning to think you wouldn't be coming home tonight, dear."

Tamara held the door to the fridge open, scanning the shelves for something quick and easy to eat.

"Well, it's a flying visit, Mum," she said, looking over at her. "The Chief Superintendent offered to supervise while I duck home for a quick bite to eat. I'll have to head back in soon."

"That's kind of him."

"Not really," Tamara said, rummaging through the salad drawers, frustrated at not being able to find what she was looking for. "He'll clock off and go home to bed when I return. He sleeps, I get the night shift."

"Ah… not quite altruism then?"

"Comes with the rank, I'm afraid," Tamara mumbled. "Mum, have you seen my vegan Camembert?"

"If it's vegan, it's not Camembert, Tammy," she said, glancing up. "You know that."

"Okay, but have you seen it? I'm sure I left it in the middle drawer—"

"Yes, I'm afraid your father and I had it at lunchtime."

Tamara sighed. "All of it?"

"Well, no. But we thought it was past its use-by because it was all dry… and a bit grey."

"That's because it's vegan—"

"Yes," her mum said, sounding exasperated with the interruptions to her puzzle work, "but we didn't realise that until after we'd disposed of it."

Tamara slowly, purposefully, closed the fridge door. "You threw it away?"

"Yes. Sorry dear. It was an honest mistake."

"Never mind."

Tamara picked up an apple from the fruit bowl and ran it under the tap. Shaking off the water, she crossed to where her mother was sitting. Francesca Greave took off her glasses and set them down beside her puzzle book, fixing her daughter with a stare.

"That's a nasty business you are dealing with today."

Tamara nodded, rolling her head on her shoulders. "I've had better days, it's true."

"Have you found that little girl yet?"

"No," Tamara said, disconsolate. She rubbed at the base of her neck, feeling a tension headache coming on. "To be honest, we don't even know if she's been abducted, let alone who by."

Her father ambled into the kitchen stifling a yawn. Spotting Tamara, he came over and put his arm around her, kissing the top of her head. She gave his arm a squeeze and smiled at him.

"Your mother's right, you do look tired," he said. "I'll pop the kettle on."

"Thanks, Dad. Make sure it's decaf for me though, please."

"Decaffeinated tea," Francesca said, shaking her head. "Borderline sacrilegious. What are you worried about; you'll be working through the night anyway?"

"Are you going back into work, Tammy?" her father said, filling the kettle. "Bit late, isn't it?"

"Always on duty, Dad," she said over her shoulder. "And I'll need to have my wits about me. I don't want to be buzzing around the ceiling when I should be paying attention."

"There's a lot to be said for expanding the horizons of the mind, Tammy. Mark my words," Francesca said. "In our youth, we were quite experimental with—"

"*Illegal substances,* Mother. I am well aware," Tamara said, leaning on the table and fixing her gaze onto her mum. "And I'll remind you how draconian you were with us when we were teenagers when it came to drugs and alcohol. Quite the hypocrite, weren't you?"

"I was not!" Francesca exclaimed. "It was a different time back then. We were campaigning for peace, an end to the Vietnam War, apartheid in South Africa... and countless other worthy causes. We wanted to be free—"

"To make use of illegal substances to get wasted." Tamara shot her mum a knowing look, well aware of how it would wind her up. Francesca was indignant.

"Things were very different back then, as you well know. The pot we were offered was far more natural, organic even," she said, raising herself upright. "*Vegan,* one might say."

Tamara chuckled. "Vegan cannabis. Now, I've heard it all."

Francesca had a point though. What was available on the streets and university campuses of Great Britain in the sixties and seventies was a far cry from the chemically engineered, mass-market drugs flooding their communities these days. The difference in toxicity was a hundredfold in many cases.

Tamara's father put a mug down in front of her. As usual, there was nowhere near enough oat milk in it for her liking, far too dark and strong, but she didn't complain, very much appreciating the gesture.

"Thanks, Pops."

"You're welcome," he said, returning to the kitchen area. "Did your man friend get in touch with you all right?" he asked absently whilst pottering around, hunting for something.

"David?"

"Yes. A thoroughly nice chap, if you ask me."

Tamara blew the steam off her tea. "I don't recall asking, no."

Francesca chided her. "Now, don't be waspy! It's not every day a man chases after you these days, is it?"

"He's hardly *chasing after me*, is he, Mum?" She chose not to mention David's invitation to dinner, the invitation she'd accepted. She sipped her drink. "He wanted to make sure I got home okay. That's all."

Francesca focussed her attention on her daughter, examining her in a unique way she'd always managed to do, particularly when Tamara was keeping something back. The woman had some kind of a sixth sense.

"Well, you'd do well to capitalise on the opportunity," Francesca said. "The path to your door isn't exactly well worn."

Tamara sighed. "I'm doing okay, just as I am."

"You need to get out more, instead of hanging around your kitchen with a couple of old fuddies like us."

"Well, if you moved into your own place, you might not cramp my style so much, Mum," Tamara said, smiling sarcastically.

Francesca scoffed. "What style? Besides, seeing as you brought it up... I've been experimenting on your behalf." She reached into the pocket of her cardigan. Tamara wondered what was coming next. She wasn't going to like it. Francesca produced her mobile phone. With it clasped in one hand, she wagged a finger at her daughter. "Now, you're not to be mad with me, okay?"

Tamara took a deep breath and smiled, wagging a finger of her own. "Well, don't do anything to make me mad with you then, okay?"

Francesca angled her head, disapprovingly.

"I took the liberty of setting you up with a dating site—"

Tamara almost choked on a mouthful of tea, managing to spit most of it back into the mug. "You did what?"

"As I said, you're not to be angry," Francesca said, waving away the protestations. "It's important."

"No, what's important is you give me space to make my own decisions, Mum." Tamara couldn't believe what she was hearing. Her father came over and sat down at the far end of the table, shaking his head.

"I told you she wouldn't appreciate it, Fran."

"Shush!" Francesca said, with a flick of her hand, and that was the end of her father's attempt at support.

"Mum!"

"Tammy, there's a reason I'm telling you now, so do pay attention. *It is important*."

Tamara rolled her eyes, cupped her mug with both hands and braced herself.

"Go on, get it over with."

"It's for your own good, Tammy. We don't want you—"

"Leave me out of it please," her father said.

Francesca sighed forcefully, and continued, "I don't want you to end up alone, Tamara."

Her ears pricked at that. Her mother never called her by her given name, not unless she was six years old and in trouble or her mum really wanted her attention.

"Go on, get it out of your system."

"You have so much to give, Tamara, and I don't want you ending up all alone..." her mother reached across the table and placed her hand affectionately on the back of Tamara's. She smiled and her mother returned it. "We don't want you becoming known as the sad old crazy lady with all the cats, do we?"

Tamara recoiled, momentarily biting her bottom lip. "Mum, the cats are yours. And believe me, when you *eventually* die, the cats will go too."

"You wouldn't kill my babies!"

"Kill them, no," Tamara said, shaking her head, "but the Cats' Protection League will find their phone ringing off the hook!"

Francesca glared at her but evidently she didn't believe Tamara was being true to her word, quickly shaking it off.

"Did you have a point in all this, Mum?"

"Yes, the dating app."

"I hate dating sites," Tamara said, quickly adding, "not that I've ever used one."

"I'm not surprised to hear you say that, Tammy. I would hate them too, if no one matched with me."

Tamara stared at her, open-mouthed. "What do you mean, no one matched?"

"Exactly that," Francesca said, logging into the app and

turning the screen for her to see. "I created a profile for you, avoiding telling people what you do for a living obviously. I'm not daft."

"Really?" Tamara asked. Francesca ignored her. "What did you say I did?"

"I said you were a civil servant." Francesca sat back, a look of triumph on her face. "It demonstrates intelligence, education and that you are a professional... of sorts, but not flaky or shallow. In retrospect, I may have aimed too high."

"Thanks."

Francesca ignored the barbed reply.

"At first, I was quite selective on who I swiped; similar age range, not aiming the bar too high on the looks front, but when no one showed interest, I had to widen it. Younger, older... further afield... it's been nearly two weeks and still, nothing—"

"Nothing?" Tamara said, wounded.

"No, love. I'm so sorry. Maybe you need to fix your hair or something."

"Give me that!" Tamara said reaching for the mobile, her mother relinquishing it under protest. "What picture did you use for my profile?" Tamara asked, trying to figure out how to use the app.

"I know it was one from a few years ago, but it was a nice one," Francesca said, looking to her husband for support.

"Yes, it is a lovely picture of you, Tammy. You are very pretty."

Tamara was dumbfounded. Not one person who'd been sent her picture had swiped to match it. No messages, nothing. It was sobering. Her own mobile rang, and Tamara put her mother's down, taking out her own. It was Eric.

"What's up, Eric?"

"I've had a response from Scarlett's mobile service provider."

"Finally! What do they have to say?"

"I know who sent Scarlett the text message, thanking her for Friday night," Eric said. "But I didn't see it coming."

Tamara's curiosity was piqued. "Anyone we know?"

"I know him, but I doubt you do; Mark Young."

"Young? Is he related to Jonny, Scarlett's estranged boyfriend?"

"His brother," Eric said, hesitant.

"What is it, Eric? What do you know about him?"

"I don't know him all that well, to be honest. He was a few years younger than us when I was at school with Jonny, and he was soon shipped off to another school anyway, one for... different kids, you know?"

"How do you mean, different?"

"I can't remember. Not sure I ever knew. He was introverted, like really insular. He didn't open up much, got frustrated and that'd lead to outbursts. Maybe he had some condition none of us were aware of. His family kept to themselves, except for Jonny who played up no end. I'm surprised that Mark could be involved, genuinely."

Tamara let the information sink in for a moment.

Eric continued, "They gave us phone mast data as well. We can track his movements for the entire night of Friday. He was in town and later... he was in the area of Scarlett's house. His phone pinged off two towers which puts him squarely in Scarlett's street by my reckoning."

"Eric, he could have come home with her, killed her and—"

"Sent the message the next day to cover his tracks," Eric said. "Yeah, that's the first thought I had too. Only... it's Mark Young... and he's not like Jonny, not at all."

Tamara took a deep breath. "Call Tom. Have him meet us back at the station as soon as possible. We'll go over everything you have then. While you're waiting, dig into Mark and see if he's come up in any other investigation over the last few years. People change, Eric. Maybe he's not the boy you knew anymore."

She hung up, putting her mobile down next to her mother's. She caught Francesca staring at her sympathetically.

"What is it, Mum?"

"Now, that Tom Janssen," she said, reaching out once more to try and touch her hand. Tamara moved it out of reach. Francesca retracted her hand. "He's a lovely man, Tom. I've said so before. If Alice doesn't want to make an honest man of him, then maybe you—"

Tamara held up her hand. "Enough! I do not want to hear any more." She stood up, went to pick up her mobile and hesitantly picked up Francesca's instead, studying it. Pursing her lips, she shook her head and exhaled heavily. Placing the mobile on the table and sliding it back in front of her mother, she tapped the screen with her forefinger.

"That's a men-only dating app, Mum. *Men only!*"

Francesca looked confused, staring at the screen. "Ridiculous! What would be the point of that?"

Tamara retrieved her own phone, grabbed her bag from the island along with a couple more pieces of fruit to go with her apple, hooked the bag over her shoulder and made to leave. "For men to meet men, I'm guessing, Mum. Nice try, though. Well done," she said, striding out of the room, making no effort to conceal her win. "Thanks for the tea, Pops."

"You're welcome, dear," he called after her. Then he looked at Francesca, slowly shaking his head.

"Well, how was I to know?" she argued, shrugging. "Have you ever heard of such a thing?"

CHAPTER TWENTY-ONE

TAMARA TRIED Tom's mobile again, but the call went unanswered, as had the previous two. Eric waited patiently, sitting on the edge of his desk, arms folded across his chest.

"Never mind," she said, "we'll just have to go without him."

"I could call his house?"

Tamara looked at the clock, it was nearly midnight, and shook her head.

"He'll be in as soon as he is. I'm not waiting. I don't want to risk waking the entire household. You and I can handle Mark Young, don't you think?"

"Yes, of course," Eric said. "He still lives at his familial address, presumably with his parents."

"How old is Mark?"

Eric scratched his head, yawning. "Twenty-three, twenty-four, maybe."

"And he's not been in any trouble with us?"

Eric shook his head, "No. As I said, he's nothing like Jonny."

"Let's go."

Tamara plucked her coat off the hook next to the entrance door and Eric hopped off the desk, hurrying to join her. Having reviewed the data provided by the mobile phone company, they'd been able to confirm Mark Young's mobile was not only in Hunstanton on the night of Scarlett's death, in the area of her house, but also that her own mobile phone was pinging the same phone masts as his and at the same time. It was reasonable to deduce that they were together. If it turned out they weren't, then Mark was stalking Scarlett, or vice versa which seemed unlikely under the circumstances.

The station was still busy for this time of the night; the call handlers were rostered on until the early hours with a couple of people scheduled to keep the lines open overnight beyond that. Even so, Tamara heard her shoes squeaking as they hurried along the corridor. Reaching the custody suite, and thereby the exit to the car park, someone called behind her.

"DCI Greave!"

She stopped. It was the Chief Superintendent. Eric looked on anxiously, his hand on the door. She nodded to him. "Get the car started, Eric. I won't be a moment."

Eric passed out into the night and Tamara turned to see her superior striding towards her. His expression was fixed as he came before her, a mixture of confusion and irritation.

"Where are you off to, Tamara?"

"Oh, Eric and I have a strong lead and it can't wait until morning," she said, glancing at the door to the yard, feeling the draught of cold night air as it swung closed.

"But you're supervising the incident room, remember?"

"Yes, of course, sir," she said, pursing her lips and avoiding the intensity of his gaze by looking around the custody suite. The desk sergeant was making a good fist of pretending not to be paying attention, although she was certain he was doing quite the opposite. "And I will, but," she leaned in to him, lowering her voice, "I need to follow this up as a matter of urgency. It won't take long." She met his eye sternly. "Do you think you could hold the fort for a few minutes longer, sir? It would make all the difference."

"Well... I..."

"You're doing a fine job, sir, if I do say so. Your quick thinking and dynamism had the incident team up and running in double-quick time. If it weren't—"

He sighed. "Spare me the bull, DCI Greave."

She smiled sheepishly. "Sorry, sir."

He thumbed behind him. She looked but there was no one there.

"I have the psychologist waiting to speak to you—"

"Valuable, sir," she said, nervously looking at the closed door and then the digital clock mounted on the wall behind the custody sergeant. "It'll not take long, sir. Fifteen to twenty minutes," she said. "You can have her go through the case files in ops while I'm out. Probably be good to do that alone anyway. Be undisturbed and all that."

"I–I suppose you're right," Watts said, glancing over his shoulder, but the look on his face implied he knew he was being played. "Fifteen to twenty minutes you say?"

"Yes, sir."

Tamara didn't wait, turning and making for the door. Pushing it open, she said, "Half an hour, tops."

She didn't hear a response even if he'd made one. Eric was waiting with the engine running. He looked at her as she got in.

"Everything all right with the chief?"

"As long as you drive quickly, yes," she said, clipping in her seatbelt. She gestured with her hand. "Go, go... drive."

Eric pulled away, turning right out of the police station and heading for Old Hunstanton on the north side of the main town. Old Hunstanton lay just beyond the lighthouse where the cliffs dropped away and the designated area of natural beauty, with its nature reserve and salt marshes, began. The long-established village, originally occupied by fishermen, was now peppered with a couple of large hotels, a handful of pubs and restaurants alongside numerous residential holiday lets. The lifeboat station could be found here with both a boat and a hovercraft available to be deployed at a moment's notice, crewed by volunteers working in the area.

Turning off the main coast road, Eric swung the car around onto Wodehouse Road, slowing as he scanned the properties on the right-hand side.

"I think it should be one of these houses here on the right."

The road was narrow, and he pulled into the kerb, parking at the rear of a line of vehicles. The properties weren't built with cars in mind and therefore many residents parked on the road itself. Scanning the flat-roofed, white-painted terrace, Eric looked for the Youngs' house. He'd never been inside their home, seeing as he and Jonny tended to steer clear of one another at school.

Each property was almost identical, built at the tail end of the Art Deco period they shared many of the design traits of the era; right angles, poured concrete and white-painted render. Each house sported pillars to the front supporting balconies accessed from the bedrooms on the floor above. A diamond pattern repeated in the wrought ironwork of the balustrades to all properties, but the original windows had long since been replaced by modern plastic double glazing. The grandeur that may have accompanied the residences at the time of their construction now looked a little tired on the eye.

"That one," Eric said pointing to a mid-terrace house.

"Good," Tamara said, "let's go."

The house was in darkness, as most were bearing in mind it was now past midnight. One car was parked in the driveway in front of the house, a battered old Ford Mondeo. Tamara rang the bell, hearing it buzz inside. She waited a moment, giving the occupants time to recognise it was their bell ringing. Then she rang again. Eric stepped back from under the cover of the balcony and looked up, seeing an upstairs light flick on.

"Someone's coming," he said, re-joining Tamara. As he said the words, the landing light came on illuminating the stairs and a figure bumbled down towards them. The light over the porch also flicked on, it was bright, and Tamara could see multiple dead flies trapped on the inside of the cover. The door swung open, and a man stood before them in striped pyjama bottoms and a white vest. He drew his dressing gown around him as the night chill reached his skin.

A rotund man, in his sixties, balding with grey hair that shot out at the sides above his ears, he glared at the two of them.

"Do the two of you know what time it is? What on earth do you want—"

Tamara brandished her warrant card. "DCI Greave, Norfolk Police. Mr Young, I presume?"

His stance softened a little, but only a little, eyeing her identification carefully. His top lip curled; his body language guarded.

"I'm Barry. I'm his dad. What's he done now?"

"What's who done?" Tamara asked.

"Our Jonny. He must have been up to something to have you knocking on my door at this time of the night."

"Actually, we're here to see Mark."

"Mark?" he said, surprised. "What do...?" he shook his head, looking back into the house. "Yes, Mark's here." He took a couple of steps back to the foot of the stairs and looked up. "Mark! Get down here. There's someone to see you."

They heard movement upstairs, floorboards squeaking and moments later a figure appeared on the landing. He stayed where he was, looking down at his father.

"Come on, son. Get down here."

Hesitantly, Mark Young descended from upstairs. As opposed to his father, Mark was a slim lad with a full head of dark hair. Cut short on the sides, it flopped to the left and he ran a hand through it as he looked between Eric and Tamara. The movement shifted his position and the light from the porch lit the left side of his face. It looked like he was sporting a black eye.

"Coppers, son." Barry put his arm around Mark's shoulder and the young man seemed to find the touch uncomfortable, shifting awkwardly in his grasp, but he allowed it, none-theless. "They're looking for you." His father pulled him in closer and grinned. "What have you been up to?"

"Nothing, Dad," he said, looking at his feet.

His father looked at Tamara. "Nothing, he says. What do you think? Do you think he's been up to nothing, DCI Grave?"

"Greave," Tamara said, correcting him.

"Sorry. What's all this about?"

Tamara smiled at him. "Is there somewhere we can talk to Mark, alone, if possible?"

"Sure," he said. "Come on in."

They were led inside to a sitting room overlooking the front of the house. It wasn't particularly large with enough space for a two-piece settee and armchair combination arranged before an open fireplace in the corner of the room.

Mark looked anxious, wringing his hands and avoiding eye contact. His father on the other hand sought to control the situation. "Right, now what's all this about?"

Tamara turned to him. "I think it would be best if we spoke to Mark alone, if you don't mind?"

He wasn't going to go easily. He folded his arms across his chest, bringing himself upright and staring at her hard. "Is that so?"

"Yes, otherwise we'll have to take Mark to the station, and you can collect him from there when we're through."

At the mention of being taken to the police station, Mark shifted nervously in his seat, his eyes darting around the room.

"All right," Barry said indignantly, looking between Tamara and Eric and lastly at his son. "But I'll be on the other side of this door, so I expect no funny business."

"Fair enough, Mr Young," Tamara said, smiling gratefully. "We will call you if we need you."

Barry Young looked at Mark, pointing at him. "If you're unsure, son, say nothing. Got it?"

Mark nodded, although he looked like a rabbit caught in the headlights. He was unlikely to offer up anything like the same levels of attitude as his father. Barry edged out of the room and Tamara inclined her head towards Eric. The detective constable ensured the door was closed. No doubt Barry would be hovering on the other side.

Tamara sat down opposite Mark, who had his hands clasped together in his lap.

"Mark, we understand you are friends with Scarlett Turnbull," she said. He nodded. "Are you aware of what happened to Scarlett last night?"

Again, Mark nodded. "Yes. I saw it on the news today."

He was on edge, it was clear.

"Mark, when did you last see Scarlett?"

He looked up at her and away again, shaking his head.

"Mark," Tamara persisted, "we know you were with her last night—"

His head snapped up; eyes wide. He shook his head again, only this time it was a half-hearted effort. "N–No, I didn't."

Tamara reached into her bag and took out a copy of the calls and texts made to and from Scarlett's mobile in the past week. Mark's mobile number was highlighted. She passed it across to him and he reluctantly took it.

"You texted her this morning, Mark." She pointed to his number on the list. He stared at the paper as if it was on fire and burning his hands and they started to shake. "You thanked her for last night."

"I didn't do it!"

"You didn't do what, Mark?"

He stared at Tamara, tears welling in his eyes, despairing. "I didn't kill her. I didn't... I–I wouldn't."

Tamara studied him. He was frightened but what of, she couldn't say. Sitting under the ceiling light as he was, the detail of Mark's face was easier to see.

"That's quite a shiner you're developing there," she said, indicating his face. Mark pursed his lips, still avoiding eye contact. "How did you come by it?"

"I don't know."

"You don't know?" Tamara said. "I find that hard to believe. Did someone strike you?"

"I–I..." Mark stammered, furtively looking at the closed door.

At that moment it opened, catching Eric on the shoulder. Barry Young bustled Eric out of the way and marched in, waving a pointed finger at Tamara.

"You've no business talking to my boy like this. Can't you see he's terrified."

"Dad, I'm really sorry, I–I..."

Barry turned on his son. "Not another word, lad. Not one more word without a solicitor present, do you hear me?"

Mark looked at the floor, unable to bear his father's wrath.

"Mr Young!" Tamara said, standing.

"Don't you Mr Young me, young lady," he barked. "My boy was home last night, with me. We had a couple of beers and watched the television until he went to bed. Now, he's got nothing to do with any of this and I want—"

Tamara cut him off. "I don't care what you want, Mr Young. Mark will be accompanying us to the station, under caution if needs be—"

"He was *with me*," Barry said, then looked at his son. "And don't you say anything different."

Mark appeared ready to cry. Eric, recovering his poise, positioned himself between Barry and Tamara. She looked at Mark. "I want you to accompany us to the station, Mark. I'd rather not arrest you—"

"Then he's not going anywhere," Barry growled. Eric placed a restraining hand gently on the man's chest. He looked down at it and then squared up to Eric.

"I don't think you'll be doing yourself or your son any favours by sitting in the cell next to him, Mr Young," Eric said calmly. It did the trick and Barry took a half-step backwards.

"Yeah, well," he said, "I'm just looking out for my son that's all."

"As are we," Tamara said. "If we have to arrest your son it will be all over the news tomorrow, or we can do this quietly. It is very much up to you."

"I'll come with you," Mark said quietly. Barry glared at his son but appeared ready to accept it was going to happen whether he liked it or not.

Unlike his father, Mark was still dressed, and Eric walked

him out and put him into the car. Barry lingered outside, Tamara beside him.

"I want to have a look around your house, Mr Young," she said.

He trained a wary eye on her. "Why would you need to do that?"

"To make sure you're not harbouring a little girl."

Barry held Tamara's gaze for a moment before scoffing and breaking eye contact. "Ridiculous." He shook his head. Gesturing with an open hand towards the house, he smiled. It was artificial. "If you must."

Tamara indicated to Eric she'd be there soon enough, and he remained by the car.

To Barry, she pointedly instructed him to stay where he was. The house wasn't large, three relatively small bedrooms and a bathroom upstairs and two down, including the kitchen. The garden at the rear was large but laid to lawn with no outbuildings to search. Maggie Turnbull wasn't here.

Returning to the front of the house, Barry sneered at her.

"Find what you were looking for?"

Tamara ignored the rhetorical question.

"Goodnight, Mr Young. Thank you for your patience."

Barry Young stood in the doorway of the house watching them drive away before going back inside. Eric was at the wheel while Tamara sat in the back with Mark for the short journey back to the station.

"Your father is a strong character, isn't he?" she said, looking out of the window.

Mark snorted, glancing sideways and flashing a smile at her. "He speaks his mind. Don't take it to heart. He doesn't mean to come across like he does. It's just his way."

"He's worried about you?"

He nodded. "Yes. He's always worrying about me."

"Why?"

Mark shrugged.

"Does he worry about your brother, Jonny?"

Mark looked at her again. This time his expression was solemn, guarded. "No, not Jonny. He can take care of himself."

CHAPTER TWENTY-TWO

ERIC TURNED the car into the police station and drove around to the rear. Tamara searched the assembled vehicles for Tom's car but didn't see it. Cassie's was there though, and she was keen to catch up with her. Mark appeared much calmer than he had been when they first met him at his home. Usually, it was when people were brought in that they became agitated or anxious having been taken out of their comfort zone. Mark was the opposite.

"Eric, why don't you take Mark through to the canteen and get him a cup of tea or something."

Eric looked puzzled but didn't question the suggestion. Something told her that Mark would be more forthcoming if they didn't put him in a high-stress situation. After all, he was still there of his own free will and so far, she hoped she was right, he hadn't given her any inclination he was a murderer. He knew something though; of that she was certain.

Eric passed Cassie on his way out of the custody suite, she smiled a greeting as she passed him clutching a piece of paper in her hands. She handed it to Tamara. It was a press release with two hand-drawn sketches of a man carrying a girl in his arms. One profile was drawn from a side angle and one from the rear.

"She didn't see his face properly?" Tamara asked.

"No, just a fleeting glimpse from the side as she drew the curtains in her bedroom. It was after he passed that she watched him more closely." Cassie shrugged. "She reckons he was five-ten to six-foot tall, white and slim build. Probably aged in his thirties but, as I say, she only caught a glimpse. It's not much, but it's the best we have."

"Okay," Tamara said, scanning the press release and hiding her disappointment. "Distinctive jacket."

"Yep, brown suede bomber style, the eyewitness reckons."

"Right," Tamara said, handing the paper back, "put that out to the media. I doubt we'll see any traction on it until tomorrow anyway. Get it out to our contacts and then you may as well get yourself off home, Cass. I'll see you bright and early in the morning."

"Tamara, good to see you back."

She turned to see the Chief Superintendent walking towards her. Cassie smiled and swiftly walked away. "He's been looking for you. Good luck," she whispered before their superior came within earshot.

"Hello, sir. I'm sorry I was a bit later than anticipated."

He waved her apology away. "That's okay. The calls seem to have dried up for now." He looked at the clock. "Probably pick up tomorrow. Now, about this psychologist—"

"Ah, I've actually got a witness to interview, sir. I don't think I'll have time tonight—"

"That's okay. You can meet in the morning. I've handed over copies of the relevant documentation and I'm as excited as you are to hear the results. Our very own expert to unlock the mind, no less!"

"Yes, sir. Excited is the word." She looked past him, keen to meet up with Eric. "I take it you'll be off home then, sir?"

"Yes, I just wanted to touch base with you first."

"I'm pleased you did," Tamara said with a smile. "If you'll excuse me?"

"By all means, DCI Greave. Carry on."

"Goodnight, sir."

Tamara excused herself and made her way through to the staff canteen. The shutters between the eating area and the kitchen were down. Apart from the vending machines, everything was locked up. Eric was sitting on the far side of the room with Mark, both of them with a drink in front of them from the vending machine. Tamara took out her mobile and rang Tom, leaving him a voicemail.

"Tom, someone better be dying," was the message she left for him. Slipping her mobile back into her pocket, she crossed the room. Both Eric and Mark looked up at her as she approached them.

"Can I get you a drink?" Eric asked.

"No, thank you," she said, pulling out a chair and sitting down alongside Mark. She deliberately chose not to sit opposite him. The psychological impact of a barrier between them, even if it was only a table, was more formal than she felt necessary. "Mark, I need to ask you about last night – Friday night – and I need you to be honest with us. Can you do that?"

Mark nursed his cup of tea, turning the plastic cup slowly on the table. He met Tamara's eye, nodding.

"Good. Now, when did you last see Scarlett?"

He bit his bottom lip, his eyes only momentarily meeting Tamara's.

"Friday evening," he said, drawing breath and clenching his hands into fists. "I saw her on Friday evening. We had a drink together."

"Was it a planned meeting?"

He nodded. "Yes," he said, smiling. It didn't last and he went back to playing with his cup. "We had a date."

Tamara looked at Eric and his expression showed he realised the significance of the comment.

"Have you dated before?"

"No, this was our first date," he said, smiling broadly. "I hoped it'd be the first of many."

"We... were under the impression Scarlett was dating your brother, Jonny?"

Mark placed an upturned thumb on the table before him, absently twisting it as if he was trying to squash something into the surface. He didn't look at Tamara.

"They split. She said so."

"You're sure?"

"I asked him," Mark said, looking up. "He said he was glad to be rid."

"And did he know the two of you were going out on a date?"

He hesitated and then shook his head.

"Where did you go, the two of you? Where did you take Scarlett?"

"Just into town." He shrugged. "She wasn't bothered; just pleased to be out enjoying herself for a change."

"Scarlett's been going through a tough time of late, hasn't she?"

"Yes," he said, bobbing his head. "Very tough. I wanted to help... to take the weight off for her, but I couldn't."

"She didn't enjoy your date?"

"No, she did," he said, grinning. "We had a great time until..." the grin faded "until Jonny turned up."

"What happened?"

Mark shrugged, staring at the table. Tamara decided to approach from a different angle.

"How did you get the black eye, Mark?"

He wrinkled his nose, shaking his head ever so slightly.

"Was it Jonny? Did he not take kindly to seeing you with Scarlett?"

Again, Mark remained silent.

"You see, here's my problem, Mark," Tamara said, thinking aloud. "Scarlett is attacked in her home shortly after returning from a date – with you – and here you are with a black eye. Now, it is conceivable to me that your brother viewed you dating his ex-girlfriend unfavourably or another theory might be that you attacked Scarlett and she defended—"

"No! I would never hurt her," Mark said. "I loved her. I always have."

Tamara cocked her head. "They say there's a thin line between love and obsession."

He met her eye, his were gleaming as he choked back tears. "I–I would never hurt her... or Maggie. I told her that. I told her on Friday that I would look after them, always."

Eric raised his eyebrows. "Even by my standards, that's one heck of a first date admission."

Mark agreed, wiping his eyes with a tissue taken from a box Tamara passed to him.

"I think she liked hearing the words, but I don't think she thought I could back it up."

"Did she reject you?" Tamara asked.

He shook his head. "No, it wasn't like that at all. I walked her home. That was after Jonny confronted us. Scarlett stepped in between us, told him to leave, but he shoved her aside. I pushed him... and he hit me." He glanced up at Tamara. "I don't think he meant to... he just sort of lashed out."

"Then what?"

Mark shrugged. "He stormed off. It was all over in seconds really. Scarlett and I walked around a bit. It was chilly, but on Friday the sky was clear, and the stars were wonderful from out by the lighthouse. We walked, listened to the waves... and then I took her home." He looked directly into Tamara's eyes. "And that was the last time I saw her."

"Tell me, did you go inside the house?"

"No, I walked her to her door – the front door – and she went in alone. I heard the babysitter speak to her just as the door was closing."

"Did anything intimate take place between you?" Tamara asked. Mark reddened around his neck and cheeks. "It's important, Mark. If you did, there will be trace evidence of you on her person and we need to know."

"She kissed me," he said quietly. "And thanked me for a wonderful evening." Mark beamed. "I–I think she liked me. I do. She treated me as an equal. Not many people do."

"And then?"

Mark looked puzzled by the question.

"What did you do then?"

"I went home," he said. "What my father told you is true. We did watch some television together."

"Then why is he so adamant that you don't speak to us?"

"Jonny came around today. He apologised for losing his temper and hitting me. We hugged it out and then... he told me and Dad that you'd be coming to see me and that I should say nothing at all."

"What time was this?"

Mark was thoughtful. "Lunchtime. Around then anyway."

"And why would he ask that of you do you think?"

Mark shook his head. "I really don't know."

Tamara and Eric exchanged a look. Tamara leaned forward, gently tapping a finger on the table in front of him.

"I'm going to have to ask a favour of you, Mark." He briefly smiled at her and nodded. "We need to look into all of this. I'm sure you appreciate how serious this situation is. I think, for your own safety, that it might be a good idea for you to stay here with us tonight. How would you feel about that?"

He looked concerned. Tamara moved to allay his fears.

"You would not be under arrest, and you can leave at any time, but until we get this ironed out, it might be good for you to spend the night here. Can you do that for me?"

"I–I suppose so," he said.

Eric shot her an inquisitive look. The conversation had been enlightening. Jonny had not only demonstrated a quick temper as well as a propensity for violence, but he was also trying to cover his tracks by manipulating his younger, arguably more naive, brother. Why he would need to do that raised many questions in her mind and she wanted answers before she was willing to release Mark back into his clutches.

Fifteen minutes later, Mark was sitting in a cell.

"I'm sorry we have to lock the door, Mark, but it is for your own safety. We have officers right outside if you need anything," Tamara said, closing the door. Mark looked fearful, sitting with his back against the wall and hugging his knees into his chest. The heavy iron door slammed shut with deafening finality, echoing through the cell block. The custody sergeant turned the key and Tamara thanked him, walking away to meet Eric in the foyer.

"Are we being too quick in ruling him out?" Eric asked. "He openly admits to being in love with her. It's likely he has been watching her, lusting after her for quite some time. And we only have his word for what happened when he dropped her home. What if he waited for the babysitter to leave and then went back?"

Tamara held up a hand to hold him there. "We're still waiting on the forensic analysis to come back. If Mark was in the house, there should be evidence of that. If the trace evidence conflicts with his version of events, then we'll have something to challenge him with. For now, I want to tread lightly. I think we'll draw more out of him that way."

"I see. Do you really think it's necessary to keep him here though?" Eric asked. "It's not like he's feeling the pressure if he thinks he's doing us a favour."

"Any time spent in one of those cells will give you time to think about what could be, and his stay is voluntary, so it won't eat into our detention time if we do need to arrest him. A decent solicitor will likely challenge that, but he hasn't requested one, so..." she shrugged. "Besides, it'll be interesting to see Jonny's reaction when he finds out."

Eric nodded. "I expect their father was on the phone as soon as we left."

Tamara agreed. "Head home and get a bit of sleep, Eric. Back here at six. Okay?"

"See you in the morning then." Eric glanced at the clock on the wall. "Later this morning," he said, correcting himself.

CHAPTER TWENTY-THREE

Tom woke with a start. For a second, he was disoriented, a book lay open on his chest illuminated by the soft blue hue of Saffy's nightlight. Another gust rattled the window within its frame. Saffy lay beside him, nestled into the crook of his arm with one of hers draped across his waist. He had no idea what time it was.

Closing the book, he gently lifted Saffy's arm away from him and slowly slid himself out from under her, getting up off the bed, careful not to disturb her. She stirred as the mattress shifted under the displacement of his weight, reached for the edge of the duvet and pulled it into her, curling up into a ball. Tom leaned over and kissed the top of her head and left the room, avoiding the squeaky floorboard that'd caught him out so many times before.

Out on the landing, he checked his watch. It was after three in the morning. He silently cursed himself for falling asleep. The wind must have blown the cloud cover away because the moonlight streamed in through the window. Creeping across the landing, he peered into the bedroom he shared with Alice. She was asleep, her chest moving in a peaceful motion.

Retreating from the bedroom, he made his way downstairs and into the kitchen.

Russell was asleep in his bed. The terrier poked his head up as Tom entered but even he closed his eyes again soon enough.

"You've got the right idea," he said, picking up his mobile phone and registering the number of missed calls from the team. Dialling in, he listened to Tamara's last voicemail. He swore again. Putting the mobile in his pocket, he went to the sink and ran some cold water, cupping his hands beneath the stream and splashing it across his face and rubbing at his cheeks to freshen himself up.

He saw a note pinned to the fridge with a magnet Saffy had insisted on buying from their visit to Norwich Castle the previous month. *Sorry not to wake you! You needed the sleep x.*

Opening the fridge was enough to rouse the dog who came to stand at his feet, looking up hopefully as Tom looked inside. He was ravenous now, hunting for something quick.

"Plastic tub, top shelf."

He looked round to see Alice standing in the doorway, pulling her dressing gown tightly around her and tying it closed. She yawned, covering her mouth with her hand.

"Sorry, I didn't mean to wake you," he said.

"You didn't. I never sleep well when you're not beside me."

He smiled. "Top shelf?"

"Your dinner," Alice said. He located the tub and closed the fridge door. She came to him and slipped a hand around his waist. "You probably shouldn't reheat it again, but I doubt it'll kill you if you do. I figured you'd wake up and head straight back into work."

"That's the plan," he said, inclining his head towards his

mobile. "I think Tamara's having an embolism at my disappearance."

Alice laughed. "She'll get over it." She pulled him to her, and he encircled her, linking his hands at the small of her back. "Besides, she gets to see more of you than I do."

"Only in the company of villains."

"And dead people."

"And dead people," he said, smiling. "Which isn't the same."

He released her from his grip, and she pointed to the book alongside his mobile phone. "What did Saffy make of the story. I heard you reading."

"Sorry about that. I've hardly seen her today, so I didn't see the harm."

Alice dismissed the need of an apology, sitting down at the breakfast bar and resting her chin on her hands. She picked up the book and inspected the blurb.

"It's different," Tom said. "It started off with the sickly child fearing death... telling his brother that the afterlife would be much better. His older brother is miserable at the thought of losing his sibling and," Tom smiled, recollecting his conversation with Alan "the little boy explains that, after he dies, he'll visit him from time to time in the form of a raven. He says he'll fly up to the window and sing to him. Whenever he hears a raven, he's to think of his little brother and smile."

"Sounds upbeat for a children's story."

Tom's expression cut a wry smile. "I think it's supposed to be reflective of society in many ways. Saffy was snoozing away pretty soon, so I must admit I was scan reading ahead. In many ways it's frighteningly prescient to the case I'm investigating."

Alice inquired with her eyes.

"Well, two brothers; one is disabled while the other is

strong and athletic. Somehow, they've ended up in a fantasy world, not sure how as I missed that part, where the disabled brother is now able bodied and goes in search of his sibling. The older one is some sort of hero standing up against tyranny; a banner for good people to rally to or something. It's not at all clear how that came about. It's all a little bit odd."

"And how does this relate to your case?"

"The missing girl is disabled… and when Saffy asked last night – if the victim was reading it to her daughter – it got me thinking. Maybe she was. The story has the disabled brother experiencing a more regular life in this fantasy land. I'm not sure whether they're supposed to be dreaming or if it is an afterlife of sorts. If it's the latter, then it's a cruel version of heaven."

"Again," Alice said, raising her eyebrows, "lovely bedtime reading."

Tom chuckled. "I know, but I researched it a bit. It's an old folk tale that's been in print now for decades, inspired television shows and there's a film in the works too apparently."

"So, just supposing our little girl, bright as she is, is on the money and it was read to offer comfort regarding an afterlife or something to look forward to, for whose benefit do you think it was read?"

"Mother or daughter, you mean?" Tom asked. Alice nodded. "Good question. Perhaps both? A double meaning, like those children's cartoons who have laughs for adults as well as the kids."

Alice yawned again. "Right, I'm going back to bed." She hopped off the stool and kissed Tom on the cheek. "I still think suffering and death is an odd subject for children."

"Scandinavian," Tom said, as if that explained everything. "They seem to have a way of challenging societal issues in interesting ways."

Alice patted the door frame as she left the kitchen. "I prefer their cars."

Tom smiled. "Goodnight."

"See you in the morning," Alice said from the hall.

Tom placed the book on top of the plastic tub with his food inside, picked up both and tucked his phone in his pocket before heading out. Taking great care to close and lock the front door with as little noise as possible, he went to the car. He decided not to phone Tamara. If she was at the station, he would speak to her then, but if she'd gone home to get some sleep, he didn't want to risk waking her. He'd spend the time getting back up to speed before the new day began.

Tom didn't see a single car between home and the station, which was why he was surprised to see a man loitering fifty yards or so away from the police station when he turned into the car park. Whoever it was seemed almost to try and hide behind an overhanging tree when Tom parked up. It struck him as strange, almost as if he was being watched as he got out of the car. Why would anyone be hanging around here in the middle of the night?

"Hello!" Tom called out, stepping onto the pavement and looking in the man's direction. He came out from under the tree, ducking to avoid the lowest branches as he tentatively walked forward. "Is everything okay?"

Tom took in his measure, as best he could under the orange glow of the streetlights at this distance. Judging by his gaunt, facial features, he was skinny, but this was hidden by weeks of wispy beard growth, unkempt hair sprouting from beneath a woollen beanie and several layers of thick clothing including an oversized winter coat. He approached Tom warily, touching his nose with fingerless glove wearing hands.

"Are you... a policeman?" he asked when he was just within earshot without the need to shout.

"I am, yes. DI Tom Janssen."

The man nodded stiffly, sniffing loudly. For a moment Tom wondered if he was homeless but his fingernails were clean and his clothes, although a haphazard combination of style, were clean. He suspected the dress sense was chosen rather than forced.

"Do you know about Scarlett's murder?"

Tom was intrigued, quickly checking their surroundings in case he needed to react to what was coming. "What do you know about Scarlett's murder?"

He shook his head. "Nothing. Like I told your colleagues yesterday... the young detective constable and that fascist stormtrooper from up north; I had nothing to do with it. I cared for Scarlett. I'd never hurt her."

Tom put two and two together. Cassie had clearly made an impact.

"Are you William?" Tom asked.

He looked taken aback but it was fleeting. "Yes. I prefer Billy, but my mum calls me William."

A gust of cold wind struck them. Billy Slegg tensed.

"You look cold, Billy. How long have you been out here?"

He shrugged. "Don't know. A few hours maybe."

Tom looked over his shoulder towards the station. "If you'd like to come inside, I can get you warmed up; a cup of tea and, you never know, a sandwich or something."

It was like Tom had threatened him. Billy took a half-step backwards, his eyes dancing around them, seeking an escape.

"It's okay," Tom said, keeping his hands passively by his side. "We can talk out here if you prefer."

Billy nodded, his eyes still furtively scanning the station in the background.

"What are you doing here, Billy?"

"I–I wasn't completely honest," he said, looking behind

him, possibly worrying about someone sneaking up on him. "I didn't mean to be, but," he inclined his head, "you're the police and all that. You can't be trusted."

"You can trust me, Billy."

Billy searched Tom's face, gauging his sincerity. After a moment, he looked down at his right hand, balled into a fist. Slowly, he dropped to one knee, keeping his eyes on Tom the whole time, and put something on the floor.

"Do something good with it," Billy said, standing up and backing away. Once he was confident Tom wasn't advancing on him, he turned and ambled across the road with an odd, uneven gait. He didn't look back, entering the alleyway between the glaziers and another industrial unit, and quickening his pace as he disappeared into the shadows.

Tom walked over and dropped to his haunches, retrieving a USB thumb drive from the ground. Turning it over in the palm of his hand, he found it unremarkable in and of itself.

"What have you given us here, Billy?" he said quietly to himself inspecting the drive. Of Billy Slegg, there was nothing to be seen. Tom was alone.

The ops room was in darkness and Tom flicked on the lights, the tubes flickering into life. Entering his office, he powered up the computer on his desk and inserted the USB drive. There was only one folder displayed in the memory and he double clicked on it. Inside were several media files. Their dates of creation were sequential with some days having only one entry whereas others had multiple on the same day. Arranging them in a list, Tom scanned down the files, selecting a random one from the previous Tuesday and played it.

It was a video file and Tom immediately recognised the location. It was Victoria Avenue, the road Scarlett Turnbull lived on, and he was looking at her house. Judging by the quality of the footage, Tom guessed it was filmed through a window of a car or, perhaps, a van from some distance down the road. It was daytime and there were cars parked on both sides of the road.

The video length was over an hour long, time coded at the beginning at eleven in the morning. Tom edged the slider forward, speeding up the images until something happened. A figure came into shot, a woman, but she continued on past Scarlett's house. The next was a man who strolled up to the front door. Tom paused the footage and moved it back, but he couldn't get a view of the face, his approach obscured by a high-sided delivery van. He was white with dark hair, wearing a baseball cap, black denim jacket and stonewashed jeans. Whoever it was entered the property shortly before midday. Tom moved the slider forward to when the door opened again.

When the man emerged, he turned back to Scarlett, dressed in a casual hoodie and joggers. They chatted briefly on the doorstep and then she hugged him, kissing him on the lips. Was it a passionate kiss or a close friend bidding farewell? With the quality of this footage, it was difficult to tell. Tom paused the video as soon the man turned to leave and zoomed in. It wasn't Jonny Young who'd paid Scarlett a visit and, even with the poor resolution footage, Tom easily recognised Tony Slater, Maggie's father and Scarlett's ex-partner.

Tom sank back into his chair, cupping his chin with thumb and forefinger.

"So, Tony, you haven't seen or spoken to Scarlett in a year to eighteen months?" he said quietly to himself. "You lying little toerag."

Opening the next file, dated on Wednesday, two days before Scarlett's murder, Tom did the same thing. This time,

Billy Slegg was parked at the other end of the street, watching Scarlett's house. A white van pulled up outside, again just before midday. The driver got out and Tom saw it was Tony Slater. He looked up and down the street before approaching the door. He didn't have long to wait before the door opened and Scarlett appeared. He moved in to kiss her, but she deflected his attentions, ushering him inside. The camera detail was better in this footage, presumably Billy didn't have to zoom in as much as he was parked much closer. To Tom's eye, Scarlett seemed on edge, looking up and down the street herself as Tony moved past her before closing the door.

Intrigued, Tom rolled on the footage. The previous day, Tony emerged within an hour. Fifteen minutes later, another figure approached the house, striding purposefully up to the front door and rang the bell. Jonny Young was far from patient, stepping away from the door when it wasn't answered and cupping his hands against the front window, peering into the interior. With no response forthcoming, he knocked on the door again and still got no answer.

"And you've been fibbing as well, haven't you, Jonny?"

Moving to the side gate, offering access to the rear garden, Jonny tried the handle, but it appeared to be locked. He made a half-hearted effort at clambering over the gate, but he couldn't manage it. Exasperated, he returned to the front door for one last attempt and hammered a balled fist against it. Up until this point, there was little sound, but Jonny began shouting. The words were inaudible, but he was visibly upset, almost working himself into a rage. Jonny hung around for a while but, with no sign of Scarlett acknowledging his presence, he appeared to walk off. The camera tracked him until he disappeared out of shot before returning to focus on the house.

Tom watched the footage play out. Tony Slater emerged

from the house half an hour later, again looking up and down the street. Scarlett was holding hands with him, releasing him after he kissed her goodbye and made his way to the parked van. Scarlett returned indoors and, as Tony opened the door to his vehicle, Jonny Young ran into shot from the right and took a swing at him. Tony ducked the punch, moving quickly to his left and avoiding the follow up as well. Undeterred, Jonny advanced on him clearly hurling obscenities. Tom heard the motor whine of an electric window engage and the glass lowered, the violent verbal exchange clear to hear.

The two men circled one another, Tony Slater holding his hands up and ordering Jonny to calm down. The repeated instructions only sought to rile him further and he attacked again. Tony's streetwise ability, no doubt honed during his time in prison, saw him more than an equal to Jonny's aggression and moments later, his opponent, over extended and off balance, threw an awkward punch that was counteracted with a swift move that left Jonny flat on his back with Tony standing over him. Jonny sought to get up, only for Tony to drive a boot into his stomach. Jonny doubled over, screaming. Tony gave him two more swift kicks to the abdomen before grasping a handful of hair and hauling Jonny upright.

Scarlett appeared from indoors, shouting at Tony to stop. Tony, fist raised, hesitated before pushing Jonny away. The latter slumped to the floor, head in hands. Tony waved a hand in Scarlett's direction and got into the van, firing up the engine and accelerating away at speed. Scarlett approached Jonny, kneeling beside him and tentatively reaching out to comfort him. Jonny pushed her away, either through embarrassment at his physical humiliation or anger with her. Tom couldn't tell. He paused playback, examining the two of them. Jonny didn't appear to be badly injured beyond a dented pride. Scarlett was crying.

Tom put his hands behind his head, interlocking his fingers. "What the hell is going on with these people?" he said, shaking his head. Billy Slegg was stalking Scarlett after all, and the footage he'd provided not only muddied the waters somewhat, but Tom was hopeful it might also provide the answers as to who killed her. He looked at the list of media files again, seeing that there wasn't one from Friday, the day of Scarlett's murder. The last file was dated on the Thursday evening. Tom hovered the cursor over it but decided to wait. "I need some coffee first."

CHAPTER TWENTY-FOUR

"I SEE it that we have two ways to go about this," Tamara said, turning away from the whiteboards and turning to face the assembled officers. "We can knock on the door, or we can kick it in."

Tom reviewed every media file handed to him by Billy Slegg prior to waking everyone up and getting them back in. Eric was the last to arrive, showing up in the clothes he'd been wearing the day before, unshaven and looking like he'd barely slept. Cassie was her usual cheery self and Tamara had dismissed Tom's apology for going AWOL the previous night.

Tony Slater had been a regular visitor to Scarlett's home in the previous weeks, showing up three to four times a week and always just before midday and leaving again by one. Reviewing Scarlett's mobile records, and with the help of the service providers, they'd been able to identify almost every number who she was in contact with on a regular basis.

There was one number, however, that was traced to a non-contract pay-as-you-go mobile which was always topped up with cash. Initially, Tom had thought this most likely belonged to the neighbour living in the street who was well known for low-level recreational drug dealing. As it turned out, he had a contract phone. Looking at when texts or calls were made to Scarlett, it was always either very late at night or during a standard working day.

In all likelihood, when someone's partner was either asleep or not around. Without a warrant, they were unable to learn of the dialogue exchanged in these text messages which were always deleted from Scarlett's mobile phone immediately after receipt. She didn't want someone, or anyone, to see them. Based on what they saw Jonny do when he confronted Tony, it wasn't difficult to understand why.

"Well," Tom said, perched on the edge of a desk, "we tried the polite approach with Tony, and he lied through his teeth. Catching him off guard is my choice."

Tamara was inclined to agree. "You lead that one, Tom." She checked her watch. She wanted to be at the respective addresses by seven o'clock. It was Sunday morning. They were both likely to be home and hopefully tucked up in bed when they arrived. "I'll take Eric with me over to Jonny's flat."

Eric looked up, bleary eyed. Whether he'd been listening was unclear.

"Right," Tamara said to the assembled uniform officers waiting patiently, "DI Janssen will allocate you roles for the coming raids. Remember, we are still looking for a missing girl, so keep an eye out for any indication of her whereabouts."

"DCI Greave, may I have a word?"

She looked towards the back of the room where Chief Superintendent Watts was trying to draw her attention. She handed proceedings over to Tom and made her way through the group.

"Good morning, sir."

"Tamara, you look like you're making progress."

"We are, sir. We'll be carrying out two raids in," she looked at her watch, "about half an hour. We're optimistic about the result."

"Information via the incident room?" Watts asked, smiling hopefully.

"It all helps, sir," she said. "I am rather busy—"

"I'd like to introduce you to our resident expert," Watts said, placing a hand on her shoulder and steering her out of the room and into the corridor. "I've lent him my office."

"Him?" Tamara asked. "Yesterday, he was a she…"

Watts opened the door and a man, sitting facing away from them stood up as they entered, turning to greet them.

"DCI Greave, meet Professor White, our expert profiler."

His warm smile faded to be replaced by surprise.

"Tamara?" David asked.

Tamara's lips moved but no words emanated from within. "I… good morning, David."

Watts glanced between them as they stared at one another. It was an awkward moment, one that he didn't understand.

"I'm sorry, do the two of you know one another?"

"Um… sort of," she said.

David White cocked his head. "A little better every time we meet, so it would appear."

The double meaning was lost on Watts, but Tamara felt a little embarrassed. Not that she allowed it to show.

"Excellent," Watts said. "Tamara, I was unaware that you'd ever used a profiler before?"

She shook her head. "Oh, I haven't, sir, it's—"

"We've met in another capacity, Chief Superintendent." David held Tamara's gaze, angling his head slightly. "Around fitness classes, I believe."

"Excellent," Watts repeated. "Well, I'll leave the two of you to get acquainted… again."

The Chief Superintendent left, closing the door behind him.

"So," David said, raising a single eyebrow, "you're *not* a fitness instructor?"

Tamara smiled awkwardly. "I don't wish to stray into pedantry, but I didn't say that I was. You made an assumption which turned out to be incorrect."

"An assumption you allowed to carry."

"Well, that's certainly true." Tamara cleared her throat. "You're a profiler. An expert no less."

David held up a hand to stop her. "I'm not a profiler, at all. I am a professor in psychology, currently guest lecturing at the UEA."

"Impressive." Tamara tilted her head. "Do you have any formal experience in criminal profiling?"

"Er... no," he said, grimacing. "But I was in the area to speak at a seminar in Blakeney and a friend of Geoffrey's... sorry, Chief Superintendent Watts, was present and suggested to him that I... well..." he held his palms wide, "help. If I can, of course."

"That's very kind of you."

He studied her momentarily. She smiled. David held a folder aloft.

"I have some preliminary insights..."

Tamara checked her watch.

"Do you need to be somewhere right now or," David bit his lower lip, "am I terribly dull?"

"You're not dull, at least I don't know whether you are or not," she said, "but I do have somewhere I need to be. We have an operation scheduled and I'm quite key to it, so I really do need to go." She smiled. "Can we go over your..."

"Insights."

"Right, yes. Your insights when I get back?"

"Yes, of course."

"Good," she said, heading for the door. "I'm looking forward to hearing them. I'm sure they'll be useful."

TOM LIFTED the radio to his mouth, checking everyone was in position. They were. The street was quiet at this time on a Sunday morning. An elderly man shuffled by them walking his dog. He looked nervous. Tom smiled and he returned it, but he quickened his walking pace, hurrying to get out of the way.

Tom took one last look at Tony Slater's house. The curtains were drawn, a car parked in front that was registered to him. He glanced at Cassie.

"Shall we wake him up?"

"His partner is pregnant, isn't she?"

"Yes."

"I probably should have mentioned this back in the briefing, but do you think it's wise to scare the daylights out of her by kicking their front door?"

Tom sighed. "It's not like you to take the fun out of the job, Cass."

"Maybe I'm growing up."

He smiled. "Okay, we'll knock politely but if the door doesn't open quickly—"

"We'll kick it in," she finished for him.

Tom was confident. Uniformed officers were waiting at the rear just in case and alongside himself and Cassie there were two more constables and a dog handler. Part of him thought this was overkill. He had no idea what reaction they would get from Tony Slater, partly because they were still unsure about his role in all of this: if he had one?

In reality, they were acting on a hunch. An informed guess. He'd lied to Tom when there had been no need to do so and that set alarm bells ringing. Cassie fell into step alongside him, and they walked up to the front door. Tom rang the bell, depressing it several times. He waited a moment and repeated the action.

Cassie stepped back and looked up at the bedroom window, seeing a curtain part and someone look down at her. She waved and gestured for them to come down and open the door.

Moments later, Tony Slater unlocked the door and pulled it open, clearly irritated.

"What are you—"

"Tony Slater," Tom said, placing a sheet of paper in his hand, "this is a warrant to search these premises."

"What the hell?" Tony said as Tom placed a hand on his chest and guided him out of the way. Cassie and the uniformed officers entered to begin the search.

"Looking for what?" Tony asked.

Olivia, Tony's partner came down the stairs, eyes wide and fearful. "Tony, what's happening?"

"It's just a misunderstanding, love. It'll be sorted out soon enough."

She stopped at the bottom of the stairs. Cassie came from the back of the house where she'd just let in the officers waiting at the rear.

"If you'll step aside, please?" Cassie asked Olivia who steadfastly refused to move from where she stood, blocking access to the first floor. Olivia looked at Tony and he shook his head.

"Just let them do their thing."

Begrudgingly, she moved out of Cassie's way, and she trotted up the stairs.

TAMARA STOOD outside the converted townhouse where Jonny Young lived in the top-floor flat. She waited for confirmation that everyone was in position before initiating the raid.

"All units, go, go, go," she said.

Eric swung the battering ram striking the latch plate of the entrance door. It was an old door and very robust; it held firm. It took several attempts before the frame gave way, the door splintering inwards with a shriek and a roar. With three other officers in tow, Eric mounted the stairs as quickly as he could, bearing in mind he was still carrying the ram.

Out of breath when he made it to the top floor, one of the others offered to take the weight and force entry to Jonny's flat. There was no way Eric was going to pass up that opportunity. This particular door offered precious little resistance, the ram virtually punching the locking mechanism through the door as if it'd been blown apart with a shotgun.

The uniformed constables bundled through, all of them screaming their presence as they made their way from room to room. Eric set the ram down and entered. Shouts went up from the far end of the flat where the bedrooms were located. Eric ran towards them. Jonny emerged from a room on the right, wearing just a pair of boxer shorts and his socks, slamming into the wall opposite before breaking into a run for the front door. Someone screamed from inside the bedroom, a howl of protest quickly morphing into anger.

Jonny's eyes met Eric's and the former's top lip curled as he charged Eric who braced himself. Jonny attempted to barge Eric aside, but Eric dropped his shoulder and stepped into the advancing man, slamming into his midriff. Eric wasn't tall but he was compact and muscular, and something of a power-house. He didn't buckle under the collision. Instead, Jonny groaned as the air rushed out of his lungs and he doubled over. Eric pressed home his advantage, pushing Jonny back. Off balance, Jonny attempted to drive his elbow down onto Eric's skull, but the impact didn't deter the detective constable, quite the contrary. Eric wrapped his arms around his opponent's waist and lifted him off the ground.

The two men stumbled, and Jonny was slammed to the floor on his back, Eric atop him. With the bit between his teeth, the wrestling manoeuvre successful, Eric attempted to pin his charge to the floor. Jonny struggled beneath Eric's frame, repeatedly striking the top of his head, first in anger and then, with each ineffective blow, an ever-increasing amount of frustration.

"Get off me! Get off me!" Jonny yelled, the pitch of his voice rising in panic as Eric grunted, working to subdue him. Eric wasn't about to let go. The ferocity of the strikes eased as Jonny's energy dissipated or as he became numb to the blows, Eric was unsure which. Another officer appeared, from where Eric didn't know but assistance seemed to have taken an age to arrive whereas it was likely to have been mere seconds. He grasped hold of Jonny and between the two of them, they soon managed to overpower and nullify his resistance. The confrontation was over.

The calm that followed the storm seemed eerily quiet. Jonny was rolled onto his front, placed in handcuffs and remained face down in the carpet, his breath laboured. PC Jenkins knelt with one knee in Jonny's back, glancing at Eric who sat back, propping himself up against the wall, breathing heavily.

"Are you okay, Eric?" he asked, looking at something on his face. Eric reached up and felt blood to the left of his eye and just above the brow. It felt superficial. He nodded.

"I'm all right."

Using the wall for support, he pushed himself upright just as Tamara entered the flat. A woman was screaming. How long she'd been screaming, Eric wasn't sure. The high of the adrenalin rush in the moment along with the fight with Jonny both having taken precedence, combining to focus the mind. She may have been screaming since they forced entry.

Tamara joined Eric and they both entered the bedroom to find Constable Dave Marshall grappling with a woman on the bed. She was naked besides her underwear, lashing out at Marshall who was trying in vain to get control of the situation. He didn't notice their presence, the woman swinging arms and legs at him, scratching, punching and even kicking out at him. The fact they were on the bed lent the scene a rather comical edge as the threat of her doing any real harm to Marshall was minimal, but also made it nigh on impossible for the officer to pin her down. The lack of clothing didn't help as he had nothing to grip, struggling as he was to take hold of her flailing arms.

"Enough!" Tamara yelled. The woman stopped, as did Marshall, both breathing heavily. Then she glared at Tamara, her eyes gleamed, bloodshot and borderline manic. Eric guessed she was high on something, which would also explain Jonny's freakish strength. Tamara raised a pointed finger at the woman. "Pack it in, now!" The stern, authorita-tive approach did the trick and she knelt there, staring at Tamara, her breath coming in short, ragged gasps. "What's your name?"

"Tina."

"Okay, Tina," Tamara said. She indicated PC Marshall. "This policeman is going to hand you some clothes. You can cover yourself up and sit down. We're not here for you but I'll be quite happy to throw you in the back of a police van if you want me to."

Tina's aggression dissipated. Marshall unceremoniously climbed off the bed. He was sweating and had multiple scratches to his face. None of them had drawn blood but he did look like he'd been wrestling a feral cat. He gathered up the nearest items of clothing to him, whether they were Tina's or not didn't matter. He threw them at her and she caught them with both hands.

"Thanks," she said without genuine gratitude.

Marshall shook his head and waited for her to cover herself up. Tamara walked back into the hall, Eric a step behind having plucked a hooded dressing gown off a hook on the back of the bedroom door. Eric assisted PC Jenkins in getting Jonny to his feet and then placed the hood of the dressing gown over Jonny's head. Patting Jonny's back, Eric leaned into him.

"Can't have you scaring the locals when we get outside, can we?"

"You're making such a mistake, Eric. You really are."

"Is that a threat?" Eric asked, not so gently shoving him forward. "We already have resisting arrest, assault on a police officer." Eric peered into the living room. The drug paraphernalia on the coffee table was readily identifiable. Blackened silver foil, a pipe and a bag of greyish brown powder were together on the glass top. Eric tutted. "I do hope you've not got enough drugs there to shift from a possession charge to one of intent to supply. It'd be a shame, for me personally, to see you facing some serious time at Her Majesty's pleasure with that list."

Jonny lurched towards the door under Eric's pressure, but Jenkins had his hand on the cuffs. If Jonny felt like making a run for it, he wouldn't get far. Although the fight seemed to have drained out of him. PC Jenkins led Jonny out of the flat. Marshall appeared from the bedroom moments later with

Tina. She was nonplussed but at least she was no longer trying to attack anyone. They stopped next to Tamara who looked the woman up and down.

"How well do you know Jonny?" she asked.

Tina shrugged. "I see him about."

"Have you seen him with a little girl, around seven or eight years old maybe?"

"Nah," Tina said, shaking her head. Tamara inclined her head towards the door and Marshall moved off, taking Tina with him.

Eric checked in the bathroom and the second bedroom but there was no sign of Maggie. He looked up to see if there was a loft hatch, but the flat was built into the eaves of the property. There was no roof space.

"Maggie's not here."

Tamara shook her head. "I've just had a message from Tom. Tony Slater is in custody but there's no sign of her there either."

"The longer this goes on," Eric said. "The less chance there is of finding her al—"

"I know, Eric," Tamara said, gently placing a hand on his forearm to stop him from saying what must be on everyone's mind. "I know."

CHAPTER TWENTY-FIVE

PROFESSOR WHITE STOOD in front of the whiteboards in the ops room. Peering over the rims of his spectacles, he occasionally paused and made a quick note in the margins of his presentation. He turned, smiling at Tamara and then broadening it as the team took their seats. She approached him.

"Are you ready?" she asked.

"Yes, yes of course. One of your colleagues advises me that you have two suspects downstairs."

"We do, yes," Tamara said. Both Jonny Young and Tony Slater were sitting in their cells awaiting interview. "But I am keen to hear your thoughts before speaking to them formally."

"I see. Good."

He sounded nervous.

"Is something wrong?"

"No, not at all. However," he said, looking down at his notes, "I have come at this trying to help you understand the mindset of the perpetrator and therefore identify him."

"And, if I'm right with either of them, then your analysis may help break them down," Tamara said, smiling.

"Yes, I suppose so. I don't really see myself involved with the *breaking* of people, though, Tamara."

She touched his elbow. "Don't worry, that's my skill set."

"One thing, Tamara."

"Yes?"

"I've had the impression... that my presence is treading on peoples' toes," he said earnestly. "It's certainly not my intention. I appreciate this isn't my profession—"

"It's not a problem," Tamara said. His eyes narrowed and she took a breath. "Honestly. Okay, this has been a fast-moving inquiry and... external input can be useful and productive... but—"

"It can also get in the way, can it not?"

She smiled but didn't wish to confirm it. Turning to face the others, the team quietened down.

"I'll do the formal introduction but I'm sure you've all had a brief chat with David at some point this morning. He's going to give us a view on the crime scene and offer us a few pointers as to the killer's motivation behind Scarlett's murder. So, take notes. They may be useful in the forthcoming interviews but also do ask any questions."

"Thank you, DCI Greave. Now, first off, I don't wish to present myself as an expert in criminology, so forgive me if I come across as if I'm patronising any of you. I focussed on the victim, specifically relating to the surrounding crime scene and how she was presented."

"Presented?" Tom asked.

"Indeed, Inspector. Yes, I believe she was presented to us... erm... to you. The killer wished her to be seen in this way. The make-up, the brushed hair... I believe her clothes were changed. Is that correct?" he asked, scanning his notes for the relevant passage.

"Yes. The clothes she was found in in her bedroom were different to those she wore for her evening out," Tom said.

"Exactly, thank you. The dress she was discovered wearing, I've deduced from the crime scene photography, was far dressier than what she wore for her date. As I understand it, the victim has no defensive wounds on her person other than some bruising that occurred some days before."

"Yes. The pathologist is carrying out the post-mortem today," Tamara said. "We have a hypothesis that her boyfriend may have learned of her striking up a relationship with her ex. Jonny is the jealous type."

"Hm... I do wonder about him," David said, seeing Tamara raise an eyebrow, he casually waved the glasses in his hand in her direction. "No matter, I'll come to that. Anyway, as I was saying, the presentation of the victim is a very personal and intimate event for the killer. He has taken the time to display Scarlett, to make her appear peaceful, almost angelic. Now, whether that is for his gratification or for ours," he made a circular motion in the air with his hand, "the general public, I mean, not necessarily the police, I do not know. I believe only the killer will know that for certain. Time is a factor in all of this. To present her in this way will have taken time. As would the act of actually killing the poor girl."

He put his glasses back on and traced his forefinger through his notes, stopping when he found what he was looking for.

"Again, supposition without the pathologist's report, but the medical examiner was confident the cause of death was asphyxiation, correct?"

"We believe so," Tom said. "We think she was smothered with a pillow."

"Yes, so I see," David said. "We have no sign of strangulation by hand, rope or flex. Again, the lack of defensive wounds suggest she may well have been unconscious when the act took place." He looked at Tamara. "She had been drinking but was not considered drunk. Is that still accurate?"

"It is."

"Then I should imagine she ingested some form of sedative; a recreational drug or something similar, willingly or receiving it under false pretences I can't say. Even if one is asleep, unless blind drunk or comatose from another substance, the body reacts to protect itself when under threat. That surge of fear to push you to the surface if you're under water and gasping for breath, the instinctive reaction to attack even the smallest of creatures if you are frightened by it, an insect for example. These are instinctive reactions. Ones we can overcome in a rational moment, but primordial reactions are seldom controlled."

"She would have fought back," Tamara said, "if she could have. Isn't that obvious?"

"Of course, sorry," David said. "The point I am making is really around the time element in this scenario. The requirements around asphyxiation as a method of murder all revolve around time; having the physical presence to subjugate your victim, the nerve to see it through, not least because the body fights back, and the mind itself will instinctively fight for survival. The muscles of the neck, too, are not weak, far from it. They are strong, and when you press or squeeze, they push back. Lastly, especially when using such a...non-lethal... weapon, in this case a pillow, it takes time itself. She would not have passed away quickly, even if she wasn't able to push back, so there is an element of commitment in the killer's psyche. A desire to see the job through."

David paused, his expression changing, almost as if a thought had occurred.

"In terms of how a killer goes about their *work*, for want of a better phrase, there are also the reactions to emotional trauma that an ordinary person goes through when they are involved in something extraordinary; be it a car crash, severe personal injury or, as we have here, committing a murder. The fight or flight principle will kick in along with the rush of adrenalin. The desire to flee from a traumatic event is very strong, even in those who have done nothing wrong or have no sense of guilt. This person, the killer, stayed at the house for a period of time. I've read about serial killers who murder their victims and then finish off the leftovers from the victim's fridge, perhaps have a beer and watch the television. These people are sociopathic or psychotic in nature. They tend not to dress their victims, seeking merely to destroy and then move on with their normal lives, hence eating or the telly. This killer had a plan, an end goal in mind."

"Which was?" Cassie asked.

David shrugged apologetically. "I'm afraid I have no idea. If you catch him, you'll have to ask him. Although, I should imagine he will be quite skilled in manipulation."

"Can you give us a profile of the killer. Any tips as to what characteristics to look out for?" Tamara asked. "That might be helpful when we move to interview."

"It really isn't my field of expertise," he said, thinking hard. "However, I would suggest that this person is of moderate or average intelligence. No doubt, he will believe he is of a higher intellect. I'm certain he will believe he is more intelligent than his pursuers," David said with a wry smile. "I would expect him to have an explosive temper, evidence of which shouldn't be difficult to find in his life, past or present. Similarly, he will likely be popular. Maybe not with everyone, but he'll carry enough charm or charisma with which to offset any instinctive fear he may engender in those around him. *Mirroring* is what we call it in the trade."

Tamara nodded as he spoke. "The ability to blend in with social groups by mimicking their behaviours."

"Absolutely, correct, Tamara," he said. "After all, it is difficult to see the devil when one is looking at one's own reflection."

Tom shifted in his seat, his expression fixed and unreadable. Tamara noticed.

"What is it, Tom?"

"Those character traits you listed arguably fit both of the men we have downstairs. You haven't mentioned where Maggie fits into all of this. I'm struggling with it. Why take her?"

"I can only speculate," David said, holding his hands up. "I agree, this is the most peculiar aspect in this scenario. From a purely psychological perspective, I find it difficult to believe the killer has any form of conscience in relation to the child. His moral compass is skewed to such an extent that protection or parental motivations are inconceivable. I don't see a saviour complex at the root of her abduction. Could he be a paedophile? Yes, that is possible, but that theory does not tie in with the murder and presentation of her mother."

Eric raised his hand and David acknowledged him. "Yes, please do ask."

"Could Maggie be a… trophy… of sorts? I mean, she is the most important element of Scarlett's life. If the killer has taken her life, Scarlett's I mean, then could he be keeping her most treasured possession for himself? If you see what I mean?"

The professor considered the theory. "I must admit, that is very dark indeed, Detective Constable." He splayed his hands wide. "I'm afraid I have no answers for you with the information I have." He looked at Tamara, disappointed. "I am sorry, but I wouldn't want to lead you astray. I am at a loss to understand how Maggie fits into this. Were it not for her disability, then I think your constable may have been on to something but I cannot for the life of me see why a killer, such as the one you are hunting, would behave in this manner. I really don't."

Tamara tilted her head to one side. "You are not alone, David. I can assure you."

CHAPTER TWENTY-SIX

JONNY YOUNG HAD his head in his hands when Tamara entered the interview room, Eric alongside her. The uniformed constable who'd been keeping a watchful eye acknowledged both officers and stepped out. Jonny glared at Eric and Tamara thought she caught a glimmer of satisfaction in Eric's expression as he took the laptop he had under his arm, set it down on the table and took his seat.

"Well, it's about bloody time!" Jonny said, staring at Tamara as she pulled out her chair.

"I take it you are refreshed and ready to progress with the interview, Mr Young?"

"Yeah," he said curtly, sneering at her. "Sooner it's done, the sooner I can go home. And you lot will get a bill for my front door from the landlord. I'll not be paying for it."

Tamara smiled. "Anything else you want to get off your chest?"

He pointed at Eric. "I want him charged with assault." Jonny pointed to the side of his face where he'd received a cut which had subsequently swollen, bruising beginning to show.

"Police brutality," he said, staring at Eric. "The press love that."

Tamara noted Eric didn't flinch. She was proud of him. Not too long ago even the hint of such an accusation would give him a night of sleepless anxiety. Although, he looked like he hadn't slept and, what with the length of history between the two men, she had to concede Eric may have been overzealous in the arrest.

"I can certainly provide the forms for you to fill at your convenience, Mr Young," Tamara said, shuffling her paper-work in front of her on the desk. "And you'll also note that the papers love murderers and child killers, too."

"What?" Jonny said, his anger subsiding, if only a little.

"They sell papers, Jonny," she said. "A lot of papers. Nothing journalists like more than feeding the public stories about wretches like you."

"Now hold on a minute," he said, sitting forward, palms flat on the table before him. He shook his head vigorously. "I've not killed anyone. Not Scarlett and not her daughter. I'm a lot of things but I'm not a child killer."

"And yet here you are, Jonny, slap bang in the middle of a murder investigation. A missing child, and you, lying to the police—"

Jonny slammed a hand on the table, lifting it and jabbing a finger at her. "You're not fitting me up with this! I'm not having it, do you hear?"

Tamara glanced sideways and Eric took his cue, lifting the lid and bringing the laptop out of hibernation.

"Now, you told us you last saw Scarlett at her home the day before her death. That was Thursday, correct?"

"Yeah, that's right. What of it?"

"You had to make up for something. That's what you

said." Tamara sat forward, fixing her gaze on him. "What did you have to make up for?"

Jonny brushed the question off with a shrug. "We had words the day before. It was all a misunderstanding. I think I told you lot this—"

Eric pressed play on the footage Billy Slegg recorded on Wednesday, earlier in the week, the altercation between Jonny and Tony Slater. Jonny sat in silence as the footage played out, hand across his mouth, staring at the screen. When the play-back ended, he shook his head.

"Like I said, a misunderstanding."

"Is that why Scarlett has bruises on her body, her arms, because you had to make up for this?" Tamara asked, pointing at the screen. "You couldn't handle Tony Slater getting the better of you in front of her, so you went back to teach her a lesson when he wasn't around?"

He shook his head, lips pursed, staring down at the table.

"It wasn't like that. You're twisting it."

"Then tell us, Jonny. Why did you have to rough Scarlett up?"

He didn't reply but his anger was growing, his lip curling with every accusation that flew at him.

"Jonny Young, the big man locally. The big man around town since school," Tamara said. "Rejected by your girlfriend in favour of her ex—"

"I told you, it wasn't like that!"

"So, your girlfriend wasn't rekindling a relationship with her ex? It looks like it from this," Tamara said.

Eric loaded another still frame taken from the video where Tony and Scarlett kissed on the doorstep. Enlarged, it certainly looked like they were parting lovers.

Jonny shook his head. He wasn't angry now. He looked upset. Upset enough to kill?

"And then we have your little brother, Mark," Eric said. "He takes her out on Friday night for a date. A romantic night out for the two of them. It must have been a surprise for you to see them together. Her bed's barely gone cold from the last time you were in it and she's out with your brother. Not only her ex, but *your brother*. That's cold, right, Jonny. It must burn inside you."

Jonny slammed a balled fist on the table and glared at Eric. "Leave my brother out of this."

"How can we?" Tamara asked. "You followed them through town and laid a hand on him, on Mark, your own blood. You don't do that if it doesn't hurt." She inclined her head, meeting Jonny's eye. "Here you are having already roughed her up for daring to see her ex and now this... your own brother. I would be so, so angry. Wouldn't you, Eric?"

"Very angry," Eric said flatly. "Angry enough to kill—"

"I didn't kill her!" Jonny barked. "She didn't want me, I realised that, and no, I didn't care for the brush off. But I'll tell you this for nothing, Scarlett didn't want Mark either."

"Then what was she playing at dating him?" Tamara asked.

He sat back in his seat and threw his arms in the air. "I've no idea. I really don't. I spoke to Mark, yesterday, after all this went down. I needed to find out if he'd had anything to do with it. With her death, I mean."

"You thought Mark could have done this?" Eric asked, failing to mask his scepticism at the suggestion.

Jonny shook his head. "No, of course not. You know Mark. He's ten times the man I am. Soft as shite, but decent. I've no idea how he's turned out so well, mind you."

"What did he say when you asked him?"

"He was scared. He took her home but didn't go inside. They kissed, or at least, she kissed him. He didn't initiate it."

"Why would she do that? It doesn't sound like Mark is her type."

"He's not," Jonny said, drawing his hands through his hair and rubbing the sides of his head as he did so. "Scarlett loved her bad boys. People like me were her weakness. The same with Maggie's father. He did a spell inside. Her old man hated both of us. He'd always be on at her about me. You know, he would never speak to me? If we were in the house at the same time, he'd pretend I was invisible. Judgemental old sod."

"You can't blame him, can you? I mean, you're not exactly a catch, are you?"

Jonny pulled a sarcastic facial expression at her. "Scarlett was lucky to have someone like me. As you saw this morning, I do all right for myself. I didn't need her and, before you say it, I'm not going to kill her because she doesn't want to sleep with me a few times a week. It's hardly a great loss to me, is it?"

"Scarlett is dead, Jonny. Does that not upset you at all?"

"Hell yeah, but not so much when you're accusing me of having done it. Look after yourself first, right?" He chewed on his lower lip and Tamara caught a fleeting glimpse of his insecurity. For all the bravado, all the posturing, he did care. He cared deeply. The veil descended quickly once more, and he sneered at her. "While you're wasting time in here with me, you could be out finding that little girl." He shook his head. "I'm not responsible and the sooner you accept that, the better it will be. For all of us. Why aren't you asking Tony Slater what he's playing at? Is it a coincidence that he comes back into her life and soon after she winds up dead?" He scoffed, laughing at them. "Not telling you how to do your jobs, but from where I'm sitting, you're not very good at this, are you?"

Tamara looked at the laptop and Eric launched another video.

"This was recorded on Thursday evening, Jonny," Tamara said. It was the last recording Billy Slegg had made. It was short. He must have been standing outside Scarlett's house, filming straight through the front window into the living room. A shout is heard from off camera and the holder turns towards it. A figure comes across the screen and a brief scuffle ensues, howls of protest and angry exchanges before someone groans, dropping the camera to the ground and the footage stopped. Tamara looked directly into Jonny's eyes. "Care to comment?"

"That weird little shit had been popping up all over the place watching Scarlett. He's lucky I didn't..."

"Lucky you didn't do what, Jonny?" Tamara asked.

Jonny sniffed, looking away. "Stalking. That's what he was doing, right? That's a crime. Why isn't he sitting in here instead of me?" He wagged an accusatory finger at Tamara. "You should get your priorities right, love."

———

TOM SAT DOWN BESIDE CASSIE. Tony Slater eyed him warily as Tom focussed on him but said nothing. The atmosphere was thick. Tony was no stranger to the police. He knew he was wrapped up in something that he could see himself being drawn deeper into. Despite his previous convictions and time spent in prison, perhaps even because of it, he was scared.

"Can you confirm for the benefit of the recording that you've waived your right to legal representation," Tom said.

"I have."

Tony was curt, monosyllabic.

"Shall we cut to the chase, Tony?"

He swallowed hard, struggling to do so. "Please."

"You lied to me, Tony. It wasn't a white lie either." Tom

opened up a folder and took out stills taken from the videos Billy Slegg supplied them with. He set them out in front of Tony whose eyes fleetingly darted to each one in turn before looking away. "You have seen Scarlett in the last year. You've seen rather a lot of her, haven't you?"

Tony nodded.

"I'm sorry, Tony but we need to hear you say so," Tom said, pointing to the recording equipment.

"Yes!" Tony said, rolling his eyes. "I'm sure you know I've been seeing Scarlett on and off, recently."

"For how long?"

"These past few weeks. No more than that."

"Why did you lie about it?"

"Isn't it obvious?" Tony looked between Cassie and Tom. "I thought the police were supposed to be brighter these days; you know, having qualifications and stuff?"

"Feel free to enlighten me," Tom said, his tone neutral, ignoring the barb.

Tony exhaled heavily, slowly rubbing his hands together. Tom wondered if he was contemplating what he was going to say or perhaps, more pertinently, what he could get away with leaving out.

"Because I am about to be married, Inspector. If Olivia were to know, then it is quite simple; there would be no wedding."

"Scarlett is dead, Tony—"

"And you think I don't know that? What would you have me do?"

Tom shook his head. "Help us to catch her killer."

Tony scoffed. "As if you haven't got me in the frame for this already."

"Lying to us and keeping a relationship with her secret is likely to do that, Tony."

"With my record, it was only a matter of time until you laid it at my door. You were speaking to me within hours." He glared at Tom. "Tell me with a straight face that I wasn't near to or at the top of the list. I dare you."

He had a point.

"Why now, Tony? Why revisit your relationship with her now?" Tom asked, softening his tone. "It's been years and, as you said, you're about to be married and you have a baby on the way. Why now?"

Tony lowered his head, rubbing at his forehead with his left hand. "It wasn't me. Scarlett came to me. She must have asked around town, found out where I was working and started showing up. At first, I wanted to stay clear of her—"

"Really? She was chasing you?"

"Yes. As difficult as you might find it to believe, she was. You think I wanted to go back to that? The relationship, I mean. We were *so* destructive to one another. I've put a lot of time and effort into starting afresh... much of it began in the nick, you know?" He pressed the heels of his palms into both eyes, letting out a purposeful groan. "I knew it. I just bloody knew it would end badly. I told her as much."

"Perhaps you can answer if I ask the same question from a different point of view. Why did Scarlett decide to come to you now?"

Tony laughed, a humourless, despondent sound. "Now, that's a question, isn't it?" He stared at Tom. "I have to admit my ego took an upturn. Even though I know we were terrible together... the lifestyle, the drugs and alcohol. The violence... It still hurt when she walked away from me. I was in prison and was powerless to stop it. Her father got his way."

"Can you blame him?"

"No, not at all," Tony said. "If she was my daughter, I'd

have done everything to get her away from the likes of me. I'll bet he was talking me down to you."

Tom didn't answer but his silence said enough.

"Thought so," Tony said with a wry smile. "Did he tell you I wrote to Scarlett from inside? Once I was enrolled on a programme, straightening myself out and looking past the drugs. Not to try and get her back, I understood that we were done, but I wanted to see my daughter." His tone turned bitter, his expression darkening. "She never answered. Not even to tell me where to go."

"She wanted a clean break, perhaps," Tom said.

"Maybe so, yes. Again, who could blame her. So, imagine my surprise when she shows up out of the blue. It threw me."

"You were saying she wanted something from you?"

He laughed. "Yeah. I thought she wanted me. Initially it was just a conversation. I told her I wasn't looking back but moving forward." He shook his head. "She kept on coming though. One thing... sort of led to another and before I knew it..."

"You were in bed together?" Tom asked. He nodded. "Amazing how that can *just* happen."

"What are you, the moral police or something? It is what it is. Adult relationships are complex... things happen. Bad things."

"So, you're telling me that Scarlett wanted to start things up again?"

"No, that's not what I'm saying. At first, I thought so but after a few days it all became about Maggie."

"She wanted you to be involved in your daughter's life?"

"No! She wanted me to take Maggie on... permanently."

Tom couldn't hide his surprise. A quick glance to his left told him Cassie's response was similar.

"Maggie was everything to Scarlett," Tom said. "Are you

really asking us to believe that she was trying to get you to take—"

"Let's get this clear, Inspector," Tony said. "She was *manipulating* me into taking Maggie off her hands. She said the child needed a stable father figure in her life, someone with prospects who could care for her."

"I'm struggling with that, to be honest with you—"

"Struggle with it, debate it, throw it in the bin, if you like, but it's the truth. As God is my witness, it's the truth."

"Why?" Tom pressed. "Why would she do that after all this time?"

Tony snarled, "I would tell you to ask her, but we can't can we?"

Of all the outcomes Tom envisaged presenting itself in the interview, this wasn't one of them. If Tony was fabricating a story, then he could have come up with something, anything, that would have more credibility than this. Perversely, it played in his favour.

"How did you respond to the request?"

Tony slumped in his seat, his shoulders sagging. "Badly. Very badly. I dismissed her. For good reason... I mean, I'm hardly equipped to cope with someone with her needs. It doesn't take a blind man to see it."

"Let me translate for you," Cassie said. "You're actually saying you *didn't want* to cope with Maggie. That's her name, Maggie. Your daughter's name is Maggie."

"I know her bloody name!"

"And yet, you kept returning to see Scarlett day after day," Tom said.

"I did," he said quietly. "On my lunch break."

"And you even purchased a burner phone to keep in touch with her."

Tony looked up at Tom.

"Yes, we know it was yours, so there's no need to deny it. Less chance of getting caught by Olivia, I suppose."

Tony nodded slowly; his lips pursed. "Yes."

"When did you last see her?" Tom asked.

"Wednesday. Her ex-boyfriend, current boyfriend... whatever came around. He came at me when I left. It wasn't a problem. I could handle idiots like him, but afterwards I realised it had to stop. Everything was getting out of hand. I texted her and told her I wouldn't be coming round anymore."

"And Maggie?" Tom asked.

Tony took a deep breath, avoiding eye contact, before sitting upright, psyching himself up to speak the words. "I said I wasn't ready. It's true, I'm not ready. Maybe, at some point in the future once Olivia and I are settled and with the new baby... then it might be different. But right now?" He shook his head. "I'm not capable. It's a shitty thing to say... to do, I know that, but I was honest." He held his hands up. "At least I was honest, right?"

Tom and Cassie exchanged glances.

CHAPTER TWENTY-SEVEN

TAMARA WAS WAITING for Tom when he came out of the interview room, arms folded across her chest. Tom could see his own emotions reflected in her expression.

"You were watching?" he asked.

Tamara nodded. "He makes a strong argument. So did Jonny Young, you'll no doubt be surprised to hear."

She turned her back to the wall, leaning against it and thinking hard.

"What do you want to do next?" Tom asked, well aware that they had nothing to link Tony Slater to Scarlett's murder or Maggie's abduction. Tamara's body language suggested the same could be said for Jonny.

"Get the witness in," she said. "The one who saw the man carrying a little girl near to Scarlett's place. If she can pick out either of them then it will give us some leverage to apply pressure with. Right now, we can't place either of them at the house in the relevant time frame. They both have holes in their movements on Friday night, relying on drunk friends or a cooperative spouse to put them away from the crime scene. It would be nice to be able to put some meat on the bones."

"Ma'am?"

They both looked down the corridor to see PC Marshall approaching. Tamara pointed at his face.

"Did you get that seen to?" she asked, indicating the scratches he'd received in the morning's raid.

"They're fine, Ma'am," he said, looking embarrassed. No doubt he'd been receiving a bit of gentle ribbing from his colleagues since they got back to the station.

"What can we do for you, Dave?"

"There's a gentleman in reception, Ma'am. He is insisting on speaking with the officer in charge."

Tamara indicated for Tom to join her and the two of them made their way to the foyer at the front of the station. Tom punched in his code and allowed Tamara to pass through the door first. A man was standing at the front desk. Dressed in jeans and a brown suede leather jacket, he looked at them hopefully.

"Are you in charge?" he asked Tom. Tom smiled and pointed at Tamara. "Oh, I'm sorry," he said, embarrassed.

"That's okay, sir. I'm DCI Greave. How can I help?"

"I understand you're looking for me," he said, concerned.

Tamara and Tom looked at one another. "I don't understand," Tamara said.

"That's my picture," he said, pointing at the artist's sketch pinned to the community noticeboard. "I think."

As soon as he indicated the sketch, Tom could see it. The hair, the build and he was wearing the same jacket. The man pointed to the seating area. A little girl was sitting there playing on a mini gaming machine, her feet dangling and swinging back and forth under the chair.

"My daughter was having a sleepover at a friend's house," he said, looking between them both.

"Where was this?" Tom asked.

"On Northgate. The parents phoned me to say she felt unwell and running a temperature." The little girl looked up at them, smiling. Her father smiled back. "Both my wife and I had had a drink during the evening and so we couldn't drive. We live nearby in Austin Street, so I walked round to collect her. She was sleeping and, what with her temperature, I didn't think it was a good idea to change her, so I wrapped her up and carried her home."

"Right," Tamara said, looking at his daughter. "Is... she okay now?"

"Yes, it was a twenty-four-hour thing. You're all right, aren't you, Chloe?" His daughter grinned, waving at them. Tamara smiled and waved back. Her father looked sheepish. "I'm sorry, I didn't realise you were looking for me. I hope I've not caused you too much trouble."

Tamara held up her hand, reassuring him. Tom could tell she was disappointed but did a good job of concealing it.

"No, no. Thank you for coming in as soon as you did." She looked at Tom. "We will need to take a statement from you while you're here. Is that okay?"

"Yes, yes of course."

"Thank you. If you could take a seat with your daughter and I'll have someone come out and see you as soon as possible."

They left him in reception and made their way back towards ops.

"Well, I didn't expect that," Tom said.

Tamara growled in frustration as she pushed the double doors into the stairwell. She stopped, looked around and made sure they were alone.

"I don't know where we go from here, Tom."

He felt it too. "We need to push for the full forensics report from Scarlett's."

"The crime scene was clean though. We will need to get very lucky, but I'm sensing whoever took Maggie didn't leave us anything to track them with."

"We might get lucky." She looked at Tom, raising a sceptical eyebrow.

"What about the autopsy?"

"Dr Paxton arrived this morning," Tom said. "But we won't have any preliminary findings until this evening at the earliest."

Tom's mobile rang and he fished it out of his pocket, glancing at the screen. "It's Kerry," he said, answering. "Hi Kerry, what's up?"

"Hi, sir. I'm sorry but I've messed up!"

Tom could hear shouting in the background. Kerry was walking, the wind noise audible down the line. The shouting ceased.

"What's happened?"

"I–I don't really know, sir. You know the house is cold... and when I got here this morning, to Alan Turnbull's, he looked frozen, so pale and unwell. He obviously hadn't had the heating on and... and I was worried about him. I asked if I could turn the thermostat up and he said no. I left it for a while, but he was shivering, so I went looking for something to help him keep warm; a blanket or a spare duvet... whatever."

"A reasonable thing to—"

"That's what I thought, but he went off on one, started yelling at me about poking my nose in and all sorts," she said, her voice cracking. Tom thought she was about to cry. "I know he wanted me to back off a bit, but I was only trying to help."

"Take a breath, Kerry, it's okay," Tom said. Tamara's curiosity was piqued, looking concerned. Tom allayed her fears with a raised hand. "What's happening now?"

"He threw me to out, sir, figuratively speaking." She was speaking very quickly, the adrenalin pumping. "W–What should I do now?"

"Come back to the station. It's been a stressful time. We'll give him some space and I'll smooth things over later on. I'll want to update him anyway."

"Okay, sir." She sounded utterly dejected. "I'm so sorry."

"No need to apologise, Kerry. Things happen. It's not necessarily about you. He's under an incredible amount of pressure." Hanging up, he turned to Tamara. "I've no idea what I'm going to say to him though."

"Investigation is ongoing," Tamara said, the phrase sounded hollow, and she knew it.

"I'll think of something," Tom said. "I'm going to visit Scarlett's house, have a dig around now the crime scene techs have been and gone."

"Get some inspiration?"

"Yes, something like that," Tom said. "What do you plan to do with the two we have in custody?"

"Three, if you include Mark, Jonny's brother." She shrugged. "At this point, we really have no grounds to hold any of them. We're coming to the end of the second day and every time we take a step forward…"

"It's two steps back. I know what you mean."

"We'll have to release them. We have zero grounds to hold them, let alone charge them with a crime. Let me know if you have an epiphany while you're at Victoria Avenue."

———

Tom PARKED outside Scarlett's house. The police cordon tape was still across the front door but aside from that, you would never know it was a crime scene. Tom remembered the book he'd borrowed was in his glove box and he took it with him. Approaching the front door, he caught sight of a few eyes watching him from their windows. The shock in the community would take some time to wear off. Catching the killer and finding Maggie would go some way to doing that. It was easier said than done.

Removing the tape stuck to one side of the door frame, he slid a key into the lock, looking over his shoulder before entering. The street looked like any other, cars parked up, televisions on in front rooms across the road. Residents watching the late afternoon kick off. The clash between such routine, everyday events and what happened here less than two days ago was not lost on him. The day he was no longer shocked would be the day he'd hand in his warrant card.

The house felt chilly. Old Victorian houses like this leaked heat and the warmth provided by merely living in them was noticeable by its absence. It was eerily quiet. The front room was silent with only the hum of a passing car to break the solitude. The rear reception room had patio doors which opened out onto a small, decked area, a couple of pot plants with forlorn-looking flowers which had seen their best days. In the kitchen he found a partially extended drawer, left open by the scenes of crime officers, he imagined. Pulling it out, he examined the contents. It was one of those drawers used to store everything that didn't have a home: pens, sticky-note pads, open correspondence and a set of earpiece headphones on top of takeaway menus, held together with a pink elastic band.

Tom took out the letters, leafing through them. One was a council tax notification of charges, another an appointment letter for the Queen Elizabeth Hospital down the road in King's Lynn. It was addressed to Scarlett. He took it out, unfolding it and scanning the details. It was a reminder for Scarlett to attend her monthly appointment this coming Tuesday. He was curious as it was her appointment and not one for Maggie. She was to report to the radiography department for a scheduled MRI scan. He was surprised no one had mentioned an existing condition and, judging by the wording of the letter, this looked like a regular appointment.

Putting the letter aside, he looked through the remaining letters. There was one unopened from social services. Tom tore open the envelope. It was written by a case handler based in Hunstanton. He read down it. Scarlett had missed a meeting the week previous to her death. She was being contacted to make another appointment or risk a referral to court. The letter didn't specify the subject matter or nature of the meeting. The wording was professional but polite. The case handler had left her contact details at the foot of the letter.

Tom sat down, taking out his mobile phone and dialled the number. Being a Sunday, he looked at his watch and saw it was after six o'clock now, and he half expected the call to go to voicemail. When a voice answered, he was surprised.

"This is Detective Inspector Tom Janssen. Could I speak to," he examined the letter again, "Mary Stuart, please."

"This is she. How can I help you, Inspector?"

"I'm contacting you regarding a case you are working at the moment. Could I ask you a couple of questions?"

"As long as it doesn't take too long, Inspector. My husband and I are about to head out for dinner. We're on a family break in Cornwall. I shouldn't have brought my work phone," she said, lowering her voice. "He hates it when I do."

Tom smiled. "I'll try not to keep you too long. It's regarding Scarlett Turnbull."

"Oh, Scarlett," she said, her voice changing as her tone turned melancholy. "This is such a tragic situation. How can I help?"

"Tragic? Yes, I would say so," Tom said. "It is difficult for everyone involved. I take it you are aware of events this weekend?"

"This weekend...? No, we travelled on Friday and have been visiting friends and... Why, whatever's happened?"

"I'm sorry to tell you like this over the phone, Mary, but Scarlett was found dead at her home early Saturday morning."

He heard her draw breath, taking in the gravity of the news. He allowed her a moment to process it. He heard another enter the room in the background and she hushed him. It must be her husband.

"Mary, I need to understand the proceedings around her case with social services. I appreciate this is out of the ordinary. Usually, I would make this request in person."

"Erm... it is highly irregular," she said, stumbling over the words.

"Scarlett was murdered, Mary, and her daughter is missing. We think she has been abducted," Tom said.

"Oh, dear Lord."

"Now, I can provide you with my identification number, you can check it and get back to me, but time is really of the essence here—"

"No, no, it is okay, Inspector. H–How can I help you?"

"Scarlett missed a meeting with you recently, is that correct? I'm looking at the letter you sent her."

"Yes, that was with a family liaison officer. We were looking to put a plan together for Maggie's care. Scarlett was... reluctant."

"I was under the impression that Scarlett was managing well with her daughter. They have daily care visits—"

"They do at present, Inspector, yes. But what will come of the girl when her mother is no longer able to care for her?"

Tom bit his lip, thinking hard, his eyes drifting over to the appointment for the MRI. "Are you referring to her medical condition?"

"Yes, what else?"

"And the nature of this condition is what exactly?"

"You're not aware?"

"No."

"Scarlett was recently diagnosed with a progressive neurological condition. She has long suffered with depression and increasing anxiety, which was understandable when you consider the health condition of her daughter."

"And what was her condition, Scarlett's?" he asked, squeezing the phone between his head and shoulder and flipping open his notebook in front of him to make a note.

"Scarlett had a rare form of primary progressive aphasia; rare because it has taken such an aggressive degeneration in one so young. Now, I'm no physician but there are several types of aphasia, and they are more common in older people or present in patients after trauma to the left side of the brain, as an aftereffect of a stroke, tumour or a severe head injury. As far as I am aware, there are very few cases in people as young as Scarlett."

"You said her case was aggressive?"

"Indeed, yes. Brutally so. People can live with this illness for many, many years and gradually deteriorate over time, whereas the progression of Scarlett's condition, bless her, was such that we needed to be involved."

"For Maggie's sake?"

"Yes, of course."

"I must admit," Tom said, "I'm not aware of this... condition. Is it debilitating?"

"The patient often maintains their faculties, Inspector. Their intelligence and powers of reasoning are largely unaffected, but it is the language and communication skills that are detrimentally affected. They may lose the ability to select the right words in their speech. They will understand which word they are trying to use but the message is lost somewhere between thought and speech. This can lead to issues around all forms of communication; speech, reading, listening and writing... even typing could be difficult."

"And what was the plan you were looking to discuss with her regarding Maggie?"

"Well... her care." Mary sighed. "As I said, a really tragic case. Maggie requires around-the-clock care and, in Scarlett's case, we couldn't wait until such time as she was incapable of looking after her daughter."

"You were looking to take Maggie into care?"

"Yes, I'm afraid so. We didn't see any other course of action. Maggie's father was not present in her life. Not that his name is listed on the birth certificate, so we were unable to contact him directly. Scarlett assured me at our last meeting that she would seek him out and ask him to become involved. Until now, Scarlett has not been forthcoming though."

"What about Alan, Scarlett's father. I understand he is very supportive. Could he not have a role to play?"

"Of course," Mary said. "We met with Alan. He strikes me as a very kindly man, and he was willing. However, at his age and with his... well... I'm afraid he would not be in a position to guarantee long-term care for Maggie. It would be a case of kicking the can down the road and, I think you'll agree, that's not good for anyone, especially Maggie."

"I see," Tom said, tapping his pen against the notebook. "Can you give me an idea about the timeline you were working to?"

"Well," Mary said, pausing, "that was for a panel to decide along with input from the family courts. We were hoping to come to an accommodation with Scarlett and present it to the court. That way, we could avoid any… unpleasantness."

"Hence the meeting?" Tom asked.

"And Scarlett's refusal to attend," Mary said. She sounded dejected. "She was dead against her daughter going into the system." She sighed. "Sometimes, Inspector Janssen, I hate my job. I really do."

"Yes," he said, glancing up at a photo pinned to the fridge by a magnet; Scarlett with Maggie sitting in her lap, both wearing huge smiles, Maggie's arms waving in the air as if she was singing along to her favourite song. "Me too."

CHAPTER TWENTY-EIGHT

TOM CLOSED the door and hurried to his car, dialling Tamara's mobile as he walked. She didn't pick up and the call cut to voicemail.

"Tamara, it's Tom. I've just had an interesting chat with Scarlett's case worker at social services. I'll explain later, but I'm heading over to see Alan now. I think I might have some answers. Call me when you get this message."

He got into his car, starting the engine and accelerating away. Alan's house was only a few minutes' drive away. He hadn't mentioned the involvement of social services or, more importantly, Scarlett's medical condition and Tom wanted to know why he'd withheld it. The closer he got to the house, the tighter the knot in his chest became.

Arriving at Alan's house, he walked up the path to the front door and rang the bell, three quick bursts. A neighbour was just setting off on an evening dog walk. He stopped and examined Tom.

"Are you a journalist?" he asked, his expression set in disgust.

"No, I'm a policeman," Tom said, taking out his warrant card. "Why do you ask?"

"Had them here earlier on," the man said, glancing at the house. "Shouldn't be allowed, badgering a sick man only a day after he lost his daughter like that. Should be strung up, if you ask me."

"Alan is unwell?"

"Oh aye. He's been battling the big C for years." He leaned on the fence, lowering his voice. "Not that he'll let on though. Tough as old boots is Alan."

"Yes. Have you seen him today?"

"Not since he gave that journalist what for this afternoon. He's in though. I saw him moving about earlier." He chuckled. "He's had a busy old day of it, has Alan. First, he was shouting at that pretty little constable you had helping him out. I don't know what she did, but she certainly got him going. He's not backward in coming forward is Alan, not when he's set his mind on something."

"Then the journalist turned up?"

"Yep. Some tabloid, paparazzi oik showed up and he got it in the neck as well."

"Okay, thanks for your help," Tom said.

"No problem. Give Alan my best, would you?"

"Of course, I will," Tom said, smiling and walking back to the front door. He rang the bell again, peering through the pane of obscured glass to the left of the door. All he could make out were shadows. There was no discernible movement inside.

Leaving the porch, he walked around to the back gate. Finding it unlocked, Tom made his way down the side of the house. The door to the kitchen was locked and the rear reception room had curtains drawn across the French doors. He tried the handle, but they were also locked. There was a gap in the curtains, barely an inch wide near the bottom of the drop and Tom had to crouch to see into the interior.

A figure sat in an armchair, with his back to the door. It was Alan. Tom knocked on the glass, but he didn't respond.

"Alan! It's Tom Janssen."

Still, he didn't move. Tom tried again, only this time he hammered his fist on the glass. With no response, he looked around the garden. Lining the edge of the patio was a dwarf wall. It was old and the mortar was in such a poor state of repair that it had crumbled, releasing several bricks which had fallen to the patio. Eyeing the glass, it was single-paned and set into a wood frame. It wouldn't take much.

Tom walked to the loose bricks, stooping to pick one up. Returning to the door, he held one hand up to protect his face and struck the edge of the glass with the brick. The first blow did nothing. The second saw the glass break, creating a hole slightly larger than a balled fist. Tentatively putting put his hand through, Tom reached to the lock and turned the key. It was a metal lock and in need of greasing, and the angle didn't help but he managed to unlock it. Carefully opening the door so as not to disturb the broken pane further, Tom entered.

He pulled back one side of the curtains to allow in a bit of daylight, illuminating the room. A ticking clock, set on the mantelpiece above the fireplace clicked back and forth, breaking the silence. Coming to stand before Alan, he reached down and felt for a pulse. There wasn't one. Alan Turnbull was dead.

Tom withdrew his hand, bowing his head and muttering a curse under his breath. A small table was set beside the armchair and on top of it was an empty crystal tumbler and a half-empty bottle of a single malt. Tom could smell the distinctive aroma of scotch in the air. An empty bottle of pills lay on its side, the cap missing. He examined the label. *Zomorph*. Tom guessed from the name that it was likely a brand name for a morphine-based prescription drug. Alan's name was printed on the label, no doubt prescribed for pain relief if he was suffering from cancer as his neighbour advised.

Tom looked at Alan, slumped in his chair, blank eyes staring up at the ceiling.

"Damn it," he whispered. He found a handwritten note and alongside it, a photograph. Tom took a deep breath, internally chastising himself as he read the words.

Leaving the room, he passed into the hall. Nothing was out of place. He glanced into the kitchen but there was nothing untoward there either. Remembering what Kerry told him earlier when she'd gone in search of a warm blanket for Alan, Tom made his way upstairs. The sound of the clock carried with him until he reached the landing. One bedroom door was closed whereas the doors to the bathroom and other bedrooms were open. Approaching the closed door, he turned the handle just as his mobile rang. Gently pushing the door open, he answered the call.

"Tom, it's Tamara. I just got your message. Are you still at Alan Turnbull's?"

He sighed, leaning against the door frame.

"What is it?" she asked, sensing something was amiss.

"You need to get over here," Tom said, quietly. "As quickly as you can."

He hung up, touching the mobile to his lips as he entered the room, crestfallen. She lay in a single bed, the duvet pulled up to just below her armpits, hands crossed, one on top of the other lying flat on her chest. She looked so peaceful that she could have been sleeping. Tom momentarily closed his eyes, forcing down the rising tide of emotion within, before reaching out to her. She was stone cold to the touch. Even in what little fading light there still was permeating the drawn curtains, the discolouration in her skin was clear to see.

Maggie Turnbull had been dead for some time.

Tom put his hand across his mouth, an image of Saffy coming to mind. He forced it away, the similarity between the two girls too much to contemplate.

"Rest easy little one," he said to her, shaking his head. He felt guilty for leaving her alone in that room. It was cold, dark and he wanted to stay with her, but there was nothing he could do for her now.

Making his way back downstairs, he returned to Alan's body. The photograph on the coffee table was a picture of a younger Alan Turnbull standing alongside Scarlett in the same vintage red dress she'd been wearing when they'd discovered her body. But, of course, it wasn't Scarlett. It was Margaret, Alan's wife. Dropping to his haunches, he reread the note in situ, only this time doing so with a far greater depth of understanding. It read, *If only I'd had the courage two nights ago. I would have saved everyone a lot of bother.*

The breeze whistled through the hole in the glass he'd made to gain entry, a solemn staccato tune accompanied by the ticking of the clock. The last line of Alan's suicide note struck him like a stab to the heart; *The ravens sing... they're calling me. One last time.*

The note was unsigned, but he didn't doubt its authenticity. Closing his eyes, Tom pinched the bridge of his nose between thumb and forefinger, grimacing at the thought of how he could have got it all so, so wrong. Despite accepting that any decision he'd made would not have changed the outcome, he still felt like he'd let them down. All of them.

What a tragic waste of life.

CHAPTER TWENTY-NINE

TAMARA FINISHED READING the pathologist's report, closing the file and setting it down on the desk to her right. Dr Paxton submitted his findings to her at midday on Monday, the lab having agreed to fast track the toxicology analysis of both Scarlett and Maggie's blood samples. Scanning the faces in the room, no one seemed to want to speak. Eric absently toyed with a pen, doodling on the pad in front of him. Cassie, usually the first, and most willing, to break the tension with a light-hearted remark, was silent.

Tamara looked at Tom. He hadn't spoken since delivering the round-up from forensics. Reaching behind him, he lifted the book he'd been reading, taken from Scarlett's bedside. He held it aloft.

"It was all here," he waved the book before tossing it down onto the nearest table. Everyone's eyes tracked it, staring at it as if it would give them the answers. "It could be the story of their lives. Two brothers, one healthy, one disabled and dying, and they travel together to an afterlife of sorts where they can both fulfil their dreams. Ultimately, they decide the afterlife is better... and together, they... they step off a cliff."

Eric had tears in his eyes. He was not alone. Kerry Palmer had a scrunched-up tissue in her fist. She spent the most time with Alan and Tom was well aware she was giving herself a hard time for not realising Maggie was upstairs.

"So, Alan took Maggie home with him that night?" she asked.

"I believe so," Tom said.

"I think we all have lessons to learn from this," Tamara said. No one disagreed. "But we approached this investigation with the right mindset, and the end goal of bringing Maggie home safely was our priority. There's no way we could have known that Maggie was already dead before we started searching." She pointed to Dr Paxton's report. "That goes some way to explaining why Alan wouldn't let you put the heating on, Kerry. It was likely he was terrified about her state of preservation. The colder it was, the longer he could hide her presence from us."

Tom looked around at the team. "Both Maggie and Scarlett were administered overdoses of sedatives. The drugs used were prescribed to Scarlett as part of her medication to help her cope with her chronic anxiety, a symptom of her aphasia. Unfortunately, the only people who know the true motivations of those concerned, Scarlett and her father, are obviously deceased. However, I would venture that they discussed their situation as a family and, facing the very real prospect of losing Maggie into the care system, along with their own degenerating health conditions... they hatched a plan to take matters into their own hands."

He folded his arms across his chest.

"It is a truly awful conclusion to come to," he said, "but, I believe, this is what they did. It's speculation, of course, but I think the plan was always for the three of them to die together that night. For whatever reason, Alan couldn't go through with it. Scarlett may well have died from the overdose in her system, but he smothered her to make sure. Scarlett, having spent one last night out with someone she knew cared for her, unconditionally, Mark Young, returned home and dressed in her best clothes; a vintage dress bequeathed to her by her mother. She then, or perhaps Alan, administered the drugs to Maggie and then herself."

Tamara nodded along. "When Alan decided he couldn't go through with it, he left for his own home. Was Maggie still alive at this point? We have no way of knowing. Did he bring her home with him to ensure that she didn't pass away alone? Again, we will never know for sure."

"I can't believe this..." Cassie said. "I mean, how messed up does the world have to be for a family to think this is their best option? The world's gone mad."

Tom couldn't argue. Tamara took a deep breath.

"Right, you lot," Tamara said, clearly forcing herself to sound upbeat. "We didn't get the result we wanted and... it was a rough weekend. They don't come much tougher than this and I hope not to see anything like it again, but it is what we signed up for, believe it or not." She looked at the clock. It was approaching three o'clock in the afternoon. "I want you all to take the rest of the day and go and do something for yourselves. Hug someone you love," she pointed at Tom, "hang out with your kid... whatever. Anything that brings a smile to your face. I'm sure we all need it!"

She came to stand beside Tom as the others set about packing up for the day. He looked sideways at her.

"What are you going to do with yourself then?" he asked.

She shrugged. "I have a sick and wounded Austin Healey to fix."

"That's not spending time with someone you love."

"Maybe not," she said, inclining her head, "but she does make me smile."

"So, you're not going to call a certain psychology professor and suggest going out on a date?"

She met his eye, then checked no one else was within earshot. "Someone's been talking."

He smiled, shaking his head. "Only David. He wanted to know what I thought about you. For someone who studies people for a living, he wasn't very good at keeping his intentions secret. I saw right through him."

"Well, we all offer other people better advice than we give ourselves, don't we?"

"That's true enough." She made to leave, but he placed a gentle, restraining hand on her forearm. "You could do much worse, you know? He's a nice guy."

She purposefully lifted his hand off her arm, setting it aside. "I will consider your recommendation carefully."

"You'll do no such thing," he said, bringing a smile out of her. "You'll hide under your car as usual."

She laughed. "That... is also true. What about you? Are you going to spend some time with Alice and Saffy?"

"Saffy is at school, or better be. I do have plans though."

ERIC SHUT down his computer and picked up his keys. Kerry intercepted him as he was leaving ops. He tried to bypass her, pretending not to realise she was deliberately blocking his path.

"Eric?"

"I–I'm sorry. I need to get home to—"

"Yes, about that," Kerry said, her face flushing, "and

before... I shouldn't have said what I did. I didn't mean to... well, I did, but I shouldn't have. I'm so sorry."

He stopped, looking into her face. She was apologetic, almost ashamed. He felt guilty then for thinking so harshly about her.

"It's okay," he said. "You care about me." She nodded, looking down. "And that's lovely... but I have a family and they are who I should be with."

"I know," she whispered, turning and hurrying out of the room. Cassie came to stand beside him.

"What was that about?" she asked.

"I don't know," he said. She looked at him and he knew she didn't believe him. He shrugged.

"Play nicely, Eric," Cassie said, "and tread carefully. There are trip hazards all over the place."

She walked away before he could say anything, pushing thoughts of Kerry's advances aside and thinking of George and Becca instead. He saw Tom watching him from inside his office. Eric waved to him, setting off, and Tom returned it.

"YOU'RE HOME EARLY," Alice said as Tom walked into the kitchen.

"Yes, Tamara thought we should have some time together."

"Tamara thought, did she?" Alice asked, amused.

"You know what I mean," Tom said, crossing the room and turning her to face him. He pulled her in close and kissed her.

"Did she tell you to do that as well?"

"Nope," he said, smiling and settling his hands on the small of her back. "That was all me."

She smiled broadly up at him. "I like Tom Janssen in the

middle of the day. Not so much the evening Tom Janssen, but he's still pretty cool."

"What's wrong with evening Tom?"

"He's often brooding... tall, handsome and attractively vulnerable... but he is moody."

"Well, in that case, I should come home early more often."

"And what are we going to do with this extra time you'll be offering me?" Alice asked, raising her eyebrows inquisitively.

"Well, for starters, I thought we could plan our future together. A proper plan, as a family. What do you think?"

"Sounds good," Alice said. "Almost as if you are planning on sticking around for the long term."

"Maybe I am," he said, smiling.

"You'll be proposing next."

He released her, bringing his hands to her sides and focussing on her intently. "It's funny you should say that because—"

"Yes!"

"What?"

"Yes, I will marry you," Alice said, confirming her decision with a firm nod.

"I know I've only done this... less than a handful of times," he said with a wry smile, "but I'm sure the convention is that you should wait until formally asked prior to answering."

"But you are asking, aren't you?"

"I'm not so sure I will now, no," he said, playfully.

"We'll have to check with Saffy anyway," Alice said, looking past Tom. He turned around to see a pair of eyes peering over the arm of the sofa, watching and listening intently.

"I thought she'd be at school."

"She was a bit upset, this case you've been working has got

her all worked up. I've tried to keep the worst of it from her, but it's been all over the telly this weekend," Alice said. "I figured she could take today off and spend it with her mum watching cartoons. You don't mind, do you?"

"No, not at all." He let go of Alice and walked into the front room, lowering himself to Saffy's level. "What do you think, Saffy? Would you be okay if I were to marry your mum?"

She thought about it for a second, scrunching up her face. "Would that mean you could be my dad?"

He glanced at Alice, waiting pensively in the kitchen.

"If you want me to be, Munchkin, yes."

Saffy beamed, scrabbling off the sofa and hurling herself into his arms. For such a slight girl, she packed a punch. He lifted her up and she wrapped her legs around his waist, arms around his neck. Alice came through and they had a three-way hug.

"Out of any bad situation, you can always find something good," Tom whispered. "On occasion, you just have to look hard for it, that's all."

FREE BOOK GIVEAWAY

Visit the author's website at **www.jmdalgliesh.com** and sign up to the VIP Club and be the first to receive news and previews of forthcoming works.

Here you can download a FREE eBook novella exclusive to club members;

Life & Death - A Hidden Norfolk novella

Never miss a new release.

No spam, ever, guaranteed. You can unsubscribe at any time.

Enjoy this book? You could make a real difference.

Because reviews are critical to the success of an author's career, if you have enjoyed this novel, please do me a massive favour by entering one onto Amazon.

Type the following link into your internet search bar to go to the Amazon page and leave a review;

http://mybook.to/the-raven-song

If you prefer not to follow the link please visit the sales page where you purchased the title in order to leave a review.

Reviews increase visibility. Your help in leaving one would make a massive difference to this author and I would be very grateful.

THE SONG PLAYING on the radio was distracting. It was a tune he remembered his mother enjoyed. She used to hum it while she was preparing tea. Well, she used to hum a few bars of it and then voice the first line of the chorus over and over again. His mum wasn't someone who could be described as having a sound memory. For faces, yes, but as for lyrics...

He turned the key in the ignition and the engine died followed by the music just as the melody faded out and the DJ spoke. Late-night radio. The oldest songs were the cheapest to play as royalty payments must be next to nothing for songs that old. Momentarily regretting being so quick to turn it off, he knew that tune was going to bug him until he remembered the title if not the singer. *Was it Dusty Springfield?* He couldn't even picture her in his mind's eye, but he could remember his mum tunelessly repeating that one line over and over. It brought a smile to his face as he got out of the van, locked up and made his way towards the office block.

The night was overcast, muggy. The threat of rain was ever present as thunderstorms were forecast. With a bit of luck, it would hold off until he'd finished his rounds. Once back in the relative sanctity of the office, the heavens could open. It wouldn't matter by then. Most people would believe the rain would drive the opportunists away, keep them at home. After all, no one particularly likes to be out at night in a storm. Decent people don't at any rate. Thieves see it differently. Two sites had been broken into in the past three days alone, stripping the copper from the on-site transformers and making off with it for scrap value.

He was half expecting to find someone charred to a crisp one of these days. It was more luck than judgement that it hadn't happened already. The increased rounds were a by-product. Not that he minded. The overtime rate was decent, and the money would definitely come in handy.

A sound carried in the night air and he stopped, turning towards it. Peering into the gloom, he struggled to make out a shape. Was it his mind playing tricks on him? Unhooking the torch from his belt, he angled the beam into the shadows. More movement. This time he was certain.

"Hello? Who's there?"

No answer.

He tried to sound commanding, "Whatever you're doing back there—"

A figure stepped out into the beam. She was blinded by the light, raising a hand to shield her eyes from the glare.

"Ben. It's me."

He redirected the beam away and focussed on her. "Angie?" he squinted as he eyed her. "What are you doing here?"

She tentatively took a step towards him. The pitter patter of raindrops struck the gravel at his feet, quickly growing in intensity. Angela was dressed only in a loose cami-vest top, cut away denim shorts and trainers. She pulled her arms close to her as the rain increased. Ben hurried to her, taking her by the hand and leading her to the nearest building. They took shelter in the doorway while he fumbled with his keys. It wasn't much but it was better than being caught out in the open.

The storm was breaking upon them and eventually Ben found the right key, unlocked the door and the two of them bundled inside out of the rain. It'd only been a matter of seconds but the two of them were virtually wet through. Ben looked upon her. Angela's shoulder-length blonde hair was soaking wet and stuck to the side of her face. She deftly moved it aside, away from her eyes, tucking it behind her ear. Her mascara had run but she didn't seem too bothered, smiling up at him as he wiped the warm rain from his own face. Her top clung to her chest revealing the contours of her body. They were close. He could smell a sweet, flowery fragrance on her.

Was it the conditioner in her hair or was it her perfume?

The room was lit by the night lights, every fourth strip light above them was on; enough to see by but the darkness ventured deeply in between casting odd shadows all around them. Angela smiled at him.

"What are you doing here?" Ben asked again. "You'll get in trouble—"

"I'm here to see you, you idiot!"

"Me?"

He was taken aback.

"Yes, you!"

She reached out and grasped his shirt at the waist, drawing him towards her. Confused, he mumbled something, but it faded out as their bodies touched. He swallowed hard, staring into her blue eyes. They gleamed in the scant light as she gazed upon him and he felt self-conscious, scared of saying the wrong thing or making a mistake.

"I wanted to say thank you," she said.

"T–There's no need."

She reached up and placed the point of her forefinger against his lips, silencing him. His mouth ran dry, and his nerves were set ablaze. On her tiptoes, she leaned in and kissed him, allowing the touch to linger for a few seconds. Unsure of how to respond, he didn't. He felt lightheaded and dizzy, but in a good way. He would never be able to explain it any better than that, no matter how hard he would try. She drew away from him, smiled again, and he found himself returning it. She tasted of strawberries.

"Thank you," she said quietly.

"T–That's okay," he said, instantly regretting the tone. In his head, he sounded feeble, pathetic.

She touched his cheek, slowly tracing her fingers down the side of his face and placing her palm flat against his chest.

"I can feel your heart beating," she whispered.

He nodded, dumbstruck.

What should he do now?

"Thank you, Ben," she repeated, releasing him and stepping back. The realisation that this was his moment, and it may have passed struck him. She moved to the side and reached for the door handle behind him. They were still touching.

He should make a move… but how? Do something. Anything.

Suddenly he felt inadequate. The hinges on the door shrieked as she opened it, the sound of the rain striking the ground beyond carried inside. Angela passed out into the storm. Ben hesitated and then followed, calling after her.

"Angie… wait!"

It was a decision that would play over and over again in his mind – and in the mind of the jurors – in the months to come. It was a real sliding doors moment. A decision that Ben Crake would forever regret.

BOOKS BY J M DALGLIESH

In the Hidden Norfolk Series

One Lost Soul

Bury Your Past

Kill Our Sins

Tell No Tales

Hear No Evil

The Dead Call

Kill Them Cold

A Dark Sin

To Die For

Fool Me Twice

Life and Death *FREE - visit jmdalgliesh.com

In the Dark Yorkshire Series

Divided House

Blacklight

The Dogs in the Street

Blood Money

Fear the Past

The Sixth Precept

Boxsets

Dark Yorkshire Books 1-3

Dark Yorkshire Books 4-6

Audiobooks

In the Hidden Norfolk Series
One Lost Soul
Bury Your Past
Kill Our Sins
Tell No Tales
Hear No Evil
The Dead Call
Kill Them Cold
A Dark Sin
To Die For
Fool Me Twice

In the Dark Yorkshire Series
Divided House
Blacklight
The Dogs in the Street
Blood Money
Fear the Past
The Sixth Precept

Audiobook Box Sets
Dark Yorkshire Books 1-3
Dark Yorkshire Books 4-6